NIGHT FALL

Also by Frank Smith

The Chief Inspector Paget Mysteries

ACTS OF VENGEANCE
THREAD OF EVIDENCE
CANDLES FOR THE DEAD
STONE DEAD
FATAL FLAW
BREAKING POINT
THE COLD HAND OF MALICE
A KILLING RESURRECTED
IN THE SHADOW OF EVIL
NIGHT FALL

Other Novels

DRAGON'S BREATH
THE TRAITOR MASK
DEFECTORS ARE DEAD MEN
CORPSE IN HANDCUFFS
SOUND THE SILENT TRUMPETS

NIGHT FALL

A DCI Neil Paget Mystery

Frank Smith

This first world edition published 2013
in Great Britain and in the USA by
SEVERN HOUSE PUBLISHERS LTD of
19 Cedar Road, Sutton, Surrey, England, SM2 5DA.

British Library Cataloguing in Publication Data

Smith, Frank, 1927-
Night fall.
1. Paget, Neil (Fictitious character)--Fiction.
2. Murder--Investigation--Fiction. 3. Police--Great
Britain--Fiction. 4. Detective and mystery stories.
I. Title
813.5'4-dc23

ISBN-13: 978-0-7278-8271-4 (cased)

Typeset by Palimpsest Book Production Ltd.,
Falkirk, Stirlingshire, Scotland.
Printed and bound in Great Britain by
MPG Books Ltd., Bodmin, Cornwall.

PROLOGUE

Monday, 29 August

Rain spattered the tinted windows. It was late, but there was still a lot of traffic on the road. They'd been ready to leave Chester by eight o'clock, but the driver of the bus hadn't returned to pick them up until after ten, so now it would be midnight or later before they got home. Ben, his name was, the driver. Funny little chap, but he had a way with the girls. He said he'd met an old mate and the time had just slipped by, but it was probably a girl.

They'd spent the time in the pub while they waited. Celebrating. And why not? After all, they'd come third, hadn't they? Third out of twenty-six entries was pretty damned good – far better than they'd expected when they set out this morning – so most of the adults were feeling no pain by the time they got on the bus, and some had continued to drink as they left Chester behind.

There'd been some boisterous celebratory singing on the bus as well, but drink and the strains of the day had finally taken their toll, and it had been quiet for the last half hour or so. Except for the pair in the front seat. Voices had been rising and falling, but now there was a sharp crack like the snapping of a dry twig, and suddenly Meg Bainbridge was on her feet, hands busily brushing down her rumpled skirt.

Her companion half rose in his seat beside her, one hand holding the side of his face. 'For Christ's sake, sit down, Meg!' he ordered hoarsely. 'It's just a bit of fun.' He made a grab for her arm and tried to pull her down.

'Well, it's not my kind of fun!' Meg snapped as she snatched her arm away, 'so you can keep your hands to yourself, Mike Fulbright.' She set off unsteadily down the aisle towards the back of the bus to look for an empty seat.

'Then you shouldn't have put it on offer,' he called after her.

Furious, Meg turned to reply, but a small man in the third seat from the front grabbed her hand. 'Good for you, Meg,' he said loudly for Fulbright's benefit. 'He's a very dangerous man, is our Mike. It's a good thing you're on a bus and not—'

'Shut it, you!' Fulbright snapped, glaring at the man.

'Or what, Mike?' the little man demanded cockily, emboldened by the drink. 'Do you know what day this is, Mike? Well, do you?'

Meg, clearly puzzled, frowned down at the man, then pulled her hand free and moved on.

'I know you've got a big mouth,' Mike sneered, 'and I'm telling you to shut it.'

'Or what, Mike?'

Conscious that others were listening, Fulbright lowered his voice. 'I'm just telling you to think about it,' he grated. 'In fact, I'd think long and hard about it if I were you.' He slid down into his seat.

The little man stared at the open can of beer in his hand, then tilted his head back and drained it. 'Think about it?' he muttered. 'I've never stopped bloody thinking about it!' Tears glistened in his eyes and spilled over.

The man beside him stirred. 'Perhaps not the wisest thing to do,' he suggested mildly. 'Antagonizing Mike Fulbright, especially when he's had too much to drink.'

The little man brushed ineffectually at the tears but remained silent.

'If you'd like to talk about it . . .?' his seatmate prodded gently. He put a hand to his mouth to smother a yawn. 'Bottling things up is rarely a good idea.'

The little man's fingers curled tightly around the empty can, eyes fixed intently on it as it crumpled and collapsed beneath the pressure. 'Why not?' he muttered in a voice barely above a whisper. Then, more boldly, 'Why bloody well not!'

He turned his head to squint at the man, then tapped the side of his nose. 'But you have to promise not to tell anyone,' he warned. 'I mean it. Not ever. All right . . .?'

Farther back, Meg Bainbridge found an empty seat next to a slim, fair-haired young man by the name of Colin Findlay. Good looking lad . . . well, not a lad, exactly. Married, two kids. Meg rather fancied him, but he was as straight as they come. Straighter. Didn't drink; didn't smoke; probably only had sex once a week if that, and he was the only man on the bus who was wearing a suit and tie. Bernice, that was his wife's name. Pretty little thing but a bit of a prude in Meg's estimation. Thin lips and disapproving eyes, and *very* possessive. Meg had wondered how Colin had come to marry her. Probably got her pregnant, then 'did the right thing'.

'Don't mind if I join you, do you, Colin?' she asked, continuing without giving him a chance to answer. 'Mike can be a lot of fun when he's sober, but he can be a proper bastard when he's had too much to drink.' She leaned closer and giggled beneath her breath when she felt Findlay flinch and try to pull away from the pressure of her breast pressed hard against his arm. 'And he's not too pleased with you either, Colin, love,' she confided. 'Not after today's performance, he isn't, so you'd better watch your back in future.' She squeezed his arm. 'And me sitting here with you isn't going to improve his temper,' she added brightly, 'so like I said, you'd better watch it, love.'

He tried to ease away, but the seat was narrow and there was nowhere to go. The heady fragrance of Meg's perfume was overpowering. He turned his head away and tried to breathe more shallowly, but there was no escaping it.

'I didn't expect to win,' he said plaintively. 'I mean I didn't set out to upset Mike. It's just that—'

He stopped abruptly as Meg reached out and pressed her fingers against his lips. 'I know, Colin, love,' she said, 'but I'm tired and I don't want to talk any more.' She yawned, then snuggled down and laid her head on his shoulder and closed her eyes. 'You don't mind, do you, love?' she murmured sleepily. Her long black hair felt soft and warm against his cheek.

Findlay breathed in deeply. 'Not at all, Meg,' he croaked huskily. 'Really, I don't mind at all.'

ONE

Friday, 30 September

The town hall clock was striking eleven when the front door of a house on Thurston Street opened and a small group of men stepped out into the night. They paused in the act of pulling hoods over their heads, surprised to find it had stopped raining. Then, with mutterings of 'G'night,' they made their way to their cars and drove off.

Billy Travis, alone on the pavement, thrust his hands in his pockets and turned towards home. It was dark; street lights were few and far between in this older part of town, but home was only a few streets away.

It had been a good session. The highlight of the night had been a demonstration by Ted Grayson of special effects that could be achieved *without* using a computer. Not everyone had found it as fascinating as he had, though. They were all computer mad these days, quick to use every new-fangled piece of software that would – what was the word? Enhance! That was the word they were so fond of using. Enhance their pictures. Well, that might be all right for some, but to him it was no different than cheating, and he had found Grayson's presentation refreshing. This obsession with manipulating pictures using Photoshop and other devices . . . Billy shook his head. Not that he was dead set against them; he'd made use of them himself at one time or another, but he'd been brought up the old way, helping his dad in the darkroom, watching images appear on a piece of blank paper, lifting them out of the tray with tweezers when his dad said, 'Now, Billy. Now!'

He liked Ted Grayson, liked going to meetings in his house with all the black and white pictures on the walls and the collection of old cameras in the back room. Grayson himself was something of a character. Gaunt-faced and pale, he was tall and thin, and with his straggling pony-tail and his addiction to weed, he looked – and sometimes acted – like a hippie from the sixties. But what Grayson didn't know about cameras wasn't worth knowing, in Billy's opinion.

The smell of weed was still with him. It was the same every time; it clung to his clothing, and he'd never been able to convince his father that he hadn't been smoking the stuff himself.

He'd be in bed now, his father. The fitful weather of the past few days was playing havoc with his arthritic knees, and he'd been going to bed early and taking a sleeping tablet to get some relief from the pain. Fifty-seven years old and he was hobbling around like a man of ninety. He was—

'*Aahhgg!*' Billy gasped as he collided with the figure of a man stepping out of a dark doorway. He stumbled and would have fallen if the man hadn't reached out and grabbed his arm.

'Sorry,' the man said. 'My fault. I should have looked where— Billy? Billy Travis? Is that you? Good God, man, fancy bumping into you like this. Are you all right?'

'Just scared the shit out of me, that's all,' Billy said shakily. Heart racing, he drew a deep breath as he peered at the man. 'What brings you over to this side of town anyway?'

'Stopped in to see a friend and didn't look where I was going when I came out,' the man said apologetically. 'You sure you're all right? On your way home, are you?'

'That's right.' For some reason, Billy felt he should offer an explanation. 'I've just been to a meeting of the photographic society. We meet every other Friday.'

'Keeping up with your work, then,' the man said approvingly. 'Always something new, I suppose; something else to learn. Good for you, Billy.' He looked up and down the deserted street. 'Look, my car's right here. The least I can do is drive you home after almost knocking you down.'

'Thanks, but there's no need,' Billy said. 'It's no more than five minutes from here.'

'Nonsense!' the man said as he took Billy's arm. 'Come on, get in.'

'No, really . . .' Billy began again, but the man had opened the door of the car, and it seemed pointless to resist the offer of a ride.

'Best buckle up,' he said as Billy got in. 'Can't be too careful, can we? Watch your arm now.' He closed the door, then paused to survey the silent street once more before opening the back door. 'Just bear with me for a minute,' he said, as he climbed inside. 'Something's been rattling around back here and I want to sort it out before it drives me mad.' He picked something up off the floor, then, settling himself in the seat directly behind his passenger, he chuckled. 'I think I should lower the headrest for you while I'm here,' he said. 'Just sit up straight, Billy, and put your head back while I do that.'

Billy chuckled himself as he pushed himself up in his seat. 'At least there's not much chance of getting whiplash when you're my size,' he said. He sat up straight and put his head back. 'See, I'm still too short.'

'Very true,' the man said quietly as he slipped the noose over Billy's head and the headrest and pulled hard on the slip-knot. Billy opened his mouth to cry out, fingers clawing at the rope that bit deep into the flesh. His eyes bulged; his feet hammered against the floor, and blood streaked his neck where his nails were digging into the flesh.

The pressure eased. His throat rattled as he gulped air, and it flashed across his mind that this must be what they were talking about when they spoke of the death rattle. The rope tightened again. He could feel himself slipping away. He was only thirty-three years old, for Christ's sake, and he was about to die! Tears streamed down his face; he tried to scream, but there was no sound except the roaring in his ears.

The pressure on his throat eased slightly. 'Talk to me, Billy,' the man said softly. He could feel the man's breath against his ear. 'I want to know every last detail. A full confession. Think of it as cleansing your soul before you meet your Maker.'

TWO

Saturday, 1 October

Grace Lovett was putting on her wellingtons at the back door when the phone rang. She groaned. Not today, *please* not today, she thought as she pulled the boots off again. They'd had it all planned. Today was to be devoted to sorting out the garden, and Neil was already down at the shed bringing out the tools. The weather forecast was for showers in the afternoon, hence the early start. With any luck at all they could have the whole thing done by lunchtime.

Depending, of course, on who was on the other end of the phone, she thought grimly as she went back into the house.

Three minutes later Grace stepped outside again. 'Put 'em all back, Neil,' she called. 'We've both been called in to work. Suspicious death on the tracks under the bridge at the Lessington Cut.'

They travelled to the site separately in their own cars. As a member of SOCO, the crime scenes investigation team, Grace would probably be spending her time at the site itself, whereas there was no telling where DCI Neil Paget would be by the end of the day.

The Lessington Cut, as it was called locally, lay some four miles north of Broadminster. The cutting was about a mile long, slicing through a fold in the land, and the bridge carrying a little-used country road was roughly halfway along the ridge.

It was an unusually subdued DS John Tregalles who greeted Paget when he arrived at the scene. The sergeant's eyes were grave, and his normally expressive features were set in rigid, sombre lines. 'It's a bad one, boss,' he said quietly as they walked from the car to the bridge overlooking the tracks. 'Never seen anything quite like it.'

'No chance it was an accident or suicide, then?'

Tregalles grimaced and shook his head. 'You'll see,' he said grimly.

They clambered down the steep bank to where white-suited members of the crime scene squad were setting up their equipment. A photographer was already at work, crouching down to get shots of the body from different angles, while two men stood waiting for him to finish before setting a plastic screen in place around the body.

'Be finished in a minute,' the photographer called over his shoulder as he took another shot.

'Who found the body?' Paget asked.

'The engine driver of the seven forty-five out of Broadminster spotted him and radioed in,' Tregalles told him. 'PC Whitelaw and his partner were first on the scene, and Whitelaw recognized the victim. His name is William Travis, and that's been confirmed by his driving licence and other things in his wallet. He's a photographer, or he was. He and his dad have a shop at the top end of Bucknell Street. Pokey little place. You've probably seen it; they do wedding photographs and passports and such. His dad did our wedding photos.'

Paget nodded. He'd never been in the shop, but he knew where it was.

'SOCO reckons he came over about there,' Tregalles said, pointing to the stone parapet of the bridge, 'and if that is the case, then he would have fallen on the tracks, so he either managed to drag himself off the tracks to where you see him now, or someone pulled him off. But with the head injuries he has, I don't see how he could have survived the fall.'

Paget eyed the distance from the parapet to the ground. 'Must be at least fifty feet,' he said. 'You're suggesting that whoever pushed him over came down and dragged him off the tracks?'

'Well, I could be wrong, but it looks to me like his neck's broken, and if that's the case, I don't think he could have made it off the tracks by himself.'

The photographer got to his feet and nodded to indicate that he was finished for the moment. He'd be back again to take more pictures once the doctor arrived.

The two detectives moved closer, and for the first time Paget got a good look at the body. He felt his stomach begin to tighten up, and he had to clamp his lips together and take several deep breaths before he could trust himself to lean closer. He'd never actually been sick when viewing a body, but he had come close on more than one occasion.

The man lay on his side, hands behind his back, wrists bound with self-locking plastic cable ties that had cut deeply into the flesh. A strip of duct tape covered his mouth, and the head lay at an awkward angle, suggesting, as Tregalles had said, that the neck was broken.

The top of the head and the face were caked in blood, and there was more blood on the hooded jacket. But in the middle of the man's forehead was a square white medical dressing held firmly in place with another strip of duct tape.

'Weird, isn't it?' Tregalles said, anticipating Paget's question. 'I was tempted to lift it to see what's underneath, but thought I'd better wait until the doc gets here. Apart from that, it looks like a gang killing to me. Tape over the mouth, plastic handcuffs.'

'But why bring him all the way out here? And why drop him on the tracks, then move him off, if that's what actually happened? Is the constable who was first on the scene still here?'

'Whitelaw? Yes, he is.' Tregalles pointed to a uniformed constable standing halfway up the opposite bank. He caught the man's attention and waved him over.

'I'm told you know the victim,' said Paget as Whitelaw approached. 'How well did you know him?'

'Used to know him better when we were kids,' the man said. 'I see him around town now and again, but I can't remember the last time we spoke.'

'Do you know any of his friends?'

'No, although I doubt he had many. Billy was always a bit of a loner. Lives with his dad above the shop; at least he did, and probably still does. His mum died when he was a kid.'

'Billy . . .?'

Whitelaw smiled. 'Nobody ever called him Bill or William,' he said. 'It was always Billy. I think it was because he was so short and scrawny as a kid.'

'I see. Tell me, what did you make of it when you first saw him?'

Whitelaw took off his cap and scratched his head. 'Tell you the truth, sir, I didn't know what to make of it. Never seen anything like it before.'

'Was he ever in a gang? Anything of that sort?'

'Billy? In a gang? Like drugs, you mean?' The constable dismissed the idea with a shake of the head. 'Can't see it myself, sir. Not Billy. Too timid for one thing, and, like I said, he was a loner. He wouldn't last five minutes in a gang.' He frowned as he looked at the body. 'You think this is a gang killing, sir?'

'It's one possibility.'

Whitelaw made a face that clearly said he disagreed. 'Unless it was a case of mistaken identity?' he ventured. 'Could be they got the wrong bloke.'

Tregalles looked thoughtful. 'He was a photographer,' he said slowly. 'Perhaps he took a picture of something he shouldn't. On the other hand—'

'On the other hand, speculation isn't going to get us anywhere,' Paget broke in, 'so let's see what the doctor can tell us.' He nodded in the direction of a grey-haired man clambering down the bank. He was followed by a uniformed constable carrying the doctor's heavy medical case.

'Morning, Reg,' Paget greeted Reginald Starkie as he slid the last couple of feet down the slope, almost losing his balance in the process. 'I hope you appreciate the fact that we didn't call you in the middle of the night this time?'

'Could have picked a better location, though,' the doctor growled. 'Got grass stains on my trousers, and stains like that never come out, so don't be surprised if it's included in the bill.'

'Not my call any more,' Paget told him. 'You'll have to take that up with Superintendent Pierce.'

'Ah, yes, I heard.' Starkie's voice softened. 'I'm sorry,' he said brusquely. 'I thought that job was yours. Is she here?'

'Comes in on Monday.'

'And I doubt if she'll be best pleased to have this on her plate on her first day,' Tregalles observed. 'Still, if she's going to get her feet wet, she might as well go in the deep end.' He sounded almost cheerful at the prospect. He, too, had hoped that Paget would get the job.

Starkie grunted. 'So let's see what she does have on her plate,' he said. He turned to the constable still holding the medical case. 'Well, don't just stand there, man,' he said testily. 'Set the damned thing down and get that sheet out of the way.'

With gloves on and sheet stripped away, Starkie bent to the task of examining the body while the three men moved back to watch and wait in silence. 'Don't expect too much,' he warned over his shoulder after a cursory examination. 'He's cold and wet from the rain in the night, which doesn't help. Now, I need help to turn him over. You'll do,' he said, focusing on Whitelaw. 'Here, take this pad to protect his face, then take his head and shoulders and ease him over when I tell you to.'

A few minutes later, the doctor rose to his feet and stripped off his gloves. 'Considering the conditions out here,' he said, 'the best I can do regarding time of death is sometime between midnight and three o'clock this morning. I *may* be able to narrow that down later, but I'm making no promises. As for his injuries, he suffered severe trauma to the head, skull fractures in several places, broken neck, and what looks like rope burns around the neck. Possible broken shoulder, and there's bound to be some internal damage. The grazing and bruising on the upper body could have come from being shoved over the parapet, and I think he might have been alive when he went over. Killed on impact. But that's not the only thing. Take a look at this.' Starkie bent down and peeled back the tape and dressing on the forehead. Paget and Tregalles bent closer, with Whitelaw peering over their shoulders.

Starting just below the hairline and ending above the eyebrows, the letter A had been carved in the forehead of Billy Travis. The cuts were deep and were meant to be seen. Starkie lowered the sheet. 'And that was done while the man was still alive,' he said quietly.

Behind them, PC Whitelaw turned away and vomited into the grass.

* * *

'That mark on his forehead is one piece of information I don't want made public,' said Paget as he and Tregalles climbed the bank to the road. He brushed himself off, then led the way to the middle of the bridge. 'Find anything?' he asked one of the men in white.

'Bits of fibre and what may be blood on the stones where he went over,' the man said. 'And there's a partial footprint in the soft earth at the base of the parapet, but it could be anyone's. The road surface is too hard to hold tyre tracks, but chances are whoever brought the victim here parked off road, so we'll be looking for impressions on both sides of the road leading to the bridge.'

Paget thanked the man, then turned to Tregalles. 'Len Ormside won't be back from leave until Monday,' he said, 'so I want you to go back to Charter Lane and start setting up the incident room. This place is so isolated I don't think there's much point in setting up a mobile unit out here, so we'll work from town. And since it's the weekend, just bring in a skeleton crew to get things started, then alert the rest and tell them to be ready to come if we need them before Monday.' He paused to look around at what was mostly open country, and grimaced. 'Not a house in sight,' he said, 'but there must be at least half a dozen farmhouses between here and the main road, so I want them checked out. Someone may have seen or heard something. Meanwhile, I'd better go and break the news to his father, and since there may be leads to follow up after talking to him, give DS Forsythe a call and tell her to meet me at the shop.'

THREE

Bucknell Street was in one of the oldest parts of town. It was a narrow street of terraced houses, beginning at King George Way and ending at Church Lane, where half a dozen houses had been converted into shops. *G. Travis & Son, Photographers – Weddings – Portraits – Passports*, was the third shop from the corner, and DS Molly Forsythe was waiting for him by her car when Paget arrived. This was not what she'd been planning for the weekend, and to make matters worse, she had just begun to wash her hair when Tregalles rang. Her hair was short, but even so a bare five minutes with the hairdryer was not enough, and it still felt damp and stringy against her scalp.

'Tregalles fill you in, did he?' Paget enquired as she joined him.

'He did, sir. Sounded pretty gruesome. Is it true that the victim had the letter A carved in his forehead?'

'I'm afraid it is,' Paget told her as he led the way across the pavement to the door of the shop, 'but keep that bit of information to yourself. I've given instructions that it's not to be released.'

The shop window was small, the glass needed a good cleaning, the paint on the sill and surrounding woodwork was peeling, and the pictures on display looked as if they had been there for a long time. The sign on the door said *Open*.

The shop was empty, but a buzzer sounded somewhere in the back, so Paget went to the counter and waited. There were pictures on the walls: weddings, portraits of children, dramatic head-and-shoulders close-ups, but while they were very well done, Paget had the feeling that they were from a distant age, and he couldn't help wondering how a business such as this had managed to survive in the electronic age where almost every gadget could take pictures, and software made everyone an artist.

A curtain behind the counter was swept aside and a grey-haired man appeared. His face was lined and he walked stiffly with the aid of two canes, but he greeted Paget and Molly with a smile and a cheerful 'Good morning, and what can I do for you today?' He perched himself on a stool and hung the two canes on the edge of the counter.

Paget introduced himself and Molly, then held up his warrant card for inspection. 'And you are Mr Travis, are you?' he asked.

The man frowned. 'That's right,' he said cautiously. 'I'm George Travis. Why do you want to know?'

'And your son is William Travis?' Paget wanted to be

absolutely sure he was talking to the right man before telling him his son was dead.

The look on Travis's face turned to one of concern. 'Billy? Yes. Why, what's happened? Is he hurt? Has he been in an accident?'

'I'm afraid it's more serious than that, Mr Travis,' Paget said quietly. 'I'm sorry to have to tell you that your son Billy was killed earlier this morning.'

Travis sucked in his breath. 'Killed . . .?' he whispered. 'How? . . . Where? . . . What happened? You *sure* it's Billy?'

Paget took out Billy Travis's driving licence and handed it to his father. George Travis took it, hands shaking as he stared at it. 'Car, was it?' he asked numbly. 'Where is he?'

Choosing his words carefully, Paget began to explain what had happened, but when he mentioned the Lessington Cut, George Travis shook his head violently and said, 'No! That's not right. That can't be Billy. What would he be doing out there at the Cut? You've got it wrong.' He thrust the driving licence back into Paget's hand. 'Someone else got hold of his licence. They must have. It's not Billy. He went to the society meeting last night, so how could he get out there?'

'I don't know the answer to that,' Paget told him, 'but one of our constables has known Billy since he was a boy, and he identified him as well. I'm truly sorry, Mr Travis, but it is your son who was killed, and while I know this is the worst possible time, I need to ask you some questions.'

George Travis started to shake. The tremors became so violent that Paget came around the counter to steady him. No sound escaped the man's lips, but he clung to Paget for support, and his fingers dug so deeply into Paget's shoulder that the marks were visible for days afterwards.

They stood like that for several minutes before the shaking stopped and Travis drew a deep if shaky breath. 'I'm all right,' he said in a firmer voice. 'Really, Chief Inspector, I'm all right. You said you wanted to ask me some questions, so you'd better come through to the back.'

He rose to his feet and grasped the two canes to steady himself, then lifted one of them to point it at the shop door. 'Better put up the closed sign and lock the door,' he told Molly.

'Last thing we need right now is a customer coming in.' He twitched the curtain aside and led the way into the back room. 'Coffee's been on for a while now, so it might be a bit strong, but you're welcome to some if you like. I know I need it, and the stronger the better.' In control of himself now, there was a grim determination about the man as he led the way past the framing tables to a small room beyond.

'I went to bed about ten,' he said as he busied himself with the coffee, 'so I didn't know Billy hadn't come home until I got up this morning. I thought there must have been a change of plan, and he'd stayed over at Trudy's after all. Trudy Mason is his girlfriend,' he explained. 'She lives around the corner. Gordon, her husband, is on the road a lot, and Billy stops there overnight when he's away.'

Paget and Molly Forsythe exchanged glances, both wondering if they had heard correctly. 'A change of plan, Mr Travis . . .?' said Paget.

Travis nodded. 'Billy told me Gordon was going to be home this weekend, so he wouldn't be going round, but when I saw he hadn't slept in his bed, I thought things must have changed.'

'I see,' said Paget, although he wasn't sure he did see. 'How long has this arrangement been going on?'

Travis thought. 'Two, maybe three years now.'

'Does Trudy's husband know about this?'

'Christ, no! And I've warned Billy there could be trouble if he finds out, but he doesn't listen. He won't be told—' The words caught in his throat as he realized what he was saying. He sat down heavily and set his coffee aside. 'Do you reckon it was him? Gordon? Came home and found them together?'

It was a possibility. A jealous husband coming home unexpectedly to find his wife in bed with another man. It had certainly happened before. But Paget still held the image of Billy Travis's broken body in his mind's eye, and he couldn't see a jealous husband going to those lengths no matter how enraged he might be. 'We don't know, Mr Travis,' said Paget, 'but we'll be doing everything in our power to find out who did this. You said Billy went to a society meeting last night? What society was that?'

'Photographic society,' Travis said. 'Well, they call it that, but it's really just a bunch of people who like to get together at Ted Grayson's house on Thurston Street. Grayson used to be one of the top photographers around here. He's retired now, but he still keeps his hand in.'

'I'll need his address. And that of Trudy Mason as well.'

'I can tell you where Grayson lives,' said Travis, 'but I don't think it would be a good idea to go round to Trudy's, not if Gordon's home. But I can get her to come round here if you like. Let me give her a bell.' Before Paget could object, Travis took a phone from his pocket and punched in a number.

'Don't say anything about Billy's death,' Paget warned.

Travis stared at him blankly for a moment, then swallowed hard and nodded. 'Trude . . .?' he said into the phone. 'George. Are you alone?' He listened for a few moments, then said, 'Good, because I've got a bit of a problem and I need your help. Could you pop round here now? It's important. Right. Good girl. See you in a few minutes then.'

He put down the phone and looked at Molly. 'Better go to the door to let her in,' he instructed. 'She only lives round the corner, so she'll be here in a couple of minutes.'

Trudy Mason turned out to be something of a surprise. Paget had expected her to be about the same age as Billy, but this woman had to be in her middle forties if not older. Small, a bit on the plump side, she wasn't beautiful or even what one might call good looking, but there was a vitality about her that Paget found compelling. It was her eyes, he decided. Dark, almost mischievous eyes, and the way her mouth crinkled at the corners when she smiled. But Trudy Mason wasn't smiling now; her eyes were red with weeping. 'I can't believe it,' she said for perhaps the fifth time. 'I mean, how could that happen to Billy?'

'That is what we're trying to find out,' Paget told her, 'so tell me, when was the last time you saw Billy?'

'Thursday dinner time,' she said promptly. 'Saw him in the street and told him Gordon would be home for the weekend, so he'd know not to come.'

'And your husband did come home?'

'That's right.'

'When did he arrive?'

Trudy thought. 'Must have been about six or maybe a bit after,' she said. 'He's a long-distance lorry driver and he was just back from Antwerp yesterday afternoon. He'll be off again come Monday.'

'He was with you all last evening?'

'That's right.'

'Did you go out at all?'

'We went round to Gordon's mum's for about an hour to pick up some chutney she'd made for him. I'm not all that fond of it myself, but he loves the stuff. Takes it with him on his trips.'

'What time would that be?'

'Eight, maybe a bit later. Can't say exactly.'

'And you stayed about an hour. Did you come straight home?'

'Stopped at the Three Crowns on the way back. Stayed till about eleven, then came home.'

'Did you or your husband go out again?'

'Not till this morning, no. He went off with his mates just before George rang. Why do you want to know all this?'

'He's wondering if it was Gordon who killed Billy,' Travis said quietly.

Trudy's eyes opened wide. 'Gordon? Kill Billy? Why would he. He likes Billy. Besides, he never went out. He was at home with me all night. That's ridiculous!'

'He *likes* Billy?' Paget echoed. 'Would he like him as much if he found out Billy was sleeping with you when he's out of town? It seems to me he would have good reason to go after him. And I must warn you, Mrs Mason, if you're protecting him, it could mean very serious consequences for you.'

But Trudy Mason was shaking her head. 'You don't understand,' she said, 'so I suppose I'd better explain. Just don't tell Billy, George, because—' The words died on her lips and her hands flew to her mouth. Tears welled in her eyes once again. 'It was a game,' she said shakily. 'Well, sort of a game.' Trudy paused to dab at her eyes and blow her nose. 'Gordon knows about me and Billy; he has done from the very beginning.'

She turned to face Travis. 'Remember that accident four

years ago, George, when Gordon was laid up for the best part of six months? Smashed himself up when he went off the road trying to avoid a kid who ran out in front of him,' she explained for Paget's benefit. 'Did a lot of damage, that did. Pinned inside the cab for four hours before they were able to get him out. They fixed him up all right, well mostly. Enough for him to go back to driving and that, but not so good on the home front, if you know what I mean. Like he's never been able to . . . well, you know . . . get it up since then.'

'He's impotent?' said Paget.

'That's it. But I'm not. Impotent, I mean in a manner of speaking, and Gordon always felt guilty about that. I mean, I still love Gordon and he loves me, but it did put a bit of a strain on things with him not being able to . . . like I said. So when I met Billy, and we got on so well together, I asked Gordon if he was all right with me and Billy getting together every once in a while. To relieve the tension, as you might say.'

Trudy Mason turned back to Travis. 'You know how it was with Billy before that, don't you, George?' she said softly. 'He'd never had a real girlfriend; I was his first. I know it's hard to believe, but he told me he'd never had sex before, and I believed him, so it was doing him good as well as me. But I didn't want to go behind Gordon's back, so I explained the way it was, and he agreed.'

Trudy made a face. 'To be honest, Gordon did have a bit of trouble with it at first,' she admitted, 'but he came round in the end. Actually, I think he was relieved in a way, because he didn't have to feel guilty any more. But he did insist on us having a couple of rules. He never wanted to see the two of us together when he came home, at least not in that way, and I wasn't to tell Billy that Gordon knew. Which was all right with me, because as long as Billy thought we were meeting in secret, it kept him excited. And, to be honest, with me being a good ten years older than him, I wanted it to stay that way.' She bit her lower lip hard as she fought back the tears. 'God! But I'm going to miss him,' she whispered. 'Who in his right mind would do something like that to Billy of all people?'

* * *

Billy's bedroom was at the back of the house. It was quite a large room with a ceiling that sloped towards a narrow window overlooking the back yards of the terraced houses in the next street. The linoleum on the floor was old, and it crackled beneath Paget's feet as he moved to the centre of the room, then paused to look around and mentally catalogue the furniture.

Billy's bed, neatly made, faced them from across the room. The wall above it was covered in pictures: everything from still life to street scenes and landscapes. Pictures of bicycles, cars, a woman hanging out washing on a line, two men loading or unloading a removals van. There were close-ups of small children, of a young couple holding hands, and the faces of old people with wrinkled necks and weathered hands.

And every one was in black and white.

Lying on the seat of a wooden chair beside the bed was a large photograph album. Paget picked it up and opened it. It was filled with pictures of Trudy Mason. Dramatic head-and-shoulders shots for the first few pages, but they became more and more revealing as Paget turned the pages.

'Good body for her age,' Molly observed archly, peering over Paget's shoulder. 'And very nicely posed. Quite tasteful, really, don't you think, sir?'

'Quite,' he said, closing the book.

A chest of drawers, a wardrobe, and a large bookcase crammed with magazines took up much of the wall opposite the window. Paget pulled out magazines at random. Every one of them concerned photography in one form or another. He looked around the room. It appeared that Billy Travis had been passionate about only two things in life: photography and Trudy Mason, possibly in that order. So what had he done to deserve such a death? Perhaps the answer was in the laptop on a shelf above the desk beside the window.

'That's odd,' said Molly, who had been cruising the room. 'Have you noticed, sir? There are no family pictures. None at all. You'd think with father and son both being photographers, there would be some family photos among this lot.'

Paget pulled the laptop off the shelf. 'That is a bit odd,' he agreed absently. 'Perhaps this will tell us something more about the man.'

Molly bent to peer under the bed, then got down on her knees and pulled out a small suitcase. It was covered in dust. Clearly it had not been opened for a very long time. She expected it to be locked, but the latches sprang open as soon as she pressed them.

Inside were photographs, scores if not hundreds of them, all of the family, but most of them of Billy himself. Billy as a baby; Billy as a toddler with his mother; Billy on a tricycle; Billy on his birthday. His mother was in most of them, so it was a reasonable assumption that his father had taken the pictures. Molly shuffled through them and found a cheeky one of Billy as a boy. He was grinning broadly as he pointed to what must have been a recent 'buzz cut'. He looked awful, but he must have changed his mind – or he'd had it changed for him – because Molly found another picture of him with a full head of hair, and looking positively angelic as a choir boy, taken a year or so later.

Molly had been passing the pictures to Paget as she sorted through them, but now Paget set them aside. 'There are none of his mother after about the age of five,' he said slowly. 'PC Whitelaw said Billy's mother died when he was young, and it doesn't look as if any pictures were taken of the boy for several years after that. Have you seen any of him from about the time he was five to something like ten?'

Molly shook her head. 'You're right,' she said, shuffling through the pile. 'It looks as if there were none taken for several years. Nor can I find any pictures of him from the time he was seventeen or eighteen. Not a single picture. I wonder why that was?'

'Perhaps his father can tell us,' Paget said. 'I'm taking the laptop with me, but you might as well put the case back under the bed for now. SOCO can go through it later.'

'Funny, but I never realized it had gone on that long,' George Travis said bleakly when Paget asked him. 'I suppose I fell out of the habit of taking pictures of the boy after his mother died. She was the one who was always after me to take Billy's picture. She couldn't get enough of them; always pestering me to take more, so I probably thought we had enough, and just stopped taking them.'

'What about later? We couldn't find a single picture of him after the age of seventeen or eighteen.'

Travis shook his head in a bewildered sort of way. 'I think it might have been earlier than that,' he said. 'I don't know what got into him, but all of a sudden he went camera shy. I thought he was joking at first, but I soon found out he wasn't when I tried to take a picture of him. Dead serious, he was, so I let him be.' His face clouded. 'Come to think of it, I don't have a picture of the boy since then.'

He raised troubled eyes to meet those of Paget as the realization hit him. 'Not one!' he repeated. 'Me, a photographer, and I don't have a single picture of my son as a man!' His lips quivered, and he turned his head away to hide the tears in his eyes.

'Perhaps Trudy Mason might have one,' Molly suggested, but Travis shook his head. 'I know she tried,' he said, 'but she told me he grabbed the camera off her and got so upset that she never tried again. He took lots of her, though.'

With Ormside away until Monday, Paget was anxious to get back to Charter Lane to oversee the setting up of the incident room, so it was left to Molly to trace Billy Travis's movements on the night before he died. George Travis had said that Billy left the shop around seven thirty on Friday evening, so the first thing that needed to be established was whether Billy had actually gone to the meeting in Thurston Street.

Now, as she followed Ted Grayson down the hall to a small sitting room, Molly could see why George Travis had described the man as 'a bit odd' when Paget had asked about the man. Grayson had come to the door wearing ragged jeans, a multi-coloured tie-dyed shirt open to the waist, and flip-flops on his bare feet. With his gaunt face, scarecrow frame, and hair pulled tight and tied at the back in a pony-tail, he looked more like one of the street people who huddled in doorways on Bridge Street each night than the owner of a small but tastefully furnished house in Thurston Street.

'So, Detective Sergeant Forsythe,' he said brusquely as he

waved Molly to a seat, 'what's all this about Billy Travis?' Grayson pulled up a footstool and squatted cross-legged to face her. 'What's Billy supposed to have done? He was here just last night, and I can't see him getting into much trouble between then and now. *Is* he in trouble?'

Molly ignored the question. 'Do you happen to remember what time it was when he arrived last night?' she asked.

'Quarter to eight, give or take a few minutes. We try to start at eight, and Billy usually gets here in good time. And you aren't answering my question. What's he supposed to have done?'

'In a moment,' Molly said. 'Can you tell me when he left?'

Grayson remained silent, eyeing her narrowly as if trying to decide whether to answer or not. 'Eleven o'clock,' he said at last. 'Everyone left at the same time, and the town hall clock was striking eleven as they went out the door.'

'How was he when he left? Did you notice anything different about him during the evening? Or did he say anything that struck you as odd?'

Grayson got to his feet. 'I don't like playing games,' he said coldly, 'especially when it involves a friend, so no more answers until you tell me what this is about. So, either you tell me or we've finished here.'

'Unfortunately, it's not a game,' Molly told him. 'I'm sorry to have to tell you that Billy Travis died last night.'

'Died?' Grayson stared at her for a long moment, then sat down heavily in a leather armchair. 'How?' he asked in a low voice. 'What was it? Some idiot run into him? Billy always walked home. Is that what happened?'

'No, Mr Grayson, it wasn't an accident. Billy Travis was murdered a few hours after he left here.'

'Murdered?' Grayson repeated. 'Who the hell would want to murder Billy? Are you quite sure we're talking about the same man? How?'

'I'm sorry, sir, but I'm not at liberty to give you any details at this point,' Molly said. 'You say Billy was a friend?'

Grayson nodded slowly. 'I just can't believe it,' he said. 'I mean, Billy of all people? He was such a harmless little guy. Good photographer. Did some good work in black and white, especially. A traditionalist, that was Billy when it came to photography.' He drew a deep breath and let it out again slowly. 'So, what do you want to know?'

'Did he seem worried or agitated last night? Did he say anything that struck you as odd? Or did he say anything to suggest he might be meeting someone when he left here?'

Grayson shook his head. 'Billy's more of a listener than a talker. I mean he will join in, especially when it's something near and dear to his heart, but he doesn't put himself forward or indulge in small talk, if you know what I mean. So all I can tell you is that he seemed perfectly normal when he left here.'

'You said he usually walks to and from these meetings. Do you know if anyone else was going his way last night?'

'No one was. All the others came by car. In fact, come to think of it, he's the only one who lives in that direction, so he'd be walking alone. Not that he had far to go; just down to the end of the road to Dunmore Lane, then straight on from there. Ten minutes at the most.'

Grayson gave Molly a list of names and addresses of those who had been at the meeting the night before, but said he doubted if they would be able to shed any more light on what had happened than he could. When Molly asked if Billy had been particularly friendly with any of the other members of the group, Grayson shook his head. 'Billy was a real loner,' he said. 'In fact, I can't think of anyone he was close to, other than his father, of course. He and George were very close. Billy lost his mum when he was a kid, so they only had each other. God!' he exclaimed, 'this is going to hit poor old George hard.'

'What about girlfriends?' Molly probed, wondering if Grayson and others were aware of Billy's relationship with Trudy Mason. But Grayson was once again shaking his head. 'Never heard him speak of one,' he said, 'in fact some of the members of the club were convinced he was gay.'

'And what did you think, Mr Grayson?'

Grayson snorted. 'Billy was a loner, and he didn't mix well with women, but I can assure you he wasn't gay.'

'How can you be so sure?'

Grayson's lips twisted into a sardonic grin. 'Let's just say it takes one to know one,' he said softly. 'Or hadn't you worked that out yet, Detective?'

Molly checked for CCTV cameras as she drove back over the route Billy had probably taken the night before. She found one in Dunmore Lane. It was pointed at the doorway of the corner shop. But had it been on last night? More to the point, was it a real CCTV camera? Some of them were no more than dummies, mounted by the shopkeepers themselves in the hope that they would deter anyone who might be thinking of robbing their shop.

Real or not, it wouldn't make a scrap of difference to some of the hoodies who spent their time slouching around the streets, looking for an easy mark. Molly got out of the car and crossed her fingers as she entered the shop.

FOUR

Monday, 3 October

Paget left the house earlier than usual on Monday morning. It had been a busy weekend, and he felt confident that everything that could be done had been done, but he wasn't looking forward to the arrival of his new boss, Detective Superintendent Amanda Pierce. It would have been difficult enough if everything had been normal, but with the death of Billy Travis, today would be anything but normal.

Trudy Mason had accompanied George Travis to make a formal identification of the body on Saturday afternoon, and Starkie had been surprisingly cooperative by offering to perform the autopsy later that day. There were no real surprises. There were some internal injuries as a result of the fall, but as he said, they were of little consequence considering that death had occurred on impact.

He'd found nylon fibres embedded in the front and sides of the neck, but none around the back of the neck. 'In other words,' he told Paget, 'he wasn't hanged or partly hanged. He was choked. There was a bruise on the back of his head, so the rope may have been slipped around his neck and his head pulled back sharply against a post or something like that. There were marks on his ankles, indicating that they were bound at some point, probably with plastic ties like those on his wrists. I won't have the toxicology report back until at least Tuesday, but I'd be surprised if there's anything unusual about it. Regarding the time of death, I've narrowed it down a bit, and I think it's safe to say he died between one and three o'clock Saturday morning. As for the capital A carved in his forehead, there was no tearing of the skin, so I'd say the instrument used was very sharp, such as a razor, a box cutter blade, or possibly a scalpel.'

'But why put a dressing over it?' Paget had asked.

'The only reason I can think of, is that he wanted it to be seen as something separate from the injuries due to the fall. I suspect it may be a message of some sort, but that's your department, not mine.'

'Which may be why he was dragged off the tracks,' said Paget. 'The killer didn't want his face messed up by a train. But what's the message, I wonder?'

'As I said, not my problem,' Starkie said cheerfully. 'You're the detective.'

Much of Sunday had been taken up with chasing down and taking statements from everyone who had been at the meeting in Grayson's house on Friday night, to no avail. They all appeared to be stunned by the news of Billy Travis's death, and all said much the same thing. The last they had seen of him was when they left the house together at eleven o'clock on Friday night. As for the movements of Trudy Mason and her husband that night, everything checked out up to the time they said they had returned home, but from that point on it was simply the word of each of them that neither had left the house again until the following morning. Gordon Mason confirmed, albeit reluctantly, that he knew about his wife's arrangement with Billy, and claimed to have had no problem with it.

But, as Tregalles suggested when he and Paget met in the

car park and entered the building together, while Gordon Mason might have gone along with the arrangement initially, it was the sort of thing that might fester and prey on his mind during those long trips abroad. 'It could build up a lot of jealousy and resentment,' he said. 'He may have wanted it to end, but perhaps his wife didn't. He probably knew about Billy's Friday night visits to the camera club, and if Trudy Mason's a sound sleeper, it would be a simple matter to slip out of the house and lie in wait for Billy as he walked home.'

'Except for the timing,' Paget pointed out. 'I mean if Billy was walking home just after eleven, and if Trudy is telling the truth about the time she and her husband got home and went to bed, the opportunity would be gone.'

'Any chance that his wife could have been in on it, and is lying about the time?'

'I think her grief was genuine when Billy's father broke the news,' said Paget. 'And what would be her motive? From what I saw, she didn't want the relationship to stop. No, I'm sure the news of Billy's death came as a complete surprise. If it was Gordon Mason, I'm sure he acted alone.'

Tregalles nodded. 'It's a motive all right,' he agreed. 'All that time on the road, thinking about another bloke banging his wife every time he goes away, especially one who's ten or fifteen years younger than her. I can see him getting pretty worked up about it. But why take him all the way out to the Lessington Cut and carve an A in his forehead, for God's sake? Unless it's A for adulterer, do you think?'

'That might make more sense if it was his wife who was killed,' Paget said. 'But you're right about the Lessington Cut. It would mean being out of the house for several hours, and I don't think he could count on his wife not waking up at some point during that time.'

Early as Paget and Tregalles were that morning, Len Ormside, fresh back from holidays, was there ahead of them. They found the grizzled sergeant hunched over his desk, with a steaming mug of coffee beside him, reading the statements gathered over the weekend.

'Coffee . . .?' he offered when he saw Paget.

'Thanks but no thanks, Len,' said Paget. You needed a strong stomach to take Ormside's coffee first thing in the morning. 'How was the holiday?'

'It was all right. The wife enjoyed it,' the sergeant said, 'but I'm glad to be back at work. You've been busy while I was gone, haven't you?' He indicated the statements in front of him. 'Not much to go on, though, is there? What about this bloke Mason? I've heard of some odd things in this job, but I've never heard of a bloke going along with the idea of his wife having a toy boy on call while he was away.'

'That's what we're led to believe,' Paget told him. 'Tregalles and I were just discussing him on our way in, and he is a suspect, but I have the feeling the motive for this killing is more complicated than a jealous husband. This wasn't some random or spur-of-the-moment killing; this was planned. Someone went to a great deal of trouble to snatch Billy Travis off the street and kill him in a particular way.'

'Looks that way to me, too,' Ormside said. 'I've looked at the copy of the CCTV tape Forsythe brought in and there's no sign of Travis on it, so it looks as if the killer got to him before he got that far. This chap Grayson and the others who were at the meeting, would know Billy Travis would be walking home alone, so they're all suspects as far as I'm concerned, and we'll be digging into their backgrounds as well. Grayson's got form, but that was at the beginning of the 'nineties. He was arrested during the Poll Tax riots for defacing a public building, and for being in possession of a controlled substance, but that was twenty years ago and we've had nothing on him since. As for the others, we'll have to see. But there's something . . . I don't know . . . something not exactly *local* about this killing, if you know what I mean? Specially with that A carved in his forehead. Find out what that means, and we'll have our killer.'

Paget raised a quizzical eyebrow as he looked at Ormside. 'Just what time *did* you come in this morning, Len?' he asked.

Ormside shrugged. 'Not all that early,' he said, 'but when Tregalles rang me last evening to put me in the picture, I popped in for a couple of hours. Well . . .' he continued defensively as Paget continued to look at him, 'I didn't want to come in cold this morning. I knew there'd be more than enough to do without me having to waste time catching up, and Forsythe was here, so she helped fill me in.'

'I appreciate that,' Paget told him, 'but really, Len . . . I mean, just back from your holidays? What did your wife have to say about that?'

'After two weeks in a caravan together, she was glad to see the back of me,' Ormside said. 'Not that it wasn't good to get away for a change, but a week would have been enough. The rain that second week wasn't much help, either, so I think we were both happy to come home.'

The door opened and Molly Forsythe came in carrying a bottle of orange juice and a sandwich wrapped in a paper napkin. Knowing the sort of day it was likely to be, and that Ormside would most likely be at his desk, she had left the flat without stopping for breakfast. She was followed by several others, who filled their coffee mugs from the urn in the far corner of the room before moving on. Normally they would have lingered to talk about their weekend, but with Paget there, they cut the Monday morning ritual short and settled in behind their desks.

The door opened once again, and a woman entered. It seemed that everyone knew instinctively who the newcomer was, and conversation died. She stood there for a moment, pausing to look round. Tall and slim, she wore a plain white blouse, straight skirt of navy blue, and matching jacket, loosely open. Her hair, short and closely styled, was brown, and the eyes that met and held those of Paget were grey.

Amanda Pierce . . . *Detective Superintendent* Amanda Pierce, Paget reminded himself, and his new boss. He had been expecting her, yet her appearance still managed to surprise him. Thirty-nine years old, and she was still a very attractive woman. A little fuller in the face, perhaps, but still as trim and fit as he remembered. The sight of her brought back memories. Twelve years . . . He drew a deep breath, trying not to be too obvious about it as he stepped forward and said, 'Superintendent Pierce. Welcome to Charter Lane.'

Amanda Pierce acknowledged the invitation with a nod and a somewhat guarded smile, and said, 'Thank you, Chief Inspector. Am I too late for the briefing on the Travis case? If not, I would like to sit in, if I may?'

'Of course. But first, perhaps I could take a couple of minutes to introduce you to everyone here?' He was trying to strike the right note, but he knew the words sounded stiff and formal.

'Of course. I would appreciate that very much, Chief Inspector,' she said.

Beginning with Ormside, Paget led her around the room, and in each case the superintendent was the first to extend her hand and repeat the name. Each response was stiff, bordering on the awkward, but Amanda Pierce pretended not to notice. She paused in front of the whiteboards and looked at the information and the pictures posted there, then turned to Ormside. 'I understand you've just returned from holidays, Sergeant. Too bad you had to come back to this.'

Clearly taken by surprise, Ormside flashed a questioning glance at Paget, who shrugged and shook his head. 'I might say the same about you, Ma'am,' Ormside blurted. 'Coming in at a time like this, I mean.'

Amanda Pierce smiled tightly. 'Not quite the way I would have preferred to start,' she agreed, 'but neither of us have much choice, do we?' She turned to Paget. 'Now, if you would like to start the briefing, I'll sit at the back and listen. And when you're free, please come to see me in the office, and we can get started on the handover.'

The briefing didn't take long, so it was less than half an hour later when Paget followed Superintendent Pierce upstairs to her new office. Fiona was on the phone, but she threw Paget a questioning, almost pleading glance as he went by. He nodded reassuringly. Fiona was worried about her job. Senior officers who had become accustomed to working with a particular secretary sometimes brought the person they favoured with them when they moved to another job or were promoted, and Fiona was afraid that her job could be in jeopardy.

Once inside the office, Amanda Pierce waved Paget to a seat, then closed the door and sat down behind the desk to face him. She sat there for a moment, not quite sure how to begin. She'd prepared herself for this moment – at least she thought she had, but now, sitting here facing him, what seemed like a lifetime of memories tumbled through her head. He looked older, but then he was: twelve years older, and the lines around his mouth were deeper. His eyes were sharper than she remembered, but perhaps that was because he was facing her across a desk where he thought he should be sitting.

'First,' she said quietly, 'I would like you to know that I had no idea I would be in competition with you when I put my name in for this job, and in that sense I'm sorry it turned out this way. I know how it must look to you. Here we are competing on the same level; you should have had the inside track because you're familiar with the system and you're qualified for the job. However, I know as well as you do that I was chosen because pressure was coming from the local police authority to move a woman into a senior position. Your chief constable . . . I suppose I should say *our* chief constable, as good as told me so in that rather patronizing way of his.

'But the point I'm trying to make, Neil, is that I am qualified. I've worked damned hard to get where I am, but everything here is new to me, so I'm hoping we can work together and put the past behind us. I know what you must think of me, and I don't expect you to change your views, but if working together is going to be a problem, then I would like to know that now.'

'Put the past behind us?' Paget repeated softly, and shook his head. 'If only it were that easy,' he said quietly. 'But it isn't, is it, Amanda? You weren't there to see what your leaving did to Matthew, and what his death did to Jill, but I was.' He shook his head again. 'No, I'm sorry, Amanda, but I can't erase that memory from my mind.'

The muscles around Amanda's mouth tightened. 'I don't expect you to believe me,' she said quietly, 'but I had no choice. It was the only way.'

'If that was the case, then an explanation would have been nice. If you'd even come to the funeral . . .'

'I was at Jill's funeral,' she said quickly. 'I just didn't stay. I was told you were in hospital. The shock . . .?'

'That wasn't the funeral I was referring to,' Paget said coldly. He was about to say more, but held back. What was the point? Whether he liked it or not, they were going to be working together, so they would have to make the best of it. He was prepared to do that on a professional level, and so, probably, was Amanda. But on a personal level . . .? *That* was something else again.

'As far as the job's concerned,' he said carefully, 'you will have my full cooperation and I won't let you down, so let's leave it at that, shall we?'

'I can live with that,' Amanda said stiffly, 'and I'll do my best to work with you and your team. However . . .' Her voice hardened and the lines around her mouth deepened. 'I want to make one thing very clear. I'm well aware that I'm coming into what might be called a hostile environment, and I'm very much aware that there will be resentment. I could feel it downstairs as I went around this morning. I know you have quite a following, and I understand that. But this job will be hard enough without having to worry about people undermining me, so I want you to understand that if I do find anything like that going on, I won't hesitate to deal with it. Is that understood?'

Paget's eyes were icy as they met those of Amanda Pierce. 'Understood,' he said. 'So where would you like to start?'

Molly Forsythe put on her seat belt and checked the address once more. One of the men at Ted Grayson's house on Friday had been out when she called round yesterday, but his wife had suggested that Molly catch him at work today.

She repeated the address to herself as she set off, but her mind was already drifting to other things that had been bothering her for days.

Molly had been a sergeant now for exactly two weeks. She'd been over the moon when she'd first heard the news of her promotion, and the next few days had gone by in a sort of blurred euphoria. But more and more, these past few days, her thoughts had turned to David Chen and what the future might have in store for each of them.

David was the nephew of Dr Starkie's wife, Ellen, and he'd just returned from a three-year stint with Doctors Without Borders when she met him. They'd hit it off immediately, and when David said he was considering taking a job in Broadminster hospital, Molly was thrilled at the prospect.

But suddenly everything changed. David's ex-wife, Meilan, living in Hong Kong with their daughter, Lijuan, had been seriously injured in a traffic accident on her way to work, and David had flown to Hong Kong to join his daughter at her mother's bedside, arriving only hours before Meilan died.

Once the funeral was over, and conscious of the fact that the offer of a job in Broadminster would not remain open indefinitely, his immediate reaction was return to England to make arrangements for his daughter to come back to live with him. But once there he began to have second thoughts. Lijuan, he told Molly, had been born in England, but after spending the last six years in Hong Kong with her mother and maternal grandmother, he wondered how fair it would be to take her away from everything she knew to start afresh in England.

'I know she's happy there,' he said. 'Her friends are there; she enjoys school and she's doing well. And she and her grandmother are very close. I'd like to have her come and live with me, but it would mean that she would have to leave everything and everyone she's known for the past six years, and I really don't know how well she would adjust to a totally different lifestyle. England's changed since she was here before. I've only been away for three years, but I notice it, and I'm not sure it's for the better. And fourteen is such a critical age. What do you think, Molly?'

She hadn't known what to say, but David was looking at her so hopefully that she felt she had to say something. 'I'm afraid that's one decision that only you and Lijuan can make,' she'd said. 'From what you've told me, your daughter sounds like a very level-headed girl, and I'm wondering if it wouldn't be better to give her some time to get used to the fact that her mother is gone before making a decision of any kind. Then sit down with her and talk it through. I know how much you would like your daughter with you; that's only natural, but it's *her* life and her future that will be affected most of all.'

His eyes had remained fixed on her for what seemed like ages before he nodded slowly and said, 'You're right. I've been so focused on what *I* want that I was in danger of forgetting that.' David had reached out to take her hand in his.

'Thank you for reminding me, Molly. I'm so glad I have you to talk to.'

He was gone the next day, back to Hong Kong, and Molly had been wondering ever since if the advice she had offered was self-serving. Leaving his daughter with her grandmother, at least for the time being, would allow him to come back to take up the new job in the hospital, and they could resume their relationship without the distraction of the resettlement of Lijuan. A daughter, she thought guiltily, who might see her as competing for her father's affections, and might well resent her.

The traffic lights ahead turned red. Molly slowed and stopped. Perhaps she was being silly. Perhaps there was no 'relationship'. Perhaps she'd misread the signs because she so wanted them to be true.

The lights changed. Molly gave herself a mental shake, annoyed for letting her mind wander, especially when she should be concentrating on her job. As a new detective sergeant, she couldn't afford to make any mistakes; this was not a time to be daydreaming on the job. But one thought in particular kept niggling away at the back of her mind. She didn't know why it hadn't registered before, but now that Paget would *not* be moving up, she wondered what her chances were of staying here. Tregalles was firmly entrenched as Paget's number one sergeant, which meant there really wasn't a place for her, and she could be transferred to almost anywhere in the Westvale Region. She might also be encouraged – or forced – to take a position outside the region altogether.

So, even if David did feel the same way about her as she did about him, and he did take the job at the hospital in Broadminster, where would that leave them?

One thing she knew: she did not want to leave her job. She had worked too hard and too long to give up now. She enjoyed her work and she was good at it, and if Superintendent Pierce could make it that far up the ladder, then why couldn't she do the same? As for the immediate future . . . it would appear that her fate lay in the laps of seemingly whimsical gods.

* * *

Tregalles dropped into a chair next to Ormside's desk, raised his hands above his head and stretched. 'You have anything new for me, Len?' he asked wearily. 'I'm no further ahead than I was this morning.'

'Same here,' said Ormside. 'Nothing from the door-to-door enquiries along Travis's normal route, so I'm going to broaden the area tomorrow in case he took another way home. I can't see why he would, but we'll do it anyway just to be sure. I've had men out talking to the farmers and people who travel the road out to Lessington, but no one seems to have seen or heard anything out of the ordinary.'

'I just don't get it,' Tregalles said. 'This Billy Travis lives and works with his father. He's not much of a drinker; he doesn't smoke; he doesn't gamble; and about the only socializing he does has to do with the church where he sings in the choir and attends the odd Saturday morning men's breakfast, where he sometimes makes the tea. He doesn't seem to have any close friends. None of the members of this camera club he goes to say they see him at any other time, so all that leaves is his dad and Trudy Mason. As for Gordon Mason, I think he might have gone along with this arrangement in the beginning out of a feeling of guilt, but once he got out there on the road and had time to think about what was going on back home, I don't think he'd like it, and he would want it to stop. Maybe he tried to get her to stop, but she wouldn't, so he decided to do something about it himself.'

'I thought you and Paget had decided the timing was wrong, and Mason couldn't have done it?' Ormside said.

'We did, at least *he* did,' Tregalles agreed, 'but I still think there's something weird about a man who would agree to something like that. So he's still a suspect as far as I'm concerned.'

'And he's still on my list as well,' Ormside conceded, 'but it seems to me that this is more like a ritual killing. I put out a request for information of any similar style killings anywhere in the country, but I've had no response.'

'Maybe it has something to do with a picture he took?'

Ormside frowned. 'Picture? What picture?'

'Dunno, but he was a photographer, so maybe he took a

picture of someone or something he wasn't supposed to and he was killed for it.'

Ormside looked sceptical. 'You think he was *blackmailing* someone and they turned on him?' He shook his head. 'Doesn't fit the profile I have of him,' he said. 'His bank account, such as it is, doesn't show any unusual deposits or withdrawals.'

'So maybe he wasn't into blackmail, but perhaps he'd taken someone's picture when they didn't want it taken, and they wanted it back?'

'Someone . . .?' Ormside challenged. 'Such as . . .?'

'I don't know *who*, exactly,' Tregalles said irritably. 'I'm just throwing out ideas. All I'm saying is it *could* be something like that.'

Ormside shook his head. 'There's more to it than that,' he said flatly. 'The killer wanted Travis to be found, and he made sure we would notice the A on Travis's scalp by preserving it under a strip of tape.'

'Which, if you're right, brings us back to a gang killing,' Tregalles countered as he got to his feet, 'and I can't see Travis as a gang member, no matter how hard I try. Trouble is, I can't think of any other motive that makes sense.' He smothered a yawn. 'Anyway, that's enough for one day. Maybe we'll have better luck tomorrow.'

FIVE

When Paget opened the front door and stepped inside, Grace was waiting for him with a full glass of wine in her hand. 'I thought you might need this,' she said as he took off his coat and hung it up. 'First day with the new boss and all that. Although it couldn't have been all that bad, because you're home early for a change. How *did* it go?' Her tone was light, but there was an undercurrent of tension in her voice.

Paget looked thoughtful as he considered the question. 'Surprisingly well, considering,' he said slowly as if reluctant to admit it. 'At least as far as work's concerned. Amanda's changed. It's almost as if she's a different woman from the one I remember, and if today is any indication, she has what it takes to do the job.' His face clouded and the muscles around his jaw tightened. 'But I find it hard to look at her without remembering what she did and what it did to Jill's brother Matthew. And to Jill herself.'

'You said she's changed,' Grace probed cautiously as they made their way into the living room. 'In what way?'

Paget settled into his chair and sipped his wine before replying. 'Just . . . different,' he said. 'I don't mean physically, although she's looking a lot better than she was the last time I saw her twelve years ago. She's more assertive, more in control of herself than I remember, and hard as it is for me to say, I think she may turn out to be very good at her job. She's a quick learner and extremely sharp. Mind you she always was, and if it had been anyone else, I would have said it was a pleasure to work with her today.' He twirled the glass in his fingers as he looked off into the distance. 'But I don't think I shall ever be able to say that about Amanda Pierce, no matter how much she may have changed or how well she may do her job.'

Grace kicked off her slippers, tucked her feet under her, and settled herself into a corner of the sofa. 'I know this is a sensitive subject for you, Neil,' she said, 'and if you don't want to talk about it, that's your choice. But it would make it a lot easier for me if you would tell me what this woman did that was so terrible. Then, perhaps I could understand why you feel the way you do towards her.'

Paget stared into his glass for a long moment, before draining it and setting it aside. 'Amanda Pierce was Jill's best friend,' he said. 'They were at school together; they joined the Service together; trained together. They were like sisters. I liked her. In fact, when a group of us first started to go around together, it was a toss-up between Jill and Amanda as to which one I liked best. In the end, of course, I married Jill, but we all remained good friends, and when Amanda and Jill's younger brother, Matthew, started seeing each other, Jill and I were both very happy about it. Amanda was a detective constable in Muswell Hill at the time, and Matthew was still at university, but he didn't seem particularly satisfied with what he was doing there, and he'd talked of quitting. So when he and Amanda announced their engagement, and Matthew said he'd decided to stay on at uni, Jill was thrilled. She thought Amanda was just the sort of woman Matthew needed to settle him down. They were married and everything seemed to be working out beautifully . . . at least at first.'

Paget paused, frowning. 'I don't know what happened, or when we first became aware that things had changed,' he said slowly. 'I know it took Jill and I a while to realize that they seemed to be avoiding us. In the past, before we were married as well as after, the four of us had always mucked in together. Our jobs and odd working hours kept us apart a lot of the time, so when there was an opportunity to get together, it would be a spur-of-the-moment thing. Jill might call Amanda and say something like, "Neil picked up a nice bit of fish on his way home but it's more than we can manage, would you like to come and help us eat it?" and they'd be there in half an hour. Or Matthew might ring up and say he was fed up with homework, so how about joining them in the pub? Or one of us would be doing a bit of painting or wallpapering, and the others would drop in to give a hand and have a beer afterwards. You know the sort of thing.'

Paget looked at Grace. 'What I'm saying is that it had been like that from the time we first met. We enjoyed each other's company, so we'd get together whenever we could. But then, as I said, it changed. If we rang them, they would make excuses: Amanda was working an extra shift, or Matthew was studying hard for another exam, or "things are a bit hectic at work right now. Perhaps next week." But we would learn later that there was no extra shift, and there was no exam, and they never called us back. We saw less and less of them, and when we did it was as if we were strangers. Jill tried to talk to Amanda, tried to find out what was wrong, but Amanda acted as if she didn't know what Jill was talking about. So Jill tried talking to Matthew. She and Matthew had always been very close, but, like Amanda, he insisted that nothing was wrong, and became quite angry and defensive when she tried to push him. Jill and I talked about it endlessly, trying to come up with a reason. Had we done something wrong? Something to offend them? We wondered if they had money problems. With Matthew at university, they were living solely on Amanda's salary. They'd both agreed there would be no children, at least for the first few years, but we wondered if Amanda was pregnant, and they were worried about how they were going to manage.'

He paused, eyes focused on some distant image from the past as he said, 'It was late at night, a Thursday, the twentieth of May, when Matthew rang to ask if Amanda was with us. When we told him we hadn't seen her, and asked if anything was wrong, he said no, Amanda was probably working late, and apologized for calling so late at night. Jill asked him why he thought she might be with us, and he said Amanda had said she might call in, and no, he didn't know the reason, and he'd better go because Amanda might be trying to call him, and he rang off. But something didn't sound right. Neither one of them had set foot in our place for six months or more, so Jill tried to call Matthew back, but she kept getting the engaged tone.'

Paget made a face. 'To be honest, Jill was more concerned than I was,' he confessed. 'Matthew was only a couple of years younger than Jill, but she'd taken on the role of mother after their parents died, and even though he was now a big, six-foot-two bear of a man, Jill still treated him as if he were her baby brother. I thought she was worrying needlessly, but just in case there was something amiss, I stopped by their flat on my way to work next morning. Matthew, all bleary-eyed and looking like he'd been up half the night, came to the door in his pyjamas. He smelled of drink. But when I asked him if everything was all right, and if Amanda had come home, he said, "Oh, yes, she got home just after midnight, so she's sleeping in this morning." When I told him Jill had been worried, and asked why he hadn't let us know, he said he thought it was too late to call, and apologized for having troubled us at all.'

Paget's lips twisted into a wry smile. 'But Jill still wasn't satisfied. She sensed *something* was wrong, so she kept going after Matthew until he finally broke down and told her that Amanda had left him for another man. Neither Jill nor I could bring ourselves to believe it . . . that is until we found that Amanda had put in a letter of resignation weeks before she disappeared. I spoke to her boss myself, a DI Joan Baxter in Kentish Town, where Amanda was working at the time, and she said Amanda's letter of resignation came out of the blue. No warning; no indication that she was thinking of leaving. She said she'd asked her if it had anything to do with the job, but Amanda said no, it was a personal matter. She regretted having to leave, but a situation had come up concerning a close member of the family who needed her, and since she would be away for an extended period of time, it was best that she resign. So everything was arranged for Amanda to leave at the end of the month, but suddenly she was gone ten days before that. No warning; not a word to anyone. She just failed to come in one day, and Baxter said she hadn't seen or heard from her since. I asked her when, exactly, Amanda had failed to come into work, and she said it was Thursday, May the twentieth.'

Paget's eyes were bleak as he looked at Grace. 'Matthew went to pieces,' he said. 'He told us he'd suspected Amanda was having an affair with someone at work for months, but neither I nor Jill could find anyone who'd worked with her who believed that. They said they were sure they would have known. As one co-worker put it, "you can't keep something like that secret for very long around here." But, true or not, Matthew had convinced himself, and there was no arguing with him.

'Matthew had always liked his drink,' Paget continued, 'but from that point on he *really* started to drink heavily. He resisted every attempt we made to help him, and three months later he was dead. Walked straight out into the street in front of a bus in Kensington High Street. Killed instantly. The driver never had a chance to stop. Everyone who saw it said it was quite deliberate on Matthew's part. Jill was devastated. Not only had she lost her brother, but she felt betrayed by her best friend, and she never forgave Amanda for what she'd done.'

* * *

They had spoken very little during dinner, avoiding any more talk about Amanda Pierce, but once the washing up was out of the way, and Grace had made a fresh pot of coffee, the talk turned to the death of Billy Travis.

'We may learn more once we dig deeper into the man's background,' Paget said, 'but he just doesn't seem to fit the profile of a man who would be killed in such a specific way. This is more like the sort of thing we used to see now and again in the Met – a killing designed to send a message to a rival gang. But Billy Travis certainly doesn't fit that picture. Mind you, it was a very dark night, raining on and off, so he could have been killed by mistake, but the gangs we have here don't operate at that level. At least they haven't up to now. Tregalles suggested it might have something to do with a photograph Travis took of someone or something, either deliberately or by accident, and someone took exception to it. But if that were the case, I would have expected to see the shop or his room ransacked, and Billy Travis shot or stabbed or strangled. This business of taking him out into the country and dropping him off a bridge, and carving the letter A on his forehead, just doesn't make sense.'

'I'm afraid Tregalles may have picked that up from me,' said Grace. 'Charlie thought his death might have had something to do with his work, so he had me and Lyle Kruger, our forensic photographer, spend the day going through Travis's files. We ignored anything taken more than five years ago, assuming that, if such a picture had been taken, it would have to be a fairly recent one to provoke that kind of reaction.

'But we soon realized it was a pretty hopeless task. Even if such a picture existed, chances were we wouldn't recognize it. I take it you've ruled out Trudy Mason's husband, Gordon, as a suspect?'

Paget hesitated. 'I had more or less dismissed him,' he said, 'but another possibility just occurred to me. Mason is a long distance lorry driver. Trudy said he'd just come back from Antwerp. What if he's involved in smuggling, as some of them are, and Billy Travis found out about it? Through pillow talk, perhaps?' He shook his head. 'Do I sound as if I'm clutching at straws?'

Grace didn't answer directly. 'Where's Mason now?' she asked.

'We had no reason to hold him or take away his passport, so he's back at work.'

'So, what will you be doing tomorrow? Is there anything more we can do? I'm sure I can square it with Charlie if there is.'

'Thanks, but I don't think there is at the moment,' he said. 'As for what I'll be doing, I'm afraid I'm going to be stuck in the office with Amanda for the next week or two until we get things sorted. With Alcott leaving so abruptly, and then with me trying to do his job as well as my own, a lot of things were shoved to the bottom of the pile, so she's going to need me there until things settle down a bit.'

'So you are prepared to work with her, then?'

Paget spread his hands in a gesture of resignation. 'Regardless of what I think of her, I can't ignore the fact that both she and I have a job to do, and we can't afford to let personal feelings get in the way. So, yes, I'll work with her, but don't ask me to like her or forgive her for what she did.'

Later that night as they lay side by side in bed, both pretending to be asleep, Paget's mind drifted back to those dark days of twelve years ago. Jill had taken Matthew's death extremely hard. 'I thought she was my friend!' he recalled her whispering fiercely at the graveside. 'Matthew was so in love with her. She as good as killed him, Neil, and I can never forgive her for that!'

Friday, 7 October

The morning briefing was not going well. A small army of men and women had spent the best part of a week knocking on doors and talking to people in the streets. Cars passing through the area were stopped and drivers questioned: had they been in the area last Friday night or Saturday morning? If so, what had they seen? What had they heard? Did anything unusual occur?

Although Travis had been a member of the All Saints church choir for many years, there was no one who claimed to be a particular friend of his. As one member put it, 'Billy always seemed to be anxious to get home. He came to services and choir practice and sang with the rest of us, then he left. He did his bit when it was his turn to brew the tea for the Saturday morning men's club, but even then he spent most of his time in the kitchen.'

Superintendent Amanda Pierce had authorized an appeal for information over the local radio stations, beginning on Tuesday evening, but apart from the calls from the usual glory-seekers, that, too, had failed to bring any fresh leads.

According to the toxicology report, Billy Travis's blood-alcohol level was consistent with the two beers Ted Grayson said he'd had. There was no evidence of Billy having taken drugs, and he didn't smoke. In fact, apart from being almost a stone overweight for his age and size, Billy Travis had been a perfectly healthy thirty-two year old.

His personal mobile calls for the past three months were checked. Calls made to and from the phones in the house and shop were checked. Billy's laptop was still in the lab, but if the preliminary findings were any indication, it, too, would not be much help. Tregalles and Molly Forsythe had talked again to Billy's father; they'd spoken to friends and neighbours; and they, as well as others on the team, had followed up on the jobs he'd done recently, but they had all come up empty.

'I think they got it wrong,' Tregalles declared as he stood before the whiteboards and stared at the picture of Billy Travis. 'As far as I can see, there was no reason to kill this man. None whatsoever. He's clean, so I think whoever did this got the wrong man. It was a dark night and the light's poor on those back streets. We keep coming back to the idea that this looks more like a gang killing than anything else, and Billy simply doesn't fit the picture. So, maybe the person who got the job had never seen the person he was sent to kill and he got it wrong.'

'Except we've never seen that level of violence in Broadminster before,' Paget pointed out, 'and there's nothing here that's big enough to attract the sort of gang you're suggesting.'

'They wouldn't have to be here, though, would they?'

Tregalles countered. 'They could be in any one of the big cities, but perhaps the man they were after was hiding out here, and they sent someone to kill him. But the killer got it wrong, and if he realizes his mistake, he could try again.'

'You may be right,' Paget conceded, 'but in the meantime, let's not lose sight of the fact that it was Billy Travis who was killed, and just because we haven't found a motive, it doesn't mean there isn't one.' He paused, mentally checking off the list of things they'd discussed. 'Do *you* have anything to add?' he asked Ormside hopefully.

'Sorry, boss,' he said, 'but as far as the Travis case is concerned, I'm afraid we've run out of leads.'

SIX

Thursday, 13 October

Eyes still shut, Dennis Moreland reached out with a practised hand to smother the alarm clock beside the bed. The bell was set on low, but it still sounded loud in the small bedroom. His wife, Joan, stirred beside him but she remained asleep. After so many years of her husband getting up at quarter past five each workday morning, she had learned to ignore the bell.

He lay there for a moment, eyes still closed, listening for the sound of rain in the pipe outside the bedroom window, and hoping he'd made a mistake and it was Sunday and he didn't have to get up. No sound, so that was good. But it was Thursday, and that meant he'd better get moving if he was to get to work on time.

He slid out of bed, picked up his clothes from the chair by the door and took them into the bathroom. Twenty minutes later, washed and dressed and shaved, he emerged. Michael, their ten year old, must be lying on his back again, because Moreland could hear the boy snoring as he passed his door. He paused to peep into Laura's room, then went in. All the bedclothes were on the floor, and she was curled up in a ball in the middle of the bed. Laura was eight, and a restless sleeper. He picked up the clothes and laid them gently over her, but he knew they'd probably end up on the floor again.

It was ten minutes to six when he left the house. He never stopped for breakfast – that would mean getting up fifteen minutes earlier – so he usually waited for the fresh buns to come out of the bakery at eight, then had one with a slice of Gouda and a coffee from the deli. He stood for a moment, breathing in the morning air. His hand and sleeve came away wet as he brushed past the car in the driveway. So there had been some rain in the night, and there was a nip in the air, a reminder that summer was definitely behind them. And he was sure it was darker than it had been at the beginning of the week, and only yesterday, Joan had been talking about having a look round the market on the weekend for a bit of jewellery for her sister in Australia for Christmas.

Dennis Moreland hunched into his coat, thrust his hands in his pockets and set off.

There was a van in the street halfway down the hill. The rear doors were open and there were several tins of paint and a plastic bucket sitting on the pavement beside the van. A man, wearing paint-smeared overalls and a cap, was leaning inside the van. He straightened up and flexed his hands as Moreland approached. 'Bloody ladder,' he grumbled loudly. 'Here, would you mind giving me a hand, mate? Just to get it out of the van. It's an awkward thing. Heavy. Only take a minute.'

'Starting work early, aren't you?' Moreland said as he stepped into the road.

'Got another lot to fetch as well,' the man explained, 'so I thought I'd get an early start. If you'd just lean in there and pull, I'll get in and push from the other end. All right? Mind your head.'

'Right.' Dennis Moreland bent forward to lean into the van and grasp the ladder . . .

Joan Moreland came awake to the sound of the telephone ringing. She raised herself on one elbow and squinted at the clock next to the phone on the far side of the bed. Twenty to seven. Who on earth . . .?

Not fully awake, her mind ran through the possibilities as she clambered across the bed and reached for the phone. Probably a wrong number, she told herself, but a call at this time of the morning was a bit worrying all the same.

'Hello . . .?'

'Joanie . . .? It's Norm. Is Dennis there?'

Norman Beasley, Dennis's boss. She frowned into the phone. 'What do you mean, is he here? Isn't he there?'

'If he was I wouldn't be ringing you, now would I, Joanie? Is he ill or just skiving off? Only we've got a lot on today and we need him here.'

She wished he wouldn't call her Joanie. She'd told him often enough but he still did it. It made her feel as if she were six years old. She ran her fingers through her hair, trying to bring herself fully awake. 'He's gone,' she said. 'He . . . I mean I think he has. Hang on a minute, Norman. I'll go and look.' She put the phone down and struggled into her dressing gown as she left the room.

Not in the bathroom. She took a quick look in each of the kids' rooms before going downstairs. 'Dennis?' she called at the foot of the stairs. Silence. Worried now, she went through the rooms. She opened the back door and peered out. Silly, of course he wouldn't be there. Then the front door. The car was still there. She padded out to the street and looked both ways. A man on a bicycle sped past, and a boy was delivering papers across the street, but there was no sign of Dennis. She went back to the kitchen and picked up the phone on the counter.

'You wouldn't be having me on, would you, Norman?' she asked tartly. 'I mean he went off to work same time as usual; he has to be there.'

'Well he's not, love, so when you find out what he's playing at, tell him to get himself down here. OK?'

Frowning, Joan Moreland hung up the phone, then made her way upstairs to replace the extension as well. What could Dennis be up to? Where could he have gone? It wasn't like him to go wandering off. She got dressed, then sat down on the bed to try to think what to do. He couldn't have had an accident or she'd have heard, and it was no distance at all from the house to where he worked at the SuperFair market. A two-minute walk, that was all. Dennis *must* be at work. Probably doing something in the back, and Norm hadn't bothered to check. Either that or it was some sort of wind-up by Norman Beasley. It was the sort of thing he might do and think it funny, and if that were the case, there was no point in worrying about it. She looked at the clock. Soon be time to get the kids up anyway, so she might as well start getting breakfast ready. She'd wait a while, then ring the market and ask for Dennis. Just to be sure.

Paget sat back in his chair and said, 'I'm sorry, Amanda, but it's just not possible. We're short-staffed as it is. There have been no replacements for almost a year now. On the one hand we're being criticized for our clear-up rate and the time it takes to complete an investigation, and for the amount of overtime, and now you're suggesting we cut staff by five per cent. It's a simple equation, so if this is your idea of a way to impress Mr Brock, then I suggest you find another way.'

Amanda had objected to Paget calling her 'Ma'am'. 'I don't like the term,' she told him flatly. 'Superintendent in public, but in private, when we're working one on one, I would prefer to use first names, if you have no objection?'

His instinctive reaction had been to balk at that himself. It suggested a not so subtle attempt on Amanda's part to break down the barrier that so clearly existed between them. But even as that was going through his mind, he knew it would sound petty, even spiteful to refuse. They could hardly go on addressing each other as 'Superintendent' and 'Chief Inspector' as they sat together day after day in her office, so he'd agreed.

Amanda, who had been searching for something on the screen on her desk, turned to him. 'I know you don't think much of me,' she said quietly, 'but I think even you will concede that I'm not stupid. I know as well as you do the consequences of such cuts, but I have no choice. Mr Brock made it very clear that it's not negotiable. Believe me, Neil, I've given the chief superintendent my opinion regarding where these cuts will lead, but I might as well have saved my breath, so let's stop wasting time on a fight we can't win.'

The uniformed constable facing her when Joan Moreland opened the door looked almost too young to be a policeman. 'Mrs Moreland?' he enquired. 'Constable Lowry. You reported your husband missing?'

The man appeared little more than a teenager. Joan Moreland looked past him, hoping to see someone more senior, but the man was alone and there was no one else in the police car at the kerb. She hesitated, then sighed and said, 'You'd better come in.

'I sent the kids off to school. I didn't want to worry them,' she explained when they sat facing each other in the living room. 'I wasn't too worried at first, when his boss phoned to ask where Dennis was, but after I'd phoned round and nobody had seen him, I rang the hospital, the ambulance people, then you. The car's still here, and I've been up and down the road to ask if anybody saw him this morning – that was after I rang you – but nobody had.'

'And he's how old, Mrs Moreland?'

'Thirty-two. Well, he'll be thirty-three at the end of the month.'

'Has he been worried about anything recently? Has he said or done anything unusual? Is he taking any medication?'

Joan shook her head to each question. 'No,' she said impatiently, 'and they asked me all that when I rang to report him missing.'

'If you'll just bear with me, Mrs Moreland. I know this must be worrying for you, but the more information we have, the better. You mentioned his boss. Where does Mr Moreland work?'

'He works for SuperFair down the bottom of the road. He's a butcher. I mean, what could have happened to him between here and there?' Joan Moreland's eyes were suddenly moist.

'I'm sure there's a reasonable explanation and your husband will turn up,' Lowry said soothingly. He continued doggedly through the standard list of questions. Names and addresses of friends and relatives. The name of Dennis's boss. Places he might be. Had there been any trouble at work? And, as delicately as he could, the probing questions about the state of their marriage.

'We're a very happy family,' Joan said tartly, 'and I resent the implication that we're not. Dennis is a good husband and father, so if you're suggesting—'

'But I'm not,' a now red-faced Lowry broke in hastily. 'I have to ask those questions, Mrs Moreland. It's routine. Honestly.' He rose to his feet. 'And we will do everything we can to find your husband. But before I go, I'd like to take a look around the house, if you don't mind?'

Joan Moreland bristled. 'What for?' she demanded. 'Do you think Dennis is hiding somewhere? I told you, he left the house to go to work.'

'It's standard procedure,' he said weakly. 'It's—'

'I know,' she broke in wearily as she got to her feet, 'it's routine. So what do we do now?'

'Perhaps we could start upstairs,' Lowry suggested. 'And do you have a greenhouse or a garden shed?'

Paget stayed late that evening to catch up on his own work. Not only was Amanda Pierce new to the job, she was in a completely new environment, so there was a lot to learn in a short space of time. To be fair, she grasped things quickly, and reluctant as Paget was to give her credit for anything, he had to admit that she was working very hard. But he knew it must be frustrating for her to have to rely so heavily on him, knowing how he felt about her.

He looked at the clock. Ten minutes to nine. Time to pack it in. Time, too, he told himself as he gathered up the files on his desk and locked them away for the night, to forget about Amanda Pierce, at least until tomorrow. But that was easier said than done.

In spite of everything he knew about her, Paget couldn't help but feel a grudging respect for the way Amanda was tackling her new job, but, as he kept reminding himself, that could never excuse what she had done to Matthew, and to Jill, when she disappeared without a word to anyone.

Amanda had known Matthew as long as she and Jill had

known each other, but because of the difference in their ages, it wasn't until shortly before Jill and Paget were married that Amanda and Matthew started to take notice of each other. Suddenly, Matthew was no longer just Jill's young brother, and sitting there now in the quiet of his office, Paget remembered how thrilled Jill had been when Matthew and Amanda announced their engagement.

'He needs the steadying hand of someone like Amanda,' she'd said. 'I'm so pleased.'

Paget pushed his chair back and stood up. So what had gone wrong, he wondered. How long had their relationship been in trouble before either he or Jill had become aware of it? How could this woman, Jill's best and closest friend for years, so callously and so deliberately walk away without a word of explanation, and leave Matthew in such despair that he'd committed suicide?

Would he ever know the truth, he wondered as he stepped out into the night. A few leaves scurried before a fitful wind to find refuge in a corner behind the steps, and another leaf fluttered past his face as he made his way to his car. Change was in the air, he thought . . . and not only with the weather.

Friday, 14 October

The investigation into the killing of Billy Travis had all but ground to a halt due to lack of both evidence and apparent motive. The suspicion that he had been the victim of mistaken identity was beginning to take hold, so while every facet of Billy's life was still being examined under a microscope, and background checks were being done on virtually everyone he had ever known, the case was at a standstill.

While a comprehensive search on the police national computer for crimes of a similar nature produced a number of cases involving the use of duct tape, beatings and/or killings, none included plastic cable ties or dropping the victim from a bridge or high place of any kind, nor was there any mention of a letter of the alphabet carved on the victim's forehead.

'Unless someone comes forward with new evidence, I'm dropping back to normal weekend staff levels,' Paget told

Amanda that afternoon. 'I wish there was more that we could be doing, but at least it'll keep the overtime down, so that should please Mr Brock.'

But Chief Superintendent Morgan Brock was not pleased. Sitting in his New Street office, surrounded by his beloved charts and graphs, he did not relish trying to explain the lack of progress to the chief constable.

He read the brief report from Detective Superintendent Pierce again, half hoping he would find something he'd missed, but the message was plain and simple: without a motive, without physical evidence, and without a single witness, the investigation was at a standstill. In fact there was even some doubt that Billy Travis was the intended victim.

Brock tossed the report onto his desk. Blunt words and not an auspicious start for Superintendent Pierce, he thought dourly, but then he'd had his doubts about her suitability for the job from the very beginning. But political correctness was what it was all about these days, and when your chief constable tells you, in confidence, that he's 'rather in favour of the idea', it pays to take that into consideration when casting one's vote.

The woman did have an excellent record, but under normal circumstances Paget would have been the clear choice: he had the background and he knew the job. On the other hand he could be a bit headstrong and hard to manage, and he couldn't always be persuaded to see the big picture and the need for compromise, so perhaps the appointment of Amanda Pierce had some merit after all. Only time would tell.

SEVEN

Saturday, 15 October

Ron Jackson shrugged into his coat as he came out of the house and looked up at the sky. 'Looks like a good one,' he said to his son, Jimmy. 'Ready to go, are you? Got your hammer and your goggles?'

'Here, Dad.' The boy held up a satchel. 'And Mum did me a sandwich and some water.'

'Good lad. Give your mum a kiss, then.' Ron turned and gave his wife a peck on the cheek.

'And you be careful,' Alice Jackson warned her son for at least the umpteenth time in the last ten minutes. 'And make sure you put those goggles on.' She looked across the boy's head at her husband. 'And mind what you're doing with that sledgehammer,' she said. 'Chips fly in all directions, so make sure Jimmy's well away from you when you're breaking those stones up.'

'Don't worry, love, I'll bring him home safe and sound.' He and the boy made their way to the pickup truck in the driveway and got in.

'Got your phone?' his wife called as he backed into the street. He nodded and waved.

Alice watched until the pickup turned the corner and disappeared. 'And do be careful,' she whispered as she went back into the house.

It was a short drive, three miles up the valley before taking the side road that wound its way through trees to the top of Clapperton Hill, where the paved road ended at a lookout point. But Jackson carried on, following a well-worn track across the moorland for close to a quarter of a mile before coming to a halt before a wire fence and gate. Half buried in the scrubby grass beside the gate was a rusted sign that had at one time warned all and sundry to *Keep Out*.

Jimmy jumped out and ran to open the gate, then waited for his father to drive through before closing the gate and getting back into the pickup. Jackson drove slowly along the strip of turf between the wire fence and the edge of the quarry, then began the spiral descent to the relatively flat surface of the quarry floor. Once parked, Jimmy, with goggles already in place, pulled his small hammer from the satchel and got out.

'That's where I got the good ones last time, Dad,' he said, pointing to a pile of smaller stones at the base of the cliff. 'The red ones, remember, Dad? Can I get some more?'

Ron got out and set the seven-pound sledge down beside

him while he slipped his own goggles over his head to hang around his neck as he looked around. He didn't need the small stuff, but it would keep Jimmy busy for a while. 'Right,' he said. 'But stay right there. Remember what I've told you about climbing?'

The boy nodded and said, 'Yes, Dad,' as he scampered off, hammer in hand.

Ron picked up the sledgehammer and walked over to a pile of larger stones. He'd done well here last week. Most of the stones had split without shattering; just what he needed for the rock wall he was building at home. He glanced up at the cliff face towering above him. It looked safe enough, but he was a cautious man, so he'd made it a practice to pick out the stones that looked promising, then carry them away from the base of the cliff before attacking them with the sledge.

He clambered onto one of the larger slabs to take a better look . . . and froze. He glanced back at the boy. Jimmy was hammering away quite happily. Ron Jackson picked his way carefully over the jumble of rocks until he came to the body. He looked up. The man had to be dead after a fall like that. Even so . . . He bent to take a closer look, then drew back.

The man's hands were bound together behind his back, his mouth was covered with duct tape, and his hair was matted with blood . . . Ron Jackson sucked in his breath and took out his phone.

Paget and Grace were sitting in the kitchen of a farmhouse half a mile up the road from home when the call came through on Paget's mobile phone. He and Grace had walked up the hill to pick up a fresh supply of free-range eggs, and they had been invited to stay for a cup of tea and to sample some freshly made scones. Two minutes later, Grace received a similar call, so they made their apologies and returned to the house, where Grace picked up her working gear, then followed Neil to the quarry in her own car.

Tregalles was there already, as was Superintendent Pierce. 'Looks like he came off that piece jutting out up there,' Tregalles said, pointing. 'A sixty-foot drop, give or take. His name is Dennis Moreland. He was reported missing by his wife last

Thursday. He's a butcher by trade, at least he was, and he vanished on his way to work around six o'clock on Thursday morning.' Tregalles grimaced. 'And you're not going to like this, I'm afraid, boss: he's got a dressing on his forehead like the one on Billy Travis's forehead.'

'Same initial?' Paget asked.

'Don't know yet. Doc Starkie's only just arrived and I didn't like to mess with it before he got here. I'm just hoping to God it doesn't turn out to be a B,' he added drily, 'and whoever's doing this isn't working his way through the alphabet.'

Amanda shot the sergeant a sharp glance, and, despite the gravity of the situation, Paget found himself suppressing a smile. It might take the new superintendent time to get used to Tregalles's quirky, and sometimes dark, sense of humour.

'Who found him?' he asked.

'Chap by the name of Jackson. He and his boy came out from town to get some stones for a wall he's building at home. They've been coming out here for the past three Saturdays. Fortunately, the kid didn't see the body, so Jackson got him into his pickup and drove out of here, then waited for us up the top by the gate.'

'Isn't this place supposed to be off limits?'

Tregalles shrugged. 'Has been for thirty years or more, according to Jackson, but it's never been enforced. They built a fence around it when they closed the quarry, locked the gate, then walked away and forgot about it. Jackson said he only found out about it last year, but some people in town have been coming here for stones for years.'

'So let's go and see what Starkie has to say.' He turned to Amanda. 'Superintendent . . .?'

'I'd like to hear what the doctor has to say as well,' she said, 'and I'd like to know what's under that dressing on the victim's forehead.'

Dr Starkie rose to his feet to nod in Amanda's direction when Paget introduced them. 'I won't offer to shake hands for obvious reasons,' he said gruffly, 'but congratulations on your appointment, Superintendent.' He looked down at the body at his feet. 'Pretty smashed up after hitting these rocks,' he observed clinically, 'so it may be a while before I can tell you with any certainty whether he was killed by the fall or not. But I can tell you he's been dead for at least twenty-four hours and possibly longer. Same MO as the other one a couple of weeks ago: tape over the mouth, plastic ties around his wrists, and his ankles have been bound at some point.' He bent and pulled back the dressing on the forehead. 'And another A just like the first one.'

Paget looked at Amanda. 'If we can establish a connection between these two men, it could prove to be the break we need,' he said. He shaded his eyes as he looked up to the top of the cliff, where he could see two white-clad figures taking measurements. 'So, while SOCO's taking care of things out here, I'd like to get back to the office and bring DS Ormside in, because the sooner we get our people out there asking questions, the better.'

Amanda nodded. 'Of course,' she said brusquely. 'I'm going back to the office myself.' She started to move off, then stopped and took out her phone. 'But I suppose I'd better let Mr Brock know before he hears it from some other source,' she said as she flipped through the numbers and put the phone to her ear.

Paget moved away, but he couldn't help feeling a twinge of sympathy for her. New at the job and two high-profile murders in two weeks. Not the best way to start, and he doubted if Brock would be inclined to cut her any slack.

With a whole weekend before her, Molly Forsythe had decided that this would be a baking day, or at least a baking morning, and if that went well, she might go shopping for some new tights in the afternoon. Big deal, she thought as she stacked the breakfast dishes, to be done later when she'd finished baking. How much more exciting could life get when shopping for tights was the highlight of the day?

She'd checked her e-mail messages before breakfast, but there was nothing from David. He was probably very busy, she told herself, and tried not to think about it by keeping busy herself.

She made the blueberry muffins first. Molly kept promising herself that she would make muffins from scratch, but it was so much easier to use the mix from the shop, and while the muffins were in the oven, she cut up the apples for the pie. She hadn't made a pie for ages, so this was going to be a special treat. Humming softly to herself, she rolled out the pastry, cut out a circle and lined the pie plate with it. The timer went off. She took the muffins out of the oven, then cranked up the heat in preparation for the pie.

Molly finished making the pie, trimmed off the edges, then popped it in the oven. The muffins were smelling particularly good, so she eased them out of the tin, 'accidentally' breaking one in the process, which meant the only reasonable thing to do with it was slather it with butter and eat it . . . just to be sure they were all right, of course.

The phone rang. Mouth half full of warm muffin, she swore softly to herself when she saw the calling number.

Moments later, Molly took the pie out of the oven and stood staring at it, trying to decide what to do with it. Finally, she cleared a space in the fridge and shoved the pie inside. So much for the baking morning, she thought crossly as she swept the dirty pots and pans into the sink and wiped the counter top.

She put a couple of still warm muffins in a plastic container, closed the lid and stuffed it into her shoulder bag. With one last glance around the kitchen to make sure the tap wasn't dripping and the oven was off, she let herself out. Another weekend gone sideways, she thought as she got in the car. On the other hand, she thought, trying to look on the bright side, the day should prove more interesting than shopping for tights.

'Clapperton quarry,' Ormside said thoughtfully as he and Paget stood looking at the map on the wall. 'Used to be you were really something if you had a house built of Clapperton stone, but times change. Like everything else, costs were rising, people couldn't afford the stone, so the builders looked for cheaper materials and that was the end of the quarry. Closed down around the end of the seventies, I think it was.' His blunt finger circled the area around the quarry. 'No houses,' he pointed out, 'and the closest farm must be a mile away. So the chances of finding a witness are probably next to nil, especially if Moreland was taken up there at night, so there's no point in putting the mobile unit up there. We'll have to work from here again like we did with Travis. Let's hope SOCO finds something we can use. Is it possible Moreland's the man they were after in the first place?'

'I'm inclined to think not,' Paget said slowly. 'Billy Travis was a small man. Moreland's much bigger, and he lives in a different part of town. I'm very much afraid the killer knew exactly what he was doing, so our only hope is to find the connection between the two men, and pray there aren't any more to come.'

He glanced at his watch. He couldn't put it off any longer. Someone had to break the news to Moreland's wife, and the fact that they had two young children wasn't going to make the task any easier. His gaze swept over the room, then stopped when he spotted Molly. Good. Forsythe could come along for support.

The house in Osmond Street was a semi-detached with a paved driveway barely long enough to accommodate a car. A small patch of grass with a flower bed in the middle lay like a mat beneath the bay window. Half of the flower bed was bare, the soil neatly banked and raked. The rest of the flowers looked wilted and sad, and Molly wondered if Dennis Moreland had planned to finish the job this weekend.

Paget rang the bell.

'Mrs Moreland?' he asked, holding up his warrant card when a woman opened the door. She nodded, her mouth suddenly dry. She ran her tongue over her lips and said, 'That's right. I'm Joan Moreland. Are you—?'

'My name is Paget,' he said. 'Detective Chief Inspector Paget, and this is Detective Sergeant Forsythe. May we come in?'

'Yes, yes, of course,' Joan Moreland said distractedly, retreating before him as he stepped forward.

'Are your children at home?' he asked as he and Molly followed her down the narrow hallway.

'They've gone to the shops for me,' she said over her shoulder. 'I didn't want to go out in case there was news and someone phoned.'

'Perhaps we could sit down,' said Paget when she led them into the front room. It was nicely furnished with a sofa in front of the bay window and big armchairs on either side, and a leather recliner chair next to the fireplace. A glass china cabinet took up about a third of one wall, but apart from a couple of figurines on the top shelf, the rest of the shelves were filled with cups and plaques and pictures attesting to Dennis Moreland's prowess at golf.

But Joan Moreland didn't sit down. Instead, she walked to the centre of the room, turned to face Paget and took a deep breath. 'It's not . . . not good news, is it?' she said. 'Is Dennis injured? Where is he? Is he going to be all right?'

'I'm very sorry to have to bring you this news, Mrs Moreland,' Paget said quietly, 'but your husband was found this morning in the Clapperton quarry. I'm afraid he's dead.'

Joan Moreland stared at him. 'Found . . .?' she said huskily. 'I don't understand. Do you mean he fell? In a quarry? What would he be doing there? He went off to work Thursday morning. Are you sure it's Dennis?'

'I'm afraid there's no mistake, Mrs Moreland. We do have the picture you gave us, and his wallet with his driving licence was in his pocket.'

Joan sat down slowly on the edge of the recliner chair, then looked up at him. 'In a *quarry*?' she whispered. 'Where is this place? I've never heard of it. What was he doing there?'

'It was closed down years ago,' Paget told her. 'It's about four miles from here; it's off the Cleebury road.' He sat down in one of the armchairs. 'Your husband was taken there,' he continued. 'The way it looks now is that he was attacked on his way to work on Thursday morning and taken to the quarry, where he was killed.'

'Killed?' Joan drew a deep breath and closed her eyes. Her small fists were clenched so tightly that there seemed to be no skin over the bone. 'Dennis was *murdered*?'

'I'm afraid so, Mrs Moreland.'

'But why?' Joan opened her eyes and looked to Molly as if expecting her to have the answer. 'Why would anyone want to kill Dennis?'

'We don't know,' Molly told her as she, too, sat down,

'which is why we have to ask you some questions, Mrs Moreland.' She flicked a glance at Paget, who nodded. 'I know this is the very worst time,' she continued, 'and we understand and can come back later if you don't feel up to it right now, but if we are to catch whoever did this, we do need your help. Would you like a cup of tea? I can make one.' Molly started to rise, but Joan shook her head angrily and waved her back.

'I don't *want* a cup of tea,' she snapped. 'I want Dennis! I want to know he's alive. I can't . . .' She ducked her head and began to cry.

'Is there a relative or close friend you would like us to call, Mrs Moreland?' Paget asked. 'Someone who could stay with you? We can come back at a better time, if . . .?'

Joan raised her head. 'What "better time"?' she asked bitterly. She brushed tears from her eyes with the back of her hands. 'There isn't going to be a better time, is there?' She looked at Molly. 'Well, is there?' she demanded shrilly. 'My husband's dead and you—' She stopped, mouth half open as she saw the hurt in Molly's eyes. Joan squeezed her own eyes shut and shook her head from side to side. 'I'm sorry,' she said huskily, 'I know it's not your fault. It's just that . . .'

'You'd like to scream at someone . . . anyone!' Molly finished for her.

Joan Moreland looked at Molly for a long moment. 'But it won't bring Dennis back, will it?' she said, and turned to Paget. 'You said you have questions, Chief Inspector . . .?'

Paget tried to be as brief as possible, but as time went by, Mrs Moreland's voice grew stronger and she seemed to want to volunteer as much information as possible. But the more she told them, the less likely it seemed that Dennis Moreland would be the target of a killer. 'I see your husband was a member of Broadminster Golf Club,' he said, pointing to the trophies. 'Do you know if he's had any trouble there? Any arguments or possibly threats from anyone?'

'He hasn't been for a long time,' Joan told him. 'He packed it in a couple of years ago when they put up the fees. Gave up his membership. He said he'd sooner put the money towards the kids' education. I thought he would miss it, but . . .'

Suddenly she burst into tears. 'Oh, God!' she wailed, 'what am I going to tell the kids?'

She kept shaking her head and insisting that she would be all right when Paget asked again if there was a friend or relative who could come and stay with her. She brushed every suggestion away, then suddenly jumped to her feet and said she was going to put the kettle on, and would they like a cup of tea? Molly said yes, she would like a cup, and offered to help, but Joan waved the offer away.

'We can't leave her on her own,' said Molly when the woman had left the room. 'I think I should stay with her at least until the children come back. There's no telling how they'll take the news, and they might find the two of us a bit intimidating.'

'You're probably right,' Paget conceded. 'Stay as long as you think necessary. And if you can pick up any more information, so much the better, because from what we've learned so far, I'm beginning to wonder if these are random killings.'

Once Paget was gone, Molly made her way to the kitchen where Joan was trying to set out the tea things on a tray, while brushing away tears every few seconds. 'The chief inspector had to leave,' Molly told her, 'so why don't we just sit down and have tea here, Mrs Moreland?'

Joan blew her nose, then sank into a chair and focused her attention on the teapot in front of her. 'Do you have children?' she asked abruptly. 'I'm sorry, but I've forgotten your name.'

Molly sat down to face her across the table. 'No, I don't,' she said. 'And just call me Molly, Mrs Moreland.'

Joan blinked an acknowledgement through her tears and said, 'I'm Joan.' She reached for the teapot and was about to pour when the front door banged open and a young voice called out, 'Hi, Mum. They didn't have any of the biscuits you like, but we got some other ones.' Two pairs of feet came running down the hall. 'And Mr Beasley wants to know if we've heard from Dad.'

EIGHT

It was two o'clock in the afternoon before Molly left the house in Osmond Street to walk the half mile to Charter Lane, so she had plenty of time to think.

Children were funny; you never knew how they would take things. Laura, blonde and pretty, had kept shaking her head when Joan finally managed to tell her and her brother that their father wouldn't be coming home again. 'But he has to,' she insisted stubbornly. 'He promised to take us to the pantomime at Christmas, because we couldn't go last year because Michael was ill in bed.' Joan, eyes brimming with tears, had gathered her daughter to her and tried to explain, but Laura just kept shaking her head, refusing to listen.

Michael had set the bag of groceries on the kitchen table and turned to Molly. 'Dad's really, really dead?' he asked solemnly.

Even now, Molly felt a lump in her throat as she pictured again those innocent brown eyes fixed so intently on her own. 'I'm afraid so, Michael. I'm so sorry.'

The boy had glanced at his mother rocking back and forth, head half buried in her daughter's hair, then turned back to Molly. 'Can I see him?' he asked.

'I'm afraid that's not possible, Michael,' she'd said. 'Sorry.'

'But Mum will have to see him, won't she? I mean to make sure it really is Dad, like they do on *Law and Order*?' He was a child, and yet Molly couldn't help feeling that there was someone older behind those dark, enquiring eyes. She'd said yes, that would have to be done, and asked if there was anyone who could stay with him and his sister when that happened.

'Aunt Sadie,' he said promptly. 'But she just comes in at night when Mum and Dad go out. We don't need anyone here in the daytime now I'm ten.'

Aunt Sadie, Joan explained through her tears, wasn't a relative; she was a friend and neighbour who lived three doors down. 'She's a good soul, but I don't want to bother her,' she said. 'Really, we'll be all right on our own.'

'I'm not so sure you will be,' Molly told her, 'and I don't feel I can leave you and the children here like this. This has been a terrible shock; someone should be with you, so it's either someone like Aunt Sadie or I shall have to ask social services to send someone round.'

Joan gave in, and Sadie Greenhill had come round straight away. She was an older woman, calm and motherly. 'I've buried two husbands myself,' she confided quietly when Molly let her in, 'so I know what it's like. I live on my own so it's no trouble to stay here for as long as Joan and the children need me.'

When she reached Charter Lane, Molly stopped in the cafeteria for a cup of coffee to go with the two muffins in her bag. You weren't supposed to bring your own food into the cafeteria, but Molly preferred to chance it after she saw what was left on the lunch menu.

'Please tell me you have something we can work with,' Ormside said when Molly appeared, 'because this puts a whole new face on the investigation into the Travis killing as well. What have you got?'

'Not much, I'm afraid,' Molly said as she sat down at the desk with him and opened her notebook. 'As far as his wife is concerned, Dennis Moreland wasn't worried or apprehensive about anything; their finances are in order, and he went off to work that morning as usual, and she has no idea why or how he would end up in Clapperton quarry. He has no enemies as far as she knows, and he hasn't fought or argued with anyone recently. She knew where the camera shop was, but the name Billy Travis meant nothing to her, and she was sure she'd never heard her husband mention it.'

'Didn't they see the piece in the local paper about Travis?'

'She said she recalled seeing something about a local man being killed, but the name meant nothing to her.'

'Did Moreland belong to anything, any organization that might have brought him into contact with Billy Travis?'

'Not that I could find,' Molly told him. 'Dennis Moreland was an ardent golfer for years, but Billy Travis wasn't; Billy was in the choir at All Saints, but, according to his wife, Dennis Moreland was never in a choir. They attend a different church, though I gather he didn't go as much as Mrs Moreland and the children. The only other activity Dennis was involved with was the Minster Players, the repertory theatre on Vicarage Walk. He was a volunteer there, working backstage.'

'Friends, relatives?' Ormside queried.

'Parents live in Sheffield, and he has one brother, a teacher, who lives in Cheadle. They have a number of friends, but only three couples they see on a regular basis. It doesn't look too promising, but if Dennis Moreland was in any sort of trouble he might have confided in one of those, so I have them on my list.'

Ormside grunted. 'Promising or not, if it's all we've got, then let's get on and do it. We've spoken to a number of people in Osmond Street, but we didn't get them all, so we'll keep going back until we do. There isn't anyone living within a mile of the quarry, so we're not going to get anything at that end, which means we'll have to concentrate on the street. Does Mrs Moreland work?'

'Apart from scrubbing, cleaning, washing, ironing, shopping, cooking, and looking after the house and the children, you mean, Sergeant?'

'Don't be cheeky,' Ormside admonished sharply, but a hint of a grin tugged at the corners of his mouth. 'You know what I mean, Molly. Does Mrs Moreland work *outside* the home?'

'No. She runs a quilting course at the Thread Basket in Market Square every now and then, and she's a volunteer at the local library, but that's about it.'

'A quilter?' Ormside looked thoughtful. 'The wife used to do that years ago, and I remember her saying some of the best quilters were men. Do you know if there are any men in Mrs Moreland's classes?'

'No idea,' said Molly. 'Why?'

'Just a thought,' Ormside said. 'Any sign of marital problems?'

'I think Joan Moreland and her husband were very happily married,' Molly said. 'In fact, I think they were a very close family.'

'Still, best to keep an open mind,' Ormside said. 'Granted, even if one of them *was* playing away from home, it may not have anything to do with why Moreland was killed, but it's still a possible lead, so don't be too hasty in crossing that possibility off your list.'

He looked up at the clock. 'Better get your notes written up and make enough copies for general distribution,' he said. 'And make sure you put the highlights on the boards. Tregalles is down at SuperFair market talking to the people Dennis Moreland worked with, so maybe he'll pick up a lead there. There's a CCTV camera at the bottom of Osmond Street, and two more in the car park, but we looked at them yesterday and Moreland wasn't on any of them, so it looks as if he never made it to the bottom of the street, let alone into work.'

'When will we have the post-mortem results?'

'Not till Monday, I'm afraid.'

Molly looked puzzled. 'I keep wondering how that could happen to someone like Dennis Moreland in Osmond Street. It's not a long street, and there are houses on both sides. There's no open land; there are no deep driveways or large bushes where someone could lie in wait. I suppose someone could have driven up in a car or van, grabbed him and bundled him inside. But if it did happen that way, you'd think there would have been a struggle; that Moreland would have shouted, and someone would have heard. So why didn't they? How could someone vanish in a street like that? And why him?'

'All good questions, Molly,' Ormside agreed, 'and the sooner we know the answers, the better, so—' The ringing of his phone cut off whatever it was he was about to say. He picked it up, then covered the mouthpiece with his hand. 'Paget,' he whispered. 'He's on his way in, so you'd better get on with those notes.'

Norman Beasley was a heavy-set, red-faced man with a balding head beneath a white cap, and a bulging stomach behind a striped apron. He looked every inch the butcher, Tregalles thought. They were standing outside on the loading dock, where Beasley had insisted they go to talk while he had a smoke. It had begun to rain, and there was a cold wind behind it.

Beasley sucked deeply on his cigarette. 'You're lucky to have caught me here on a Saturday,' he said. 'I'm only here because we've been a man short since Dennis went missing.' He picked a thread of tobacco off his lower lip and flicked it away. 'I still can't believe the poor bugger's dead.'

'You say he was a good worker, got on well with everybody and everybody liked him,' Tregalles summed up. 'But somebody didn't. What about women? Anything going on between him and any of your female workers?'

Beasley sucked on his cigarette. 'Not that I know of,' he said. 'I'd've noticed if anything was going on here. We work pretty closely together, and the two girls in this department are married and have kids.'

'But this is a big store and there are a lot of women working here. He must have mixed with them as well. Tea breaks and lunchtime? Social activities after work?'

'Believe me, mate, you're barking up the wrong tree,' Beasley said decisively. 'Dennis wasn't that sort, and why would he look somewhere else for his jollies with a nice little piece like Joanie waiting for him when he got home?'

'Fancy her yourself, then, do you?'

Norman Beasley butted his cigarette and leaned closer to Tregalles. 'I wouldn't say no if it was on offer, if you know what I mean,' he said. 'You've seen her, haven't you?'

'No, no I haven't,' Tregalles said, 'but I'll take your word for it. Ever been tempted? Tried chatting her up?'

Beasley shook his head. 'Not that I wouldn't have liked to,' he confided, 'but it would've been more than my life's worth to have tried it on while Dennis was around. Very protective of Joanie he was.' He paused, and his eyes grew thoughtful as he looked off into the distance. 'But he's not, now, is he?' he said slowly. 'Around, I mean, and it's going to be hard for her with those two kids to bring up, so she's going to need a friend, someone she knows.' A sly smile tugged at the corners of his mouth. 'Like they say, it's an ill wind . . .'

Tregalles pulled back to look hard at the man. 'Are you suggesting what I *think* you're suggesting?' he asked. 'The man's not been dead five minutes.'

'Which is why she's going to need some support,' Beasley

shot back. 'I'm only thinking of her, for Christ's sake! What do you think I am?'

'To be honest, Mr Beasley, I'm still trying to work that out,' Tregalles said. 'And, since you seem to be more than a little interested in Dennis Moreland's wife, you can tell me where you were last Thursday morning around six o'clock, when Dennis Moreland was on his way to work.'

Back at Charter Lane, Tregalles sought out Molly. 'You've seen Mrs Moreland,' he said. 'What's she like? Good looking, is she?'

'She is as a matter of fact,' Molly said, 'but that's a strange question to be asking about a woman who's just lost her husband.'

'No, no,' Tregalles protested, 'it's nothing like that. It's just that Moreland's boss seems to have more than a passing interest in Moreland's widow. In fact, if it weren't for the fact that there are witnesses who confirm where he was when Dennis Moreland disappeared, I'd have brought the slimy little toad in for questioning. But what about Mrs Moreland? What's your impression of her, Molly?'

'She is a very attractive woman,' Molly agreed. 'But if you're suggesting she might have been seeing someone else, I would doubt that very much.'

'Certainly not his boss, then. He's a fat slob, but there could have been others. I couldn't talk to all of the people Moreland worked with today, so I'll try and catch the rest on Monday. Anyway, that's it for me, so I'm off. See you, Molly.'

The sergeant was on his way out of the building when he was stopped by Gavin Whitelaw, the PC who had been at the scene where Billy Travis was killed. 'Got a minute, Sarge?' he asked, then lowered his voice. 'I just heard about the bloke they found out at Clapperton quarry. They're saying it looks like the work of a serial killer, because it's the same MO as Billy. Is that right?'

'That's right.' Tregalles glanced at his watch. Time was getting on and he'd told Audrey he would be home on time for dinner.

Whitelaw lowered his voice even further. 'Same sort of thing carved in his forehead, was there?'

'That information is still not being released,' Tregalles warned. He began to move away, but Whitelaw stopped him. 'Was it an A like the first one?' he persisted.

'Why are you so interested?' Tregalles asked. 'Does it mean something to you?'

Whitelaw raised his hands, palms outwards, and backed away. 'No, no, it's nothing like that,' he said quickly. 'It's just that I keep seeing the way Billy looked out there. Can't get it out of my head, and now with another one . . .' He blew out his cheeks and flicked his head from side to side as if trying to clear it. 'You think he might strike again?'

'God knows, but I hope not.' Tregalles eased past Whitelaw and was about to continue on his way, when he paused. 'And the less said about *that*, the better,' he warned. 'All right?'

'Right!' Whitelaw said. 'Understood.'

When Paget arrived, Ormside called Molly over. She repeated what she had told the sergeant, concluding by saying that if there was a connection between Dennis Moreland and Billy Travis, she hadn't been able to find it. 'I had a look at several family photos,' she said, 'but I didn't see anything by Travis and son, and their wedding photos were done by a Ludlow photographer. I'm just finishing up my notes now, if you'd like a copy before you go home, sir. Give me fifteen minutes?'

Paget looked at the clock, but Ormside spoke up before he could answer. 'Superintendent Pierce said she'd like a progress report before you leave,' he said. 'In her office,' he added as Paget reached for the phone.

Paget put the phone down. 'I don't know how long I'll be,' he told Molly, 'so leave a copy of your notes on Sergeant Ormside's desk, and I'll pick it up on my way out.'

Judging by the amount of paper on her desk, Amanda Pierce looked as if she would be there for the rest of the evening. She was wearing glasses, which surprised him; he'd never seen her with glasses before. She removed them and waved him to a seat.

'Is this normal?' she asked, indicating the heaps of paper.

'Pretty much,' he told her. 'But it looks to me as if you've taken on Fiona's job as well.'

'It's just that I feel I have to involve myself in everything, at least until I know what's going on,' she said. 'And I'm certainly not trying to take over Fiona's job. In fact it's almost the other way round. She has things so organized I almost feel redundant. I don't know what I would do without her. She's very efficient.'

'Believe me, I know,' he said. 'So you'll be keeping her on, then?'

'Absolutely. I knew she was worried about her job, but I didn't want to make any decisions until I'd had a chance to assess her work. I'm also aware she would have preferred to be working for you rather than me, so we had a chat about that at the end of last week to clear the air, and I think we have.'

'Good. I'm glad,' he said, and was about to say more, but stopped short. He was tired, it was the end of the day and he'd almost allowed himself to slip into the comfortable relationship he'd once enjoyed with Amanda. Annoyed with himself, his tone changed as he said, 'You wanted a progress report on the Moreland killing,' and proceeded to bring Amanda up to date in short, clipped sentences.

'The MO's the same,' he concluded, 'and while we haven't been able to come up with a motive in the Travis case, I'm hoping we can find a link between Travis and Moreland. But we also have to consider the possibility that there may not be a connection, and the killer is choosing his victims at random, picking them off dark streets whenever he gets the chance. It's that damned letter A that bothers me. It's clearly a message, but is he trying to tell us something, or is it meant for other potential victims?'

Paget spread his hands. 'I know that's not what you want to hear, and I'm sorry, but it's the best I have to offer at the moment.' He rose to his feet. 'Was there anything else?'

'For the moment, no,' Amanda said crisply. The abrupt change in Neil's tone and body language had not gone unnoticed, but she decided not to comment on it. 'But I want to be informed immediately if there are any developments. Night or day.'

'Of course,' he said as he made for the door.

Sunday, 16 October

Although there was no doubt in anyone's mind that the latest victim was Dennis Moreland, it had to be confirmed, so it was Molly who was given the task of picking up Joan Moreland and taking her to the mortuary on Sunday morning. 'I could send someone else,' Ormside told her before she'd left for home on Saturday, 'but she knows you, Molly, and I'm sure it's hard enough for the woman as it is.'

Which was why Molly now found herself escorting Joan Moreland through the lower corridors of the hospital to what was known as 'the viewing room'.

Starkie had done his best to clean him up, but there was only so much he could do. The right side of Moreland's face and skull had been crushed when he'd fallen some sixty feet onto the jagged rocks, and that side of the head was bandaged, while a small flesh-coloured patch covered the letter on the forehead. But enough of the face had to be exposed for formal identification, and there was little that could be done with Moreland's right eye, which had been pushed down and sideways into the side of his nose. The result was a grotesque distortion of his features, and even though Molly had been warned about what to expect, and had tried to prepare Joan, it still came as a shock to both of them when the sheet was lifted.

It was too much for Joan. She gave one long, agonizing gasp, and almost ran from the room. Oddly, though, she did not cry. Eyes closed tightly as if to wipe the scene from memory, she allowed Molly to guide her out of the building and into the car.

Joan sat slumped in the passenger's seat, eyes closed, head resting against the window. Molly waited, wishing she didn't have to ask the question, but it had to be asked and she couldn't put it off any longer. 'I know how hard this is for you,' she said quietly, 'but I have to ask you this question: was that your husband, Dennis Moreland, whom you saw just now?'

Joan lifted her head to stare at Molly. 'Why?' she asked hoarsely. 'For God's sake, why, Molly? Why would someone do this to him? He was a good man; he was . . .' Her hands fluttered in a gesture of helplessness. 'The kids . . . What am I going to do?' Suddenly it was all too much and tears streamed down her face.

Joan was still sobbing quietly when Molly started the car and drove slowly out of the gates into Abbey Road, blinking hard to keep her own tears in check. Technically, Joan hadn't answered the question, so, according to the rules governing the identification of the deceased, it should be asked again and the answer recorded. But, rules or not, there was no way that Molly could bring herself to ask that question again. It would appear as a 'Yes' in her notebook.

Later that day, a funeral service was held in All Saints church for Billy Travis. Billy had been a long-time member of the choir there, and George Travis was pleased to see that every member of the choir was present. But it was a big church and most of the pews were empty. Ted Grayson was there with half a dozen members from the camera club, and George recognized a smattering of friends and acquaintances who lived or worked near the shop. It was a disappointing turnout, but then Billy had always kept to himself. Trudy Mason stood at George's side, and they both wept openly when the last hymn was sung. Gordon Mason wasn't there.

Paget sat at the back and was one of the first to leave. He moved a discreet distance away, watching as people filed out of the church. A small, sandy-haired man dressed in dark suit and tie followed him out and stood at the edge of the path as if waiting for someone. His hands were clasped loosely in front of him and he held a small leather case about the size of a prayer book. He remained there until the last person had gone, then made his way down the path to his car. He nodded to Paget as he went by. He was one of Charlie Dobbs' SOCO team, borrowed by Paget for the occasion, and there would be a video clip and a batch of still photographs of everyone who had attended the funeral on Ormside's desk on Monday morning.

NINE

Monday, 17 October

The Minster repertory theatre, with seating for three hundred and twenty-two people and eight spaces for wheelchairs, was a funny old building that had been many things in the past, including an armoury around the time of the Boer War. Parking was a problem for patrons, but at eleven o'clock on Monday morning, Molly had no trouble.

She'd been to a few plays here, and enjoyed them. The theatre might be small, but it attracted some very good actors, and productions were always well attended. But this morning she had an appointment with a man by the name of Jamie Lester, stage manager, lighting director, scene shifter and general dogsbody, according to his own description of his position there.

He was a small, wiry man of about forty, and Molly found him in a tiny office behind the stage. 'I couldn't believe what I was reading in the paper this morning,' he told her once they were seated. 'I mean, Dennis of all people. Any idea why?'

'That's what we're trying to find out,' Molly told him. 'Do you have any idea yourself?'

'Me? God, no. Everybody around here liked him, and we appreciated all the time he put in. Pity, too, because he was really looking forward to being in *HMS Pinafore*.'

'You're saying he was an actor? I thought he just worked behind the scenes.'

Lester shook his head. 'He wasn't,' he said, 'but he had a good voice, so whenever we had a spot in the chorus where he could stay in the background, I'd pop him in, and he enjoyed that. And, like I said, he was really looking forward to *Pinafore*.'

'When did you see him last?'

Lester thought. 'Must have been last Wednesday,' he said.

'Yes, that's right, it was, and he would have been coming in again tomorrow to work on the scenery.'

'That would be the night before he disappeared,' said Molly. 'How was he then? Did he appear to be worried or preoccupied?'

'Same as usual,' Lester said. 'Mind you, we were both busy, so I didn't see that much of him, but he seemed all right.'

'Do you remember what time he left here?'

'Ten or thereabouts. He always tried to leave by then because he had to be up early in his job.'

'Was there anyone in particular he was working with that night?'

'Yes, Mary. Mary Baker. She's another volunteer. They often work together. They make a good team.'

'Where can I find her?'

'I can give you her address. She lives in Cherwell Street, not five minutes from here.' He took a card from his pocket and scribbled Mary Baker's address and phone number on the back of it.

Molly thanked him and tucked it away in the side pocket of her handbag. 'Just one more thing before I go,' she said. 'Do you know a Billy Travis?'

'Billy?' Lester looked startled. 'Bloody hell,' he breathed, 'I never thought. He was killed a couple of weeks ago as well, wasn't he? Yes, I knew Billy. He used to do our programmes and the stills for our shows. Yeah, and that reminds me,' he continued softly, 'I'll have to look for someone else to do them, won't I? I doubt if his dad'll be prepared to take them on. Can't move about the way he used to.'

'Did you know Billy well?'

Lester shrugged. 'Can't say I knew him all that well,' he said. 'Came and went. Did his job, didn't talk much.'

'Did he and Dennis ever meet here, talk to each other, perhaps?'

'I doubt it. Billy used to come round in the mornings like you're doing now, and Dennis was only here in the evenings, and the odd Saturday, of course.' He paused, frowning. 'Although, come to think of it, Billy did come round a few times in the evening to get some shots of the show and the actors, so I suppose they could have met then. Not that I ever saw them together.'

'When was the last time you saw Billy?'

Jamie Lester pursed his lips. 'Must be about four or five weeks ago,' he said. 'We talked about some changes in the programme format, but that was about it. And before you ask, he was the same as he always was as far as I could tell. You think they were both killed by the same person?'

'That's still under investigation,' Molly told him as she slipped the strap of her handbag over her shoulder and stood up. 'Is there anyone else here who knew Dennis Moreland?'

He shook his head. 'Not now, but there will be a few here tomorrow night. I don't know if they'll be much help, but you're welcome to come by and talk to them if you like.'

'I may do that,' Molly told him, 'and thank you very much for your time.'

Mary Baker came to the door wearing an apron over her ample body and a turban around her hair. Fifty or more, thought Molly, guessing at Mary's age. Certainly not a contender as the 'other woman', if there was such a thing in Dennis Moreland's life.

'I'm in the middle of doing a wash,' she told Molly as she led the way into the kitchen where a washing machine was thumping away in the corner. 'Poor thing's on its last legs, but it does not do a bad job if you keep your eye on it. Like a cuppa, would you?' Without waiting for an answer, Mary filled the electric kettle and plugged it in. 'So, how can I help you? Jamie phoned not five minutes ago to say you might be round. I couldn't believe it when he told me about Dennis. I haven't seen the papers this morning, so it came as a real shock, I can tell you. You are sure it's him, I suppose?'

'I'm afraid so,' said Molly. 'I believe you and he used to work together at the theatre?'

'That's right, love, we did. Lovely lad, he was. Do anything for you. Nice to work with someone like that. I shall miss him.'

'You and he were working together last week,' said Molly. 'Last Wednesday, I believe? Did you notice anything different about him? Did he seem worried or bothered about anything?'

Mary shook her head. 'Same as always, he was. In fact he was in good spirits. We were painting one of the sets. Worked from about seven till ten. He was a butcher you know, so he had to be up early and he always left about ten to get to bed. I used to tease him about having to get his beauty sleep.'

'Did he ever talk to you about any trouble at work, at home, or anywhere for that matter?'

'Used to go on about his boss. He didn't like him much. He used to talk about Joan and the kids; real proud of his kids, he was, and Joan, of course.'

The kettle boiled and Mary made tea. She insisted that Molly try her shortbread, but it soon became clear that she could add nothing to what they already knew. And when Molly mentioned Billy Travis, Mary looked blank. 'The photographer who does the theatre programmes and the glossy stills,' Molly prompted.

'I may have seen him about, but I don't remember the name,' she said. 'Sorry, love. Here, hang on a minute and I'll wrap up a bit of that shortbread. You can take it home and have it with your tea.'

'Just received the results of the autopsy on Moreland,' Ormside told Paget when he came into the incident room shortly after lunch. 'The summary, anyway; the detailed report won't be available until tomorrow, but it's pretty much what we expected.'

'Was he alive or dead when he went over the edge?' asked Paget.

'Starkie believes he was alive. Whether he was conscious or not, he doesn't know, but it was the fall that killed him. A lot of broken bones and internal injuries from the fall. The side of his skull was crushed when he fell, but there was one injury to the back of the head that occurred twenty-four to forty-eight hours before he died. It was a single blow with a blunt instrument such as a pipe or truncheon or something along those lines. Not enough to kill, but it would have knocked him out, and there were scrapes and bruises on his elbows and shins that occurred about the same time. Starkie thinks they may have been caused when Moreland was dragged, either along the ground, or possibly when he was bundled into the boot of a car or the back of a van.'

'Moreland was a fairly big man,' said Paget thoughtfully, 'so perhaps more than one person is involved in these killings. It wouldn't be easy to manhandle a man his size to the top of the quarry.'

'Starkie has a theory about that,' Ormside said. 'He said he noticed a chipped tooth and bruising around Moreland's mouth, and he thinks that something like a bottle was forced into his mouth at some point. He went back to his notes on Billy Travis and found similar marks around his mouth, so he thinks it's possible they were forced to drink something laced with Rohypnol or GHB, the date-rape drugs of choice these days. He says it would make the victim drowsy and compliant and much easier to handle, and it disappears within twenty-four hours, so it would be gone by the time tox got around to it in both cases.'

Paget looked sceptical. 'That suggests the killer has access to a prescription drug that's tightly regulated,' he said, 'so . . .' He stopped when he saw Ormside shaking his head.

'Starkie tells me it's not hard to get. He says there are bars in town where you can get a drink spiked for anywhere from thirty to fifty quid a pop.' He made a face. 'Sounds like the doc's done his homework. Makes you wonder where he spends his time off, doesn't it?'

'It does,' Paget agreed. 'I've been wondering how the killer managed to get his victims from where they were first attacked to where they were killed, because even Travis, small as he was, would be hard to handle as a dead weight. Is there anything else?'

'Not really. Moreland was in good health. The complete toxicology report won't be along for a day or two, but Starkie says there were no obvious signs of alcohol or substance abuse. There were marks on his ankles, suggesting they'd been tied at one point, probably with the same sort of plastic ties that were used on his wrists. The ties and duct tape were the same as the ones used on Travis, but there was one difference. At some point, Moreland had been blindfolded, using duct tape. Bits of thread and glue were found sticking to the eyelids, and hair from the eyebrows had been pulled away when it was ripped off.'

Paget winced at the image it conjured up. 'What about the capital A? Did he have anything to say about that?'

'Sharp blade, same as Travis. Starkie's best guess is a razor blade or box cutter. Box cutter would be easier to handle.' Ormside set the report aside. 'We've checked with Moreland's bank,' he said. 'He and his wife have joint accounts. No large sums in or out. No overdrafts. The house is mortgaged, and they've still got a year and a half to go on payments on the car, but both payments are well within their means. Mrs Moreland has a small savings account of her own, and Moreland had life insurance, but the amount isn't anything out of the ordinary. It'll help the wife and kids out for a short while, but hardly enough to kill for.'

'And that's about it,' he concluded as he rose from his chair to refill his mug with coffee. 'Tregalles is out talking to the rest of the staff at SuperFair, and he and Forsythe will be talking to friends of the Morelands later on.' He took a sip of coffee and grimaced when it burned his tongue. 'I don't understand it,' he said, frowning. 'There has to be something behind this ritual he goes through. The A's the clue, but what the hell does it mean?'

'If we knew that, Len,' said Paget, 'we wouldn't be having this conversation. In the meantime, we'll do what we always do. Keep digging until we find something.'

Tuesday, 18 October

PC Gavin Whitelaw opened his eyes and squinted against the light as he tried to focus on the clock. Twenty past ten, for God's sake? He threw off the covers and raised himself on one elbow. His head ached and his mouth tasted foul. He should never have finished off that bottle of Portuguese plonk last night. Thank God it was his day off.

He reached for a cigarette, lit it and sucked in a lungful of smoke and immediately started to cough. He'd been trying to quit for months, ever since the divorce, but the best he'd managed so far was two days. He swung his legs over the side of the bed and hung his head while he continued to cough. It just wasn't worth it; he *had* to quit smoking. Apart from anything else, he couldn't afford it.

Whitelaw looked around the room. The place was a mess. Clothes were on the floor; the remains of his pizza were still in the box on the table, together with the empty wine bottle and assorted dirty knives, forks, and mugs and plates. He'd had every intention of cleaning up last night, but then he'd sat down and got to thinking . . . and drinking. At least he'd remembered to hang his uniform on the hook behind the door. It might need a bit of a press, but it looked clean enough. He got to his feet, stuck the cigarette in his mouth, and made his way to the tiny bathroom, then stood there, hands on the sink, staring at his reflection in the mirror. Red eyes, pasty face . . . and there was something stuck between his two front teeth. He stuck out his tongue and shuddered. 'You look like the bloody wrath of God!' he told his image.

He stood up and tossed the half-smoked cigarette into the toilet. He knew there was something he had to do, today, but what the hell was it . . .?

Tregalles and Molly had spent Monday evening talking to friends of the Morelands, but, as they told Ormside next morning, everyone agreed that the Morelands were nice, ordinary people, and no one could think of a reason why Dennis Moreland had been killed.

'The same applies to Billy Travis,' Ormside said dourly, 'so we're no further ahead, are we?'

'I thought the killing of Billy Travis had to be a mistake,' Tregalles said, 'but now, with this second one, I don't think so. I mean, no one would mistake Travis for Moreland, even in the dark, so we have to assume the killer got the right man each time. The question is: *why* were they killed?'

'We know the *question*,' Ormside said irritably. 'What we need are answers, and I'm damned if I know where else to look. So, unless you have any other leads to follow, I could use some help around here. There was a free-for-all outside a pub last night that put three people in hospital – two with knife wounds, one with concussion. Several with minor injuries

– and all of them are women. So I've got two people tied up on that one. Also, the copper thieves have struck again. They cut out fifty feet of phone cable last night, leaving two villages and God knows how many farmhouses without a landline, so I've got two more out there. Fowler's on a course and Sorenson's on stress leave, and I've got work piling up on my desk, so I could use some help here. All right?'

Dressed in faded jeans and a heavy jacket as protection against a sudden drop in temperature and a biting wind, Gavin Whitelaw paused to look in the window of Bridge Street Motors. Next year's models were already on display, but despite the hype on TV, they looked much the same as last year's to him. Not that he could afford any of them anyway after the lawyers were finished with him.

He pushed the glass door open and stepped inside. Waving off the salesman who came forward to greet him, he was making his way towards the back of the showroom, when a woman came out of one of the offices and almost ran into him.

'Sorry,' she said as she stepped back, then said, 'Gavin . . .? Good heavens, I hardly recognized you. How are you? Sorry to hear about the divorce. Is Bronwyn and . . . Sorry, I don't remember your daughter's name . . .'

'Megan. She and her mother have gone back to Cardiff,' he said stiffly. 'So, how are you, Anita?'

'Fine,' she said, smiling brightly as if to prove it. She certainly looked fine. In fact she looked better than fine to Gavin Whitelaw. A natural blonde, blue eyes, and a great figure. He toyed briefly with the images inside his head before he said, 'How's Graham?' Graham was her husband.

'All right as far as I know,' she said with a shrug bordering on the dismissive. 'He's so busy these days I hardly ever see him. The last time I heard from him he was in Glasgow. We must get together sometime when he's home.'

She turned on the smile again. Anita Chapman had beautiful teeth, but he only had to look at her eyes to know she didn't mean it. It was just something you said when you met someone you hadn't seen for a while, and Whitelaw never had had anything in common with Graham. Funny bloke. Small, very dark skin. Going bald on top. English father, Sri Lankan mother. He was a franchise specialist, at least that was the way he described himself. His job was to guide new licencees through the intricacies of setting up a franchise, teaching them how to deal with banks and lawyers and accountants, and he was hardly ever home. Which was probably just as well, because, as almost everybody knew, Anita and Mike Fulbright had been having it off for years.

'Right,' he said mechanically. 'I'd like that. But right now I'd like to see Mike. Is he in?' He nodded in the direction of the closed door with the word *Manager* on it.

She nodded. 'Here to buy a new car, are you, now you're single again? I'm sure he can give you a good deal. Come on, I'll tell him you're here.'

Anita walked ahead of him to the door, knocked perfunctorily, then walked in. 'Someone here to see you, Mike,' she said breezily. She stepped aside to let Whitelaw pass, then stepped out and closed the door behind her.

Even sitting behind the desk Mike Fulbright looked big. Heavy set, broad-shouldered, he seemed almost too big for his chair. Not quite as handsome as he'd once been, but he was still a youthful looking man with rugged features beneath a mass of curly black hair. He wore a white shirt, collar open, and sleeves rolled up to reveal thick, muscular arms.

A big man and star performer on the local rugby team, the Broadminster Grinders.

'Gavin!' he said heartily, as he got to his feet. 'Good to see you.' He extended his hand. Whitelaw's own hand was a good size, but it was lost in Fulbright's iron grip. 'Here, take a look at these. Just had them printed up. Gold lettering. Present to myself for the best sales quarter in two years. Neat, eh? What do you think?' He took a handful of business cards from his pocket and thrust them at Whitelaw.

'Yeah, great, Mike,' Whitelaw said with barely a glance at them. 'But I didn't come to look at your bloody cards. We have to talk.'

Fulbright stepped back, frowning. 'You look upset,' he said, 'but if that's what you want, we'll talk. But take one of these anyway. Keep us in mind.' He peeled off one of the cards and shoved it into Whitelaw's coat pocket, then moved back behind his desk. 'So, sit yourself down, Gavin, and get whatever it is off your chest.'

'Everything all right, love?' Audrey asked. 'You've been a bit quiet since you came in. Something to do with these murders, is it?' Audrey was fishing. She liked to hear about what was going on at work, but with the children growing up and quick to prick up their ears, John had become more cautious about talking about work when they were around. But now, Olivia was at Guides and Brian was upstairs doing his homework, so the two of them were alone.

'No. At least not directly,' he said. 'Superintendent Pierce called me into her office this afternoon and asked me a lot of questions.'

'What sort of questions?

He frowned as if finding it hard to remember. 'It was more like a chat at first. She asked me how I liked the job, and we talked about things in general, and we talked about the murders. But then she started asking what my goals were. Where did I see myself in the service a year from now, five years from now, then ten? Then she asked me if I was finding enough study time for OSPRE.'

'Did she, now?' Audrey recognized the acronym for the Objective Structured Performance-Related Examination, which Paget had encouraged John to take if he wanted to move up to the rank of inspector. John had ordered the software, but it was still sitting next to the computer unopened. Audrey tried to keep her voice as neutral as possible as she said, 'What did you tell her?'

Tregalles shot her a guilty glance. 'I lied,' he confessed. 'I told her it was hard, considering the workload and family and all, but I was managing.'

'What did she say to that?'

'She said she understood how hard it could be, but I had a good record and DCI Paget had said I had good potential, and she was sure I wouldn't regret the hard work I was putting into my studies.'

Audrey remained silent, not quite sure what to say, or whether to say anything at all. In the end, it was Tregalles who spoke. 'I think I've screwed myself, love,' he said. 'I'm going to have to get started on that programme now whether I like it or not.'

Audrey leaned over and patted him on the knee. 'I'll help,' she said. 'We'll do it together. It'll be all right. You'll see. Maybe they'll let me sit the exam as well and we can both be inspectors.'

TEN

Wednesday, 19 October

Paget waited for Fiona McRae to catch up with him as he left his car on Wednesday morning, and they crossed the car park together. It was blustery and spitting with rain, and Fiona was holding a folded newspaper over her head. 'My hair all goes to frizz and I won't be able to do anything with it if it gets wet,' she confided.

'Why not a rain hat or umbrella then?' Paget suggested.

Fiona shook her head. 'Hats squash my hair, and I can't stand umbrellas. Fiddly things, and you can poke someone's eye out with them if you're not careful.'

'Doesn't do much for your morning newspaper, though, does it?'

'I've read all I want to read at breakfast,' she said. 'I only bring it with me for the crossword at lunchtime.'

They reached the front door and went inside. 'So, how do you like your new boss?' he asked casually as they made their way up the stairs.

Fiona cast him a sidelong glance, hesitating before she answered. 'I like her,' she said. Then, hastily, 'Not that I wouldn't have preferred to be working for you, Mr Paget, but I think you know that, don't you? But, like you, I've had to accept it, and we could have done a lot worse, couldn't we?

She knows what she wants and she listens and asks my opinion. And she's not afraid of Mr Brock.' She smiled as if at some secret joke. 'To tell you the truth, I think he might be a little bit afraid of her.'

They paused when they reached the landing on Paget's floor; Fiona still had one more to go, but she stopped and put out her hand to touch Paget's arm in a conciliatory gesture. 'I really was sorry when you didn't get the job,' she said softly, then turned quickly as if embarrassed, and set off up the remaining flight of stairs.

Paget paused to watch her go. He was fond of Fiona; she had been a great help to him when he was filling in for Alcott, and he was pleased to hear that things were going smoothly for her and she was happy to be working with Amanda. He wished he could feel the same, but then Fiona didn't know what Amanda Pierce was capable of . . . and he hoped she never had cause to find out.

Molly Forsythe finished entering the latest information into the computer and punched *Print*. One more piece of paper to add to the Moreland file. One more line on the whiteboard, but no further ahead. Another hour or so of wasted time? Or would there be something buried in there that they couldn't see now, but would prove useful later on?

Molly stared blankly at the two files on her desk. Billy Travis and Dennis Moreland. She'd been back and forth between the two, searching for a connection, but there was nothing. The two men had lived at opposite ends of the town. They didn't belong to the same clubs; they didn't frequent the same pubs; they didn't go to the same church.

The words were beginning to blur, and she found herself thinking about the e-mail she'd received from David last evening. She'd read it so many times last night and again this morning before coming to work that she knew it by heart.

> Dear Molly,
>
> Sitting here writing to you late at night, I keep remembering how much I enjoyed our time together, and I do so wish it could have been longer. I was looking forward

to settling down in Broadminster, but it seems that fate has intervened at a most inopportune moment, and I must remain here for a while longer.

Lijuan's grandmother is feeling better and she's gone back to work. She's been with the Hongkong Electric Company for almost thirty years, and she says it keeps her from thinking about what happened to Meilan. But the loss of her only daughter has hit her very hard indeed, so the last thing she wants to hear is any talk about taking her granddaughter away as well. And, as you said, Molly, it is much too early to make any major decisions regarding Lijuan's future, or, for that matter, my own as well, so I will have to be patient and give it time. Meanwhile, please keep writing, Molly; I do so look forward to your e-mails.

Affectionately, David

Much too early . . . my own as well? What did that mean, Molly wondered. Was he talking a month . . . six months . . . a year? Would he come back at all, for that matter? In her heart, Molly knew David had no choice, but that didn't make things any easier. Lying in bed last night, the thought had flashed through her mind that she might be able to get a job with the police in Hong Kong, and she'd fantasized about that for some time before more practical thoughts nudged their way in, and she told herself not to be so foolish. She knew how she felt about David, but she still didn't know how he felt about her. He'd signed off with the word 'affectionately', but what did that *really* mean? She'd gone to the old thesaurus that had belonged to her father to look it up. There were lots of synonyms to choose from: adoringly, lovingly, devotedly, fondly, tenderly, passionately . . . and several related terms: infatuation, crush, and more.

So which one was in his mind when he'd chosen that particular word? She'd still been thinking about that when she dropped off to sleep and dreamt about . . . work.

'This is getting to be a habit,' Grace observed that evening when Paget arrived home before six. 'Quiet day, was it?'

'Too quiet,' Paget told her. 'We're not getting anywhere

with either murder. Both victims seem to have led very ordinary, blameless lives. How about you?'

Grace shook her head. 'Nothing to report, either, I'm afraid. I spent most of the day looking at everything on the Morelands' computer, but I didn't find anything. He did all his banking on line, as did she, but it was all very simple and straightforward. They have no major debts, other than the mortgage on the house and the car, and they've never missed a payment. He has stacks of pictures and videos on disks and flash drives, but they were all taken by him or his wife. None of them were taken by Travis. And about ninety-nine per cent of them were of the kids: Christmas, birthdays, holidays, and everyday things from the time they were born till about a week before his death. They look like nice kids, but I was getting pretty tired of them by the end of the day. We've been through the house from stem to stern, but we found nothing of interest there either. The same as we did with the Travis household, so I'm afraid we're not much help to you.'

They had talked of other things during dinner, but it was clear that something was preying on Paget's mind, something he didn't seem anxious to discuss. 'So what's the problem, Neil?' Grace asked when everything was cleared away. 'I know something's bothering you, so why don't you tell me what it is instead of bottling it up inside?'

He shook his head. 'It's not something you can do anything about,' he said. 'It's just that I feel there should be something more I can do to move this investigation along. Everybody's working hard, but we're not getting anywhere. We have no suspects; we have no motive. In fact we have nothing, and that's what I have to tell Amanda Pierce at the briefing tomorrow morning.' He made a face. 'It's not that I have any love for the woman, but she's still my boss, and I can't help feeling I've let her down.'

'Yet you feel you've done everything you can?'

'Yes, I do, but—'

'Would you be feeling the same if it was Alcott you were briefing tomorrow morning?'

'Probably, but that's different. He wouldn't have been happy, but he would have understood.'

'You told me that Amanda Pierce has come up through the ranks, so she should know how difficult it can be. Why should it be any different when you're talking to her?'

He grimaced. 'It just is,' he said stubbornly.

'Only because it's Amanda Pierce,' she countered, 'and much as you say you dislike her, you want to impress her, don't you? You'd like to walk into her office and say, "There, it's solved. We have the killer. See how good I am at my job!" That would be nice, wouldn't it, but I've seen what you have to work with, Neil; I've been part of it and I'm just as frustrated as you are. You can't manufacture motives or suspects or evidence. All you can do is make sure you've done all you can, then be patient and wait for a break or for someone to come forward. I know it's hard, but we've all been there before, and I imagine Amanda Pierce has been there as well. So stop torturing yourself. If she's really earned that position, then she'll understand. You're quite right when you say she may not like it, but there's nothing she or anyone else can do about it until you get a break.'

Grace was right, of course, he thought later as they settled down in bed. But he was still trying to think what else he could have done when he went to sleep.

Slouched in a kitchen chair, Gavin Whitelaw shook the last few drops of beer out of the can into his mouth before setting it aside with the others. He stabbed at the remote and watched the picture on the screen fade to black. Hell of a way to spend the evening, but that was how it had been since the divorce. Bronwyn and their daughter, Megan, were well settled in Bronwyn's parents' house in Cardiff, while he was stuck here in the Freemont hotel in an area best known for its bars, drugs and prostitutes, until he could clear some of his debts and find a decent place to live.

Everybody in the place knew who he was; they knew he was a copper but they didn't see him as a threat. Thirty-three years old and still a constable, a constable who was divorced, broke and living in this pigsty, he was no better than they were, and they made sure he knew it in their not so subtle ways.

Whitelaw stood up, then grabbed the edge of the table to steady himself. Work in the morning, and he'd better not be late, he reminded himself. He'd had two warnings already, and things could get serious if he was late again.

His vision kept blurring, and he had trouble staying upright. He dreaded the coming of morning and the inevitable headache that would follow him halfway through the day. He knew he shouldn't have drunk so much, but what the hell else was there to do? His stomach growled. He was spending more on cigarettes than food. He smoked and drank because he was hungry, and he was hungry because what little money he had was spent on cigarettes and drink. The thought held his attention briefly as he undressed. He tried to concentrate on it: there was a message in there somewhere, but whatever it was, it would have to wait till morning.

His befuddled mind switched to Mike Fulbright. Fulbright and his fancy office with the leather chairs, and his gold-plated cards. All talk and bullshit. Big smile up front, but there was a vicious streak beneath that smile. Like today. *How you doing, Gavin? Here to buy a new car, are you?* Bastard! Fulbright knew very well that Bronwyn had cleaned him out, and he'd sat there with that smug smile on his face, secretly gloating. 'Or not so bloody secretly,' Whitelaw muttered as he weaved his way into the bathroom. He and Fulbright were the same age, but there was Mike, sales manager of Bridge Street Motors, and here he was, PC Whitelaw, living in this dump.

Not that Mike had come by it honestly, he told himself. The only reason Mike had that job was because he played rugby for the Broadminster Grinders. Built like a bull, he'd earned the reputation of being the dirtiest bastard on the team, but the Grinders were winners, and Bridge Street Motors was one of their major sponsors. Which was why Mike had made his way up the ladder so fast. It had bugger all to do with talent. Whitelaw's lip curled in contempt as he peered into the mirror. He pulled his lips back to examine his teeth. He couldn't get his eyes to focus properly, but his teeth looked all right; they'd do till morning. He managed to relieve himself without going too far off course before making his way to bed. The walls of the room seemed to be leaning inwards as he lay back. He closed his eyes, waiting for the room to right itself, and brought his thoughts to bear once more on Mike Fulbright. Mike had tried to persuade him that what had happened was pure coincidence, but Gavin Whitelaw wasn't buying it. Travis and Moreland, both killed in the same way within days of each other? That *might* have been a coincidence. But the letter A carved on their forehead . . .? *That* was no coincidence. So why would Mike insist there was nothing to worry about? Whitelaw struggled to bring his thoughts to bear on the question.

Unless . . .

The thought, blurred and hazy, hovered at the edge of his mind. The more he tried to grasp it, the more elusive it became, but he knew instinctively that it wasn't good. Not good at all, he told himself as he pulled the bedclothes up under his chin and rolled onto his side. Tomorrow, he promised himself. He was too tired to work it out now, and things would be clearer in the morning. He'd give it some serious thought tomorrow . . .

Thursday, 20 October

He came awake slowly, not recognizing what had awakened him until the third or fourth ring. He groaned and buried his head in the pillow. Wrong number, or somebody playing silly buggers. They'd get fed up and hang up if he ignored them.

But the phone continued to ring. Muttering, Whitelaw crawled out of bed, snatched up the phone and said, 'Yeah?'

'PC Whitelaw?' A man's voice.

'Yeah, whadyawant?'

'This is Tony. I'm a roofer and I'm on your roof right now trying to stop a leak dripping into the room above yours, but the reason I'm calling is because of what I've found up here. It looks to me like someone's stashed their drugs in a hiding place up here. I called the station, but they told me to give you a call, since you're living here. They want you to come up and take charge of them.'

'Who told you that?' He was coming awake now, but his head was throbbing and his eyes felt as if they were on fire, and the flashing neon sign on the night club across the street wasn't helping.

'Your mates at the cop shop. I rang them as soon as I found this, but they said they had a bit of a flap going on and they couldn't spare anyone, and since you lived in the building they said to ring you, and they gave me your number.'

'They shouldn't be giving out my number.' Whitelaw sat down heavily. 'Who did you talk to?'

'I don't know,' the man snapped. 'He didn't give me his bloody name. For Christ's sake, man, here I am trying to fix your bloody roof *and* be a good citizen and you're nattering on about phone numbers. Do you want these sodding drugs or not?'

'You're sure it's drugs?'

'Well, it's all in little white packages like I've seen on TV, and I don't think it's sugar. There must be ten pounds or more of the stuff.'

Ten pounds! Jesus! Whitelaw squinted at the window. It was raining steadily. 'Can't you bring it down here?'

'And have my prints all over it? No bloody way, Constable. Besides, I've got a leak to fix before the water comes through *your* ceiling, and it's pissing down up here. So get your coat on and get up here before someone comes to collect this stuff. It's making me nervous.'

'OK, OK, keep your shirt on,' Whitelaw growled. 'I'm on my way. How do I get up there?'

The ringing of the phone beside the bed woke Paget. He squinted at the calling number and groaned. Ten minutes to three? This was not going to be good news. He picked up the phone and said, 'Paget.'

'We've got another one, boss.' It was Tregalles. 'Except this time it's one of ours. Remember PC Whitelaw? He was the one out at the Lessington Cut who knew Travis.'

'I remember.'

'Same MO, wrists bound, tape over his mouth, and a dressing on his forehead. Pushed off the roof of the Freemont Hotel where he was living.'

ELEVEN

Paget drove in alone, thankful that Grace wasn't on call as well, considering the way the rain was pelting down. The less people on the road in weather like this, the better. Detour signs were in place at both ends of Prince Street, and the screens and tent had been erected by the time Paget had driven in from Ashton Prior. SOCO vans were drawn up at the side of the road; white-suited men and women were already at work, and Paget found Tregalles and Charlie Dobbs sheltering from the rain in a shop doorway.

'I was just warning Tregalles that this rain's going to make it all but impossible for us to gather anything useful off the ground or the roof,' Charlie said as Paget joined them, 'so don't expect too much from us on this one. Sorry to hear it's one of yours.'

'Funny,' Tregalles said, 'but Whitelaw stopped me the other day to ask if there was an A on Moreland's forehead. I didn't think much about it at the time, I thought he was just curious, but it looks like he might have known more than he was letting on.'

Paget pulled the hood of his rain jacket tighter as he stepped out into the street and turned to look up. 'Is there any doubt that he came off the roof?' he asked.

'One of his boots is still up there,' said Charlie. 'It looks to me as if his boots weren't laced up, and he lost one of them when he went over the parapet, then lost the other one in the fall. We found it in the middle of the road.'

Paget ducked back under cover. 'And Whitelaw was *living* here in the Freemont?' The Freemont was the sort of hotel where they rented rooms by the hour, and no police officer, no matter what his or her rank, should be living in such a place.

'He was,' Tregalles confirmed, and pointed at a dark, uniformed figure huddled against the rain by one of the barricades. 'That's Lou Bates,' he said. 'He was Whitelaw's partner for a while, and he told me Whitelaw's been living here since he and his wife were divorced six months or so ago. She and their young daughter took off for Cardiff, his wife's home town, and he was left to clear up the mess. Seems like the problem was debt. Got in over their heads, according to Bates. He sort of hinted that drink was involved as well. Anyway, he says Whitelaw was living here because it was all he could afford.'

'Who found the body?'

'A taxi driver reported what he thought was a drunk,' Tregalles said. 'He should have stopped to see if the man *was* just drunk or injured, but he said he couldn't, because he was on his way to pick up a businessman at the Tudor Hotel, who wanted to be driven to Birmingham airport, and he wasn't going to be late for a fare like that. He's been told to report to Charter Lane as soon as he gets back.'

'Right,' said Paget. 'Wait here until I've seen the body for myself, then I want to take a look at the roof and Whitelaw's room.'

'He landed right there at the edge of the pavement,' said one of the men squatting beside the body inside the tent, taking measurements. His name was Geoff Kirkpatrick, one of Grace's colleagues. 'Hard to tell if he bled much because blood would have been washed away by the rain.'

Gavin Whitelaw lay on his back. Paget remembered him from their encounter at the Lessington Cut, but Whitelaw's features were so distorted that he wouldn't have recognized the man if he hadn't been told who he was. Duct tape covered Whitelaw's mouth, and there was a dressing in the centre of his forehead. And, like the others, it was held securely in place by an additional strip of duct tape. 'Same MO,' Kirkpatrick observed, indicating the dressing. 'The killer wants to make sure the dressing doesn't come off when they land. Not that it made any difference in this case,' he continued. 'Looks like he landed on his back and the skull was pushed upwards when his head hit the ground. Shoved the bones up under the nose and rammed his teeth up to twist the mouth as well.'

Paget, never comfortable around such scenes, could have

done without the explanation. 'I take it the doctor's been informed?' he said.

'Should be here any minute.' The man looked at his watch. 'I took pictures as soon as we arrived, but Starkie will want more when he turns him over.'

'You haven't been on the roof yet, I take it?'

'No need. Fred's up there, getting soaked, I imagine.'

Paget left the tent and rejoined Tregalles. 'Let's go up and take a look at the roof, and then I want to look at his room. Do you have the number?'

'Three nineteen,' Tregalles told him. 'I've got his keys. The only thing in his pockets except for this.' He handed Paget a business card, the name embossed in gold.

'Mike Fulbright, Sales Manager, Bridge Street Motors,' Paget said. 'That name sounds familiar.'

'It should,' Tregalles said. 'Rugby player. He's been playing for the Grinders for God knows how many years. Built like a brick shithouse; they call him the Avenger. But then, you don't follow sports much, do you, boss?'

'Not much, no,' Paget said thoughtfully. 'But I do wonder why this card would be in Whitelaw's pocket when he's living in a dump like this. Can't quite see him being in the market for a new car, can you?'

The Freemont Hotel was one of the oldest, if not *the* oldest, in Broadminster, and it smelled like it; musty and sour, the pervasive odour was enough to sting the eyes. The ceiling in the lobby was high, and the light was poor. It was like entering a cave, and the mustard-coloured paint and years of grime on the walls did nothing to alleviate the feeling of gloom. The carpet in front of the reception desk was worn through to the canvas, and the top of the counter was chipped and scarred and burned. A wizened, bald-headed man, who looked almost as old as the hotel, sat dozing with his chin on his chest in a chair in the tiny office behind the counter. 'That's Mr Thomas,' Tregalles said. 'Says he didn't see or hear anything unusual when I spoke to him earlier.'

'Hardly surprising,' said Paget. 'I wonder what does pass for unusual in this place?'

The lift wasn't working, and Paget wasn't sure he would

have trusted it if it had been. The stairs were made of marble, steep and narrow and deeply worn by the passage of time and thousands of feet, and both men were breathing hard by the time they reached the roof.

Fred Chandler, another of Charlie's men, met them as they stepped out. He wore a clear plastic cape and hood over his white coveralls, and water was literally cascading off him. 'Could have saved yourself the climb,' he told Paget, 'because there's bugger all to see up here. If there was anything it's been washed away by the rain. We'll come back again when it stops raining and have another go, but I wouldn't expect too much if I were you.'

'Charlie mentioned a boot . . .?'

'Bagged and on its way,' Fred told him. He led the way to the parapet. It was no more than two feet high. 'For him to land where he did, he must have gone over here,' he explained, 'but there's no physical evidence that I can see. As I said, we'll come back when it's dry, but . . .' He shrugged and shook his head.

They stood at the edge looking down. Paget calculated mentally. Sixty feet or more to a hard, unyielding pavement. He pictured the scene in his mind and shivered.

Back inside, Paget and Tregalles made their way along an ill-lit corridor to room 319, where a WPC stood guard outside the door.

'Anyone show any interest?' Tregalles asked.

The young woman shook her head. 'Quiet as the grave, Sergeant,' she said. Her eyes flicked up and down the corridor. 'And not much different to being in one, if you ask me.'

Tregalles took Whitelaw's keys from his pocket and opened the door, then led the way inside, only to stop dead a few paces in. 'God! What a stink!' he muttered, wrinkling his nose in disgust. He pointed to the beer cans and bottles, empty pizza boxes and crisp packets spread over the table. 'The man was living like a pig!'

'Doesn't look as if there was any kind of a struggle in here,' Paget observed. 'I wonder how the killer got him up to the roof.'

'Could have been someone he knew. Someone he trusted?' Tregalles offered.

'Whoever he was, he must have been pretty damned persuasive to get him up there at that time of night in the pouring rain,' Paget said as he looked around.

'Left his wallet here.' Tregalles pointed to a jumble of objects on the top of a cardboard box serving as a bedside table. He pulled on a pair of latex gloves and opened the wallet. 'Eight pounds ten,' he said. 'Driving licence, several business cards, including two from lawyers, a two-for-one coupon from McDonald's, a library card, a business card from Kingsway Self Storage, a preferred client card from a video store, and two condoms. But no credit cards of any kind. That's a bit odd.' The sergeant listed the contents in his notebook, then put them back and bagged the wallet.

'Bring that along but leave the rest for now,' Paget told him. 'I'll get Forsythe on it.'

Tregalles bagged the wallet and stuffed it into his pocket. 'Sorry, love,' he said to the WPC when he locked the door again, 'but I'm afraid you're going to be here until we can get someone to relieve you. Shouldn't be long, though.'

The look she gave him said more than words what she thought of that.

'Quiet, isn't it?' he said as they made their way down to the ground floor. 'Any other place we'd have people out in the hallways demanding to know what was going on, but not here. It's going to be interesting to see who and what we find when we go through this place and start knocking on doors. My guess is they'll all claim to have been sleeping soundly in their beds and didn't see or hear a thing.'

'I suspect you're right,' Paget agreed, 'so let's go and see if Starkie's arrived and if Charlie's people have found anything useful.'

Mr Thomas was snoring gently as they passed him on the way to the door. Tregalles opened the door and was about to step outside, when he paused and stepped back in. 'Looks like we have company,' he said. 'Superintendent Pierce is out there.'

'So, there's absolutely no doubt now that we have a serial killer on our patch,' Amanda said. 'And this latest victim is one of our own. What do we know about PC Whitelaw, Neil? Do you have any idea how he may be connected to the two previous victims?'

Amanda Pierce and Paget had taken shelter from the rain in her car, and they were having to raise their voices to be heard above the steady drumming on the roof. They were reasonable questions, and Paget dearly wished he had reasonable answers.

'He was one of the first responders when Travis was killed,' he told her, 'although I think that was sheer coincidence, but Tregalles tells me that Whitelaw was asking questions about the way Moreland was killed, and he asked specifically about the letter A on Moreland's forehead. But until we have a chance to dig into his background and private life, I can't tell you any more than that.'

'But living here in this hotel . . .?' Amanda made a face. 'I know the pay scale could be better, but I didn't think it was quite *that* bad.'

'According to one of his colleagues, Whitelaw was recently divorced, and he was deeply in debt,' Paget told her. 'We don't know how accurate that information is, nor do we know if his situation had anything to do with his death, but we'll be following it up. As for the rest of the investigation, as I told you yesterday, we have little in the way of hard evidence. The duct tape and plastic ties can be bought anywhere; the killer leaves no tyre tracks or footprints; he leaves no fingerprints, no hairs, no fibres, nothing. As for the letter A, we don't know if this is his signature, his initial, or if it stands for something else. So far, about the only thing these men have in common is that they're about the same age. But if Tregalles is right, and Whitelaw's interest in the way Moreland died was more than idle curiosity, then Whitelaw either knew or at least suspected what that connection was. So let's hope there's something in his background, or in the things he left behind, that'll lead us to his killer.'

Amanda Pierce looked at the clock on the dashboard. Four fifty-two, and the rain-swept streets were all but deserted as she drove away from the crime scene. Too early to go into work, and too late to get much sleep if she returned to her flat in Albany Place. Three murders in three weeks! What a way to start a new job, especially when you knew there were those who were just waiting for you to fail. Was that what Neil wanted, too, she wondered. Did he hate her that much? She sighed heavily. She could hardly blame him. Reason enough with what had happened in the past, but then, to come along years later to snatch away the job he'd every right to believe was his for the taking, that *would* be hard to take.

The irony was that it was *her* future that was in *his* hands. If he didn't solve these murders, and soon . . . Amanda dismissed the thought. That was no way to think. Neil would do his job, regardless of his personal feelings towards her, because that was the way he was. But if he failed – if the killings continued – then it would be her head on the chopping block, and Chief Superintendent Morgan Brock would be only too happy to pick up the axe.

TWELVE

Paget had spent what was left of the night in his office, alternately filling in time with paperwork and dozing at his desk, but he was downstairs in the incident room to greet Len Ormside when the sergeant arrived.

'Human Resources won't be in for another hour, but I want Whitelaw's personnel file as soon as they get in,' he told the sergeant. 'It should tell us if he has any close relatives here in town who can identify the body, and his ex-wife will have to be notified. I'm told she and their daughter are living in Cardiff. If there's no one here, then we may have to ask her to come back and do it.'

'It's not as if we don't know who he is,' Ormside pointed out. 'I mean the man has worked here for something like ten or twelve years.'

'Still has to be done, though, doesn't it?' Paget said. 'And speaking of that, I want to talk to everyone he worked with. One of his colleagues hinted to Tregalles that Whitelaw was having money and drinking problems, so let's bring in his mates and his sergeant and find out what they can tell us about him. Including why he was still a PC after that many years on the job.'

The corridors were crawling with uniformed police and plain clothes detectives going from door to door when Molly arrived, but the lone WPC was still there in front of the door to room 319. 'Thank God,' she said when Molly identified herself and told her she could go. 'The rotten sods wouldn't even stand in for me when I said I needed to go for a pee. They seem to think it's funny.'

'Better get going now, then,' said Molly. 'Wouldn't want you contaminating this nice clean carpet, now would we?'

'Bloody toilet down the hall's a disgrace anyway,' the girl said. 'I took a look when I came in.' She shifted from one foot to the other. 'Any chance I could use the one in here? It's got to be better than the one down there. Besides, it's unisex and you know what some of the men are like, spraying all over the place.'

Molly hesitated. 'Do you have any gloves?' The WPC shook her head. Molly reached into her bag and took out a pair of latex gloves. 'Put those on,' she said. 'It probably doesn't matter, but try not to disturb anything while you're in there. OK?' She unlocked the door, and the girl shot past her and disappeared into the tiny bathroom.

Molly paused to take stock. The room was small. A bed, a table, two wooden chairs and a small padded armchair, a sink, a two-burner stove, an under-the-counter fridge, a shelf, a small chest of drawers, and a painted wardrobe whose door wouldn't close properly.

Molly's nose twitched as she pulled on a second set of gloves. SOCO would be coming in later to do a thorough search, and she'd mentioned that to DCI Paget, but he'd said, 'Take a look round anyway. Having been involved in the other crime scenes, you might spot something that might not mean anything to them.'

The place smelled of stale beer and smoke. She walked over to the window and tried to lift it, then saw that it had been nailed shut. So much for that idea. Slowly, she began to circle the room.

'Sarge . . .?' a plaintive voice called from behind the bathroom door. 'Is there any toilet paper out there?'

Paget closed the file and handed it back to Ormside. 'Frequently late, questionable sick leave, out of contact on numerous occasions, and still a constable after twelve years on the job?' he said. 'This man should have been disciplined if not sacked long ago. And he's not the only one,' he continued ominously. 'Someone above him has been covering for him, and I'd like to know who it is. Talk to some of his colleagues, see what they can tell us about him.' He turned to Tregalles. 'If Bates is still here, let's have him in first.'

PC Lou Bates was wet and tired, and wanted nothing more than to go home, dry off and get some sleep, so he was pleased when Paget said, 'I'll try not to keep you any longer than necessary, but we need information about Whitelaw, and I understand you were a friend of his.'

'I *was* partnered with him for a while, sir,' Bates said carefully. 'It was while he and his wife were going through the divorce, but I wouldn't say I was a friend.'

'But you knew him well enough to tell DS Tregalles that the man was in debt and had a problem with drink. Right?'

Bates nodded. 'I don't want to speak ill of the dead, but he did have a problem with drink, and it got worse after the divorce. And I know he was in debt because he used to talk about it all the time.'

'What kind of debt? Credit cards? Gambling?'

'I don't know about the gambling, but I know he was so deep in debt with his cards that they forced him into some sort of payback programme, and he said it was going to take him something like three years to clear what he owed. I believe he was having to pay child support as well.'

'So what had he been spending it on? Or was it his wife? Did she have expensive tastes?'

Bates shifted around in his chair as if suddenly uncomfortable. 'Don't know exactly,' he said, but his eyes told another story.

'I think you do,' Tregalles said, 'and this is not the time to be holding anything back. Three people have been killed, and this may be our best chance to track the killer down. So I'll ask you again: where was the money going?'

Bates drew a deep breath. 'Women,' he said. 'He couldn't stay away from them. Prostitutes mostly.' Bates hesitated. 'I don't know this for sure,' he said carefully, 'but from some of the things Whitelaw said, and from phone calls he used to make from the car, I think he was having it off with a married woman as well. In fact, I believe that was what the divorce was all about. Well, that and the debt.'

'What about the WPCs and our female civilian staff? Did he ever try it on with them?'

Bates shrugged. 'I don't know about that,' he said, 'but it wouldn't surprise me if he did. I mean he couldn't seem to help himself. He'd try it on with almost any woman given half a chance. Like when we'd stop a woman driver who was speeding or who'd shot the lights. If they were even halfway good looking, he'd chat them up. Didn't matter if they were married or not.'

'Did you bring any of this to the attention of your sergeant?'

Bates shifted uncomfortably in his seat. Paget waited, but the man remained silent. It was the old problem: misplaced loyalty. Never squeal on your partner, no matter what he or she may do.

'What about drugs?' Paget asked. 'You say he was a drinker, but was he into drugs as well?'

Bates shook his head. 'No, sir, I'm sure I would have known if he was.' He paused, frowning. 'Mind you, I can't speak for now. It's been a while since I rode with him.'

'Just one more question before you go: who would you say was Whitelaw's best friend here at work?'

Bates hesitated, then said, 'Don't know if there was one, sir. At least not that I know of. Everybody stayed clear of him, because he was always looking to borrow money, and you knew you'd never see it again.'

* * *

'Find anything useful?' Ormside asked when Molly returned to Charter Lane later that morning.

'Afraid not,' she said. 'There were no personal papers of any kind. No bank book or a will, in fact nothing much at all. Has anyone searched his locker here?'

'Tregalles is taking care of that,' Ormside told her, 'and he'll be going out to the Kingsway Self Storage lockers on Oldfield Road to see what Whitelaw has stored out there. There's a picture in his file, so make copies and show it to George Travis and Trudy Mason and Mrs Moreland, and ask them if they know him or can think of anything the three men had in common.'

'Right,' said Molly, but she looked as if something was troubling her.

'Something wrong?' Ormside asked.

'It's just that I can't understand why Whitelaw would be on the roof in the middle of the night in the pouring rain,' she said. 'They say there was no sign of a struggle; no sign that there was anyone else in the room. I don't understand it.'

'I don't either,' Ormside said, 'but I checked on calls to and from the phone in his room, and he received a call at one forty-eight from a disposable phone. The call lasted two minutes. Twenty-three minutes later, a taxi driver reported a drunk lying in the road, so I think it's a fair assumption that was when he was killed. Somehow the killer managed to persuade Whitelaw to go up to the roof where he probably knocked him unconscious, tied his hands behind his back, gagged him, then carved his initial or whatever it is on his forehead before pushing him off the roof.'

Molly shuddered. 'I just hope we can catch this maniac before he strikes again,' she said. 'A photographer, a butcher and a policeman. I just don't see the connection.'

Eileen Calder, solicitor, sat with fingers steepled as she looked at Paget over the top of her half-moon glasses. She was a short, plump woman of about forty. Her fair hair, parted in the middle, hung straight down on either side of her face like side curtains without a valance, and Paget couldn't help wondering if she had ever really looked at the result in a mirror.

'Murdered?' she said. 'How terrible.' The words were spoken without the slightest sign of emotion as she rearranged her features into a look of mild regret. 'I'm sorry to hear that, Chief Inspector, but to answer your question, I did act for Mr Whitelaw during the divorce proceedings earlier this year, but our association was very brief, so there is little I can tell you about the man himself . . . apart from the fact that I didn't like him very much.'

'Did he leave anything with you? Any papers, his will, anything at all?'

Eileen Calder shook her head. 'Nothing,' she said firmly. 'As I said, our association was very brief.'

'Do you know if he had another solicitor?' Paget took out one of the cards found in Whitelaw's wallet. 'A Brian Davey?'

'Brian is or was his wife's solicitor,' Ms Calder said, 'so I don't think you'll fare any better there, Chief Inspector.'

Paget put the card away. 'Is there anything you can tell me about Whitelaw or the divorce proceedings themselves? What, for example, were the reasons for the divorce?'

Eileen Calder thought about that for a moment. 'I suppose, since it's in the public record, it can't hurt to tell you,' she said. 'It was Mrs Whitelaw who sued for divorce and the grounds cited covered quite a wide spectrum. Neglect, infidelity, adultery, physical and mental abuse and so on. In short, Chief Inspector, your policeman was a drinker and a womanizer who abused his wife. Wisely, Mr Whitelaw decided not to contest the allegations, partly because his wife had more than enough evidence to support her claims, and partly because he wanted to keep as low a profile as possible, because he felt it could jeopardize his position in the police force if it became known. And then there was the matter of costs. His biggest asset was his car after the house was sold, and I believe he had to sell that to cover them.' The corners of her mouth turned down. 'Even then it wasn't enough, and now he's dead, I suppose I can forget about what he owes me. Not that I had much hope before, but still . . .'

'Was there anything in your dealings with him that struck you as odd or strange?'

The woman frowned. 'I'm not sure I know what it is you're after,' she said. 'Strange in what way?'

Paget shook his head. 'To be honest, I don't know myself,' he said, 'but the man was murdered in a particularly brutal way, and I'm wondering if he ever mentioned any threats or anything like that.'

'No. Our meetings were very brief. There was no time for chit-chat. He was always in a hurry, partly, I suspect, to minimize his costs.'

'You mentioned physical and mental cruelty,' Paget said. 'Did you ever get the feeling that his wife might have wanted to harm him in return?'

'I think she was just glad to see the back of him,' the solicitor said. 'She moved away, you know. Brian Davey told me she'd moved to Cardiff to live with her parents. No doubt he could give you her address if you need to contact her. In fact I can ring him if you like.'

Paget got to his feet and shook his head. 'Thanks, but that won't be necessary,' he said. 'I'm on my way to see him now.'

'Get anywhere with the lawyers?' Ormside asked when Paget returned to Charter Lane.

'Afraid not,' Paget said. 'Have you come up with anything?'

'According to his file, Whitelaw didn't notify anyone formally that he was divorced, and his ex-wife's still listed as his next of kin. Nor did he submit a change of address, though it seems that everyone he worked with knew where he was living. The South Wales Police sent someone round to break the news to his ex-wife, and to ask if she would come and identify the body. She said she'd rather not.'

'He was only in his thirties, so what about his parents?'

'Both went their separate ways when they were divorced ten years ago,' Ormside said. 'No other relatives on file. I spoke to payrolls in accounting, and they say Whitelaw's wages used to be paid into his bank account at Barclays by direct deposit, but he had that changed to payment by cheque to a PO box number four months ago, saying his current account was closed. But that's not entirely true,' Ormside continued. 'I had a word with the manager, and he said it was still open, but the most he's had on deposit for the past two months is twelve quid. He cashed his cheques at the bank, but he never banked any of it. And there's no record of a safe deposit box there either. Tregalles found his chequebook and a number of legal papers pertaining to his divorce in a cardboard box in his locker, but there's nothing unusual about them that we could see, so Tregalles has gone out to Oldfield Road to see what's stored out there.'

'We need to settle the matter of identifying the body,' Paget said, 'so see if you can persuade Mrs Whitelaw, or whatever her name is now, to come and do it.'

'Davies,' Ormside said. 'It's her maiden name. And I can give it another try, but the chap I spoke to down there said she was pretty blunt about it. She told him she never wants to see Whitelaw's face again, dead or alive, and wants nothing to do with his funeral, either. He said she was pretty bitter.'

'Try it anyway,' Paget told him. 'Apart from the formal identification, we need to talk to her, so it would be better if she could come here and we could do both at the same time. So tell her it's important that she come. It's not all that far, so she could do it and be back home the same day. You can tell her we'll pay for her travel and out-of-pocket expenses.'

'You mean there's been *another* one?' Joan Moreland said in hushed tones. 'Oh, my God! What is going on, Molly?'

'I really wish I could answer that,' Molly said, 'and that's why I'm here.' She took out a picture of Gavin Whitelaw and showed it to Joan. 'Have you ever seen this man before? Or do you know if your husband knew him or had anything to do with him? Please take your time, it's very important.'

Joan Moreland studied the picture carefully, then shook her head as she handed it back. 'I'm sure I've never seen him before,' she said slowly, 'but I suppose it's possible that Dennis might have known him through work or the theatre or something like that. Sorry, Molly, but that's all I can tell you. You say he's a policeman?'

'That's right.'

Joan looked puzzled for a moment, then stepped back a

pace, eyes narrowed as she looked at Molly suspiciously, and her voice took on a harder tone. 'I'm not sure I like the sound of this,' she said. 'If you're suggesting that Dennis and this man were involved in something . . . I don't know . . . something illegal, it isn't true, Molly. It isn't. Dennis would never . . . he was a *good* man; he loved me, he loved the kids, he . . .' Tears bubbled to the surface and spilled over.

Molly moved to her side and put a hand on her shoulder. 'I'm not suggesting *anything*,' she said quietly, 'but there has to be *something* linking these three men, and we have to find out what it is, because there may be others.'

Joan raised a tear-stained face to look at Molly. 'Well, I don't know what it is,' she said tightly. 'In fact, the more I think about it, the more I'm sure it was a mistake. I think this madman mistook Dennis for somebody else, and I don't think there ever was a connection. I'm sorry, Molly, but you're wasting your time here, because I know very well that Dennis was never involved with this policeman or the other man who was killed.'

Joan Moreland took a deep breath. 'I don't wish to sound unkind, Molly, but I'd like you to leave me alone now. The funeral's tomorrow and I have a lot to do, and I don't need this. So please go.' She shepherded Molly to the front door. 'And please don't come back again,' she said as she closed the door.

'You say he's the same one who said he knew Billy from when they were kids together?' George Travis shook his head as he looked hard at the picture again. 'No, I'm sure I've never seen him,' he said firmly. 'Billy used to tell me about who he'd seen that day and who he'd talked to, and I don't remember him ever talking about anybody called Whitelaw.' Travis sniffed hard then blew his nose. 'I miss that,' he said huskily, 'talking with Billy. He was a good lad. He didn't deserve to die like that. I miss my boy, I really do.'

It was late in the day and Molly knew she was probably wasting her time, but since Trudy Mason lived just around the corner, she decided to stop there before going home. So she was taken by surprise when Trudy took one look at Whitelaw's picture and said, 'Oh, him. Oh, yes, I remember him all right. Why do you want to know?'

'You know him?' Molly said. 'How? Have you known him long?'

Trudy chuckled. 'When I said I *know* him, I just meant I remember him from when he stopped me on the ring road. Tried to chat me up. Tell you the truth I was quite flattered, so I played along and it worked. Let me off with a caution, then rang me up the next day to ask if I'd got home all right. Cheeky sod! I told him yes, I did, and I was ever so grateful for him letting me off, and my husband was, too.' Trudy laughed. 'I didn't catch what he said before he slammed the phone down, but I don't think it was complimentary.'

'When was this?'

Trudy thought. 'Seven, maybe eight months ago,' she said. 'I don't know exactly. It was in the spring. Is it important?'

'To be honest, I really don't know,' Molly confessed. 'Why did he stop you?'

Trudy grimaced. 'I was in a bit of a hurry, and I changed lanes and almost cut somebody up. The bloke blew his horn and gave me the finger, and it just happened that the cop car was behind him and this chap saw it all.' She tapped the picture. 'Why are you asking? What's he done? Something to do with a woman, I'll bet. He's the sort.'

'He was killed this morning,' Molly said.

'Killed . . .?' Trudy repeated. Her eyes narrowed. 'How?' she asked cautiously.

'He was murdered in the same way Billy was murdered, which is why we're looking for a connection between the two. Did you tell Billy about the incident on the ring road?'

Trudy nodded.

'What was Billy's reaction?'

'We had a laugh about . . .' Trudy paused, frowning. 'Well, I did,' she continued slowly. 'I thought the whole thing was hilarious, but Billy didn't think it was funny at all. He got quite serious about it. Said someone like that should be reported. Went on about it for a while, but I finally jollied him out of it.' She lowered her voice as if afraid she might be overheard. 'To tell you the truth, I thought he was jealous, and I was quite chuffed about it.'

'Did you know Whitelaw's name at the time?'

'Oh, yes. He told me who he was. In fact he made sure I'd remember it. Thought he was God's gift. You know the sort.'

'And you told Billy who the man was?'

Trudy nodded once again.

'Did the subject ever come up again? More recently, perhaps?'

'No. After the way Billy went on, I never mentioned it again, and neither did he.'

'What about your husband? Did you tell him about it?'

'Gordon? No. He was away at the time, and I don't think I ever told him.' Trudy frowned, thinking back. 'No, I'm sure I didn't. I'd forgotten all about it by the time Gordon got home, and it was only when you showed me the picture today that I remembered it again.'

THIRTEEN

Friday, 21 October

It was Tregalles who attended the funeral of Dennis Moreland, and the same sandy-haired man was there taking pictures as discreetly as he had the Sunday before. The two sets would be compared to see if there was anyone who had attended both funerals, yet looked out of place. It was a long shot, but killers had been known to attend the funerals of their victims.

The funeral was held at the Unitarian church in Radnor Street, and Molly should have gone, but after her brush with Joan Moreland the day before, it was decided that Tregalles should go instead. The small church was almost full. Clearly, Moreland had been well liked, and Tregalles recognized several members of the SuperFair staff, including Moreland's boss, Norman Beasley. The man looked quite presentable in his somewhat dated three-piece suit, and he was almost obsequious in his approach to Joan as she and the children left the church.

Following the service, Tregalles drove out to the storage depot on Oldfield Road, where two junior DCs were loading cardboard boxes into a van to be taken back to Charter Lane. Eight boxes in all, three of which were unopened, still bound by tape, while the rest were filled with a variety of loose articles ranging from books and magazines to tools, bits of clothing, glass mugs, a toaster, and assorted mismatched plates and cups and saucers.

Tregalles took a look inside the locker. Still remaining were a chest of drawers, a small workbench, a bookshelf with one of the shelves missing, a lawn mower, garden tools, a bicycle and a rolled-up braided rug.

'Never mind the rest of this stuff,' he told the two men. 'Lock up and take those boxes in to DS Ormside, and if he asks you where I'll be, you can tell him that DCI Paget and I are off to look at cars.'

'Detective Chief Inspector Paget,' Fulbright repeated as he came out from behind his desk to shake hands. 'Didn't I see something in the paper about you a few weeks back? To do with those murders out at Bromley Manor? Surprised the hell out of me, I can tell you. Charles Bromley and his wife were clients of mine. You never know, do you?' Fulbright rubbed his hands together. 'So, what can I do for you gentlemen? Please, have a seat.' He returned to his own chair behind his desk. 'I suppose it's too much to hope you're here to buy a fleet of police cars?'

'Not today,' Paget told him. 'We're here to ask if you've had dealings with one of our officers recently. PC Gavin Whitelaw?'

Fulbright's shaggy eyebrows came down in a solemn frown. 'I heard about what happened,' he said gravely. 'I couldn't believe it. Gavin was here in this office last Tuesday, sitting where you are now. I know things hadn't been going all that well for him lately, what with the divorce and all, but he seemed all right when he was here. What happened? They didn't say on the news, so I wondered if it was suicide.'

'We're treating it as a suspicious death,' Paget told him. 'Were you a friend of his, Mr Fulbright?'

'Mike, please,' said Fulbright expansively. 'Nobody calls me Mr Fulbright.' He put the frown back in place. 'I've known Gavin on and off for years,' he said, seeming to choose his words carefully, 'but I wouldn't say we were *friends*, exactly. He bought his last car from us and he drops in from time to time, just for a look round. You know how it is with some people; they like to look at the latest models even when they know they're not ready to buy.'

'So, if not a friend, I'm wondering why he would come to you rather than one of your sales staff,' Paget said.

'Oh, I see. Well, that's simple enough. I *was* one of the sales staff when Gavin bought his first car from us, so he continues to come to me. If he's serious about buying, I turn him over to one of our sales people to close the deal. But why are you asking? What's this all about?'

Tregalles spoke up. 'We're trying to trace his movements during the past few days, and we found your business card in his pocket,' he said. 'You say he was here on Tuesday?'

'That's right.'

'Thinking of buying a new car, was he?' He nodded in the direction of the showroom.

Fulbright shook his head. 'Hardly,' he said. 'I'm sure he'd have liked to, but to be honest, I very much doubt if he could afford it, not with the divorce and all.'

'So why did he come in, then?' asked Paget.

'He was on a fishing trip,' Fulbright said. 'Fishing for a price on the car he wanted to trade in. You know how it is: you're toying with the idea of trading your car in, so you try to get a feel for the market and find out what your old car might be worth. Doesn't do any good, of course, because we never make a valuation on something we haven't seen recently, so I told him the same as I tell everyone else: bring it in and we'll take a look at it.'

'Do you recall the make and model of the car he was talking about trading in?'

'Yes. It was a Nissan X-Trail station wagon, 2006. As I said, I sold it to him myself, back then.'

'Was he going to bring the car in for valuation?'

Fulbright shrugged. 'He said he would, but I suspect he was going to try other dealers as well to see if he could coax them into giving him a price. I doubt if he would have succeeded, but people like to try.'

'Did you talk about anything else?' Paget asked. 'Other than cars, I mean.'

Fulbright shrugged. 'Not really. I'd heard about his divorce and we spoke briefly about that, but I can't remember anything else of consequence.' His frown deepened. 'But I don't understand what this has got to do with Gavin's death. Why are you asking all these questions?'

Paget got to his feet. 'As Sergeant Tregalles said earlier, we are trying to trace Whitelaw's movements in the days leading up to his death, and to establish his state of mind. Would you say he was in good spirits when he left you on Tuesday?'

Fulbright shrugged. 'As far as I could tell, he seemed to be his usual self.'

'Then thank you, Mr Fulbright. If you should think of anything else that you talked about, even if it seems insignificant, please give me a call.' He took out a card and handed it to Fulbright.

Tregalles stood up and Fulbright came out from behind his desk to usher them to the door, then handed each of them a card. 'And please do keep us in mind if you should need new cars, either personal or for business. I could give you a very good deal either way.'

'We will,' Paget assured him. He paused at the door. 'Did Whitelaw speak to anyone else while he was here?' he asked.

'Just my receptionist, Anita Chapman, when she showed him into the office.'

'Right. Then thanks again, Mr Fulbright. We'll have a word with her on our way out.'

'Not much help there,' Tregalles observed as they drove away. 'From the receptionist, I mean. Good looking woman, though. Bet she hasn't done the business any harm.'

'But she did call Whitelaw by his first name,' Paget pointed out, 'and she knew about the divorce, so I suspect both she and her boss knew the man better than Fulbright led us to believe. And, since I can't think of a reason why Whitelaw would go in there to talk about trading in a car he'd sold months ago, I think Mr Fulbright's lying about the reason for Whitelaw's visit. The question is, why, and what did they talk about? I think I'll have Len do a bit of digging into that man's background.'

Paget didn't speak again until they pulled into Charter Lane. 'What did you say they call Mike Fulbright on the rugby field?' he asked as they got out of the car. 'The Avenger?'

'That's right. He's—' Tregalles stopped. 'Oh, come on, boss. Mike Fulbright?' The sergeant sounded genuinely shocked. 'You're not thinking *he's* our killer, are you? He's the Grinders' star player.'

'Just a thought, Tregalles,' said Paget mildly. 'But the word "Avenger" does start with a capital A.'

Ormside waved both men over to his desk when they entered the room. 'I have Dr Starkie's autopsy report on Whitelaw,' he told them as they approached. 'Nothing fancy about this one, by the look of it. There was a lot of damage done to the back of the head when he hit the ground, but there was also a separate injury, a blow that left a curved indentation on the left side of the head. Starkie says the blow might have been enough to kill him, but he thinks it more likely that it merely stunned him. The weapon used was the proverbial blunt instrument, possibly a piece of one-inch metal pipe.'

Ormside tilted back in his chair and locked his fingers behind his head. 'And he could very well be right,' he concluded, 'because one of Charlie's people found just such a piece of pipe in the bottom of a waste bin inside the door leading out onto the roof. It's gone to forensic for examination, but it'll be next week before we know if there's any blood, hair or useful fingerprints on it. But it is the right shape and size.'

'So,' said Paget, 'I take it he's suggesting that Whitelaw was lured to the roof on some pretext or other, then hit on the head the moment he stuck his head out. And I think he's right when he says he doesn't think the blow killed Whitelaw, because the man's hands and mouth were taped. He was probably hauled to his feet, then frog-marched to the edge of the roof and pushed off. Also, as Starkie pointed out to me at the scene, there was a fair bit of blood on the dressing on his forehead, which suggests that Whitelaw was still alive, but hopefully unconscious, when the letter A was carved in his forehead.'

There was a memo on Paget's desk when he arrived back at the office, and a similar message on his voice mail, both from Fiona, asking him to set aside some time, following the briefing on Monday morning, to discuss staffing levels and the role of key personnel in his section with Superintendent Pierce.

'Whatever that means,' he muttered under his breath. Didn't she realize she would be wasting her time? There was no way Brock was going to budge on manpower, and what she meant by 'the role of key personnel', he had no idea. He was about to toss the memo when he remembered what Grace had said, and decided he was being churlish. If a similar message had come from Alcott he wouldn't have responded that way at all. In fact he would have welcomed the superintendent's interest in the subject, no matter what the outcome.

He looked at the clock, twenty past five. Fiona would be gone, but Amanda might still be there. He rang her number, but was greeted by her voice mail, asking him to leave a message after the tone . . .

Mike Fulbright rolled over on his back and said, 'Sorry, 'Nita, but it isn't working, is it? Too much on my mind, I'm afraid.'

Anita Chapman pulled the covers over her naked body. 'No, it's not working,' she said peevishly. 'I thought you'd died halfway through. Not exactly flattering, Mike. What's the matter? I knew there was something wrong the minute you came in. Is it something to do with the police? They were asking me about Gavin after they came out of your office. What's going on?'

'Nothing's going on,' he snapped irritably. He raised himself on one elbow and reached for the glass half full of whisky on the night table and drank. 'It's nothing.'

Anita pulled herself up in bed. 'I'm not a fool, Mike,'

she said, 'so don't treat me like one. Something *is* wrong, so tell me.'

Fulbright glared at her. 'I *told* you, it's *nothing*! As for what happened just now, I'm just tired, that's all. Anyway, it's time I left. Rachel invited some people in for drinks around eight, so I'd better be going.' He drained the glass and swung his legs out of bed.

'You didn't say anything about that when you came in. You just thought that up, didn't you?'

'So what if I did?' he snarled. 'You and your damned questions. I have to go.' He softened his tone as he began to dress. 'Sorry,' he said brusquely. 'Didn't mean to snap at you. But I do mean it when I say there's nothing for you to worry about.'

Anita eyed him stonily. She knew he was lying or at least holding something back, but there was no point in pushing it with Mike. Push him too far and you'd pay for it; she'd learned that a long time ago. But she'd seldom seen him like this. 'Will I be seeing you over the weekend?' she asked. 'I'm not at work tomorrow, remember? And Graham will be away until the middle of next week.'

'I'll have to see,' Mike said vaguely. 'I'll call you.'

But calling Anita was the farthest thing from his mind as he drove home. It looked as if Gavin had been right after all, but he'd dismissed the warning. Now Gavin was dead, killed in the same way as the other two. But an A carved in their foreheads? Bullshit! That was an invention of Gavin's, it had to be. There'd been no mention of anything like that in the papers or on radio and TV. Gavin must have made that up to try to convince him.

But the fact remained that all three men were dead. The first two *could* have been a coincidence, and that was what he'd told Gavin, but three . . . He couldn't ignore that. An involuntary shiver ran through his heavy frame. He wasn't afraid, he told himself. If anyone wanted to have a go at him, they'd find him a tougher nut to crack than Billy Travis, or Dennis, or Gavin. But it was worrying, just the same. And why now?

* * *

'Oh, no, not again,' Grace groaned. 'You can't keep doing this to yourself, Neil. You have to take some time off. You're going to make yourself ill if you keep working at this pace, and I'm sure it would do you more good to get out in the fresh air instead of spending the day in the office. The weather forecast's good and it's been months since you were last out. We're doing the circular route, beginning and ending in Clun, so I'll have to get to bed early if I'm to be up and on the road by six thirty. Starting time is eight o'clock. I'm sure you'd enjoy it, Neil. It's a reasonable distance, roughly nineteen kilometres – eleven and a half miles, if that sounds better. It's a mixed group, so we'll be going at a leisurely pace, and I know you haven't done that route before. What do you say?'

'Believe me, Grace, I'd like nothing better than to be out there on a walking tour with you, but with this serial killer on the loose, and having to spend so much time with Amanda, my own paperwork's been piling up and I'm so far behind I can't put it off any longer.'

'Then do it Sunday. It doesn't matter which day it is as long as it gets done, does it?'

Paget looked sheepish. 'I wasn't going to mention it tonight, but I planned on working Sunday as well. I wasn't kidding when I said there's a lot to do.'

Grace shook her head and sighed in weary resignation. 'I'd come in and help you if I could,' she said, 'but as I told you, it's a new group and I'm team leader, so I have to go.' She looked at the clock and got to her feet. 'Anyway, it's twenty to ten now, so I'd better start getting ready for bed. There's nothing worth watching on TV, so why don't you come up as well and have an early night for a change?' She stretched out her hand. 'And perhaps I can persuade you that there are better ways to spend your time than working all hours.'

FOURTEEN

Monday, 24 October

The Monday morning briefing was depressingly short. Ormside reported that he had spoken to a number of Whitelaw's colleagues. 'As you can imagine, there was a reluctance to speak up against one of their own, but the picture I came away with was that, even though he was still only a PC, Whitelaw used his seniority to intimidate the junior officers. He borrowed money from them, none of which he ever paid back, and I think there's little doubt he was hated by the WPCs and female civilian staff alike. We also know from the record of his divorce that he was unfaithful, abusive and addicted to gambling, so if we're looking for a motive for murder, we shouldn't have to look far.

'However,' he continued, 'while we can't ignore those as potential lines of enquiry, the fact remains that the manner of his death matches the MO of the two previous deaths of Travis and Moreland, so that still remains front and centre as far as motive is concerned.'

'Could be a copycat killing,' one of the men suggested. 'Someone smart enough to take advantage of the way the other two were killed. Throw us off the track.'

'Except for the letter A on his forehead,' Ormside said. 'That still hasn't been made public. No, I don't think so.'

'But it was known by a lot of us,' the man persisted, 'and you said yourself, Sarge, there were people who hated him.'

'Fair point,' Ormside conceded. 'All right, we'll keep it in mind.'

The boxes from the storage locker had been emptied, their contents examined, catalogued, and then repacked and sent to the evidence room. Except for one box containing files and legal papers that had yet to be examined.

Hardly a promising start to the week, thought Paget grimly as he made his way upstairs. And the thought of having to tell

Amanda Pierce, once again, that they were no closer to finding the killer than they had been on day one did not sit well. He'd had dry spells on other cases, but somehow it had been different when Alcott was in charge. This time it wasn't just different; it was personal as well.

'Surely it can't be that bad, Mr Paget?'

Startled, he looked up to see Fiona sitting at her desk. So immersed in his own concerns had he been that he had all but walked right past her. 'Sorry, Fiona,' he said, forcing a rueful smile. 'I'm afraid I was miles away, and I'm afraid the answer is yes, it *is* that bad.'

'The serial killer?' Fiona said. 'I know. I was downstairs a while ago, and you could cut the atmosphere with a knife. But I'd better not keep you,' she said briskly, with a flick of the head in the direction of the closed door. 'Superintendent Pierce is expecting you, so you can go in.'

Amanda was standing by the window, looking out. She held a mug of coffee in both hands as if to warm them, and she turned to face him as he entered. She wore a stylish two-piece tan-coloured suit, and a crisp white blouse with a high collar under the jacket. She looked very smart, very cool, every inch the executive as she turned to greet him. 'Good morning, Neil,' she said, and waved him to a seat.

'Good morning,' he said stiffly as he settled into the chair.

'Would you like a coffee before we begin?' she asked.

He shook his head. 'I had some downstairs,' he said, 'so thanks but no.'

Amanda walked over to her desk and sat down. 'I think we can dispense with a report on this morning's briefing,' she said tersely, 'because I had a word with DS Ormside earlier, and he told me where we stand. It's not good, and I don't like it, but there's nothing to be gained by my taking my frustration out on you. So let's deal with things we can do something about. But first, a question: after you left the Met, you came into Westvale Region as an inspector, but when you were promoted to chief inspector, the position you left behind was never filled. Can you tell me why that was?'

'In theory, the job's still open,' he said, 'but if you have any thoughts of posting it, I suggest you forget it. It'll die on

Mr Brock's desk. It's his way of cutting costs, and I don't think there ever was an intention to fill it. In effect, the two jobs were combined.'

Amanda nodded. 'I did wonder if it was something like that,' she said. Then, 'You were working here all through the weekend, weren't you?'

'That's right,' he said, 'as were you, I believe?'

'True,' she said, 'but in my case I'm coming into a new job and I have some catching up to do. But I don't intend to keep it up, and neither should you. How many weekends have you had off in the last six months, say? Complete weekends, Saturday and Sunday.'

'It's a nice thought,' he said, avoiding the question, 'but with the way work's piling up and with a serial killer running loose, it's just not possible.'

Amanda sat back and clasped her hands together. 'Then perhaps we should be making use of the resources we have to better advantage so it is possible,' she said. 'I've been talking to your sergeants,' she continued, then waved a hand in the air as she saw he was about to speak. 'No, I wasn't going over your head, Neil. I just wanted to get to know them a little bit better and let them get to know me as well.'

Amanda leaned forward to rest her arms on the desk. 'You have some good people,' she said quietly. 'In fact, with the recent promotion of DS Forsythe, we seem to have a surplus of sergeants, at least for the foreseeable future, and I think we should take advantage of that while we can, because I'd like you to spend less time out in the field and more time doing what you're supposed to be doing as a DCI.' She held up her hand as he started to protest. 'That isn't a criticism,' she said. 'I can imagine what it must have been like around here following Superintendent Alcott's departure. You've been trying to do this job as well as your own, and you've been spending far too much time out in the field doing the work of others. Tell me, what is your honest assessment of DS Tregalles? Is he ready to take the next step to inspector?'

Paget wasn't sure where this was leading, but Amanda had asked a fair question. 'Yes,' he said, 'I think he is, *if*, and I emphasize the *if*, he buckles down to studying for the exams.

I believe he could handle the job, but he's been dragging his feet on the studies.'

Amanda nodded. 'I had a talk with him about that the other day,' she said, 'and I think I may have persuaded him that it would be for the best if he did get on with OSPRE. And if, as you say, he is capable of doing the job, I suggest we start using him as we would an inspector, and allow you to spend more time doing your job. You have an excellent man in DS Ormside, and you have a promising DS in Forsythe, who has nowhere to go at the moment. And with everyone cutting staff, her chances of getting a permanent posting are slim, at least for the time being, so let's use her.

'In short, what I'm suggesting, Neil, is that we even out the load.'

'And telling me that I haven't been doing my job?' he said thinly.

A hint of steel crept into Amanda's next words. 'What I'm saying, Neil, is that you haven't been *allowed* to do your job because of so many pressures from all sides. When you took on the responsibilities of a DCI, the vacancy you'd left behind wasn't filled, so, as you said yourself, you took that workload with you. Then, when Superintendent Alcott left so suddenly, you ended up trying to do all three jobs.'

Amanda sat back. 'I believe we can correct that situation if we redistribute the workload. Give Tregalles more responsibility; let's see what he can do when he has to make some of the decisions you've been making. Give him a chance to come out from under your shadow, and let's see what Forsythe can do as well. I don't see this as a formal arrangement – there are no acting positions, no extra pay is involved. In fact, I don't think we should even tell them what we're doing. I suggest we simply do it. Just gradually shift responsibilities onto their shoulders and see how they respond. It'll be good training for them, and it'll relieve you. I know how much you like to be out there on the front line, but you can't do it all, Neil. You have to let the others shoulder some of the load and responsibility.'

Paget remained silent, elbows on the arms of the chair and fingers steepled, as he tried to decide whether he was being reprimanded for not doing his job, or if Amanda was genuinely interested in evening out the workload. It would mean spending more time in the office while more interesting things were happening in the field, and he would miss that part of the job. On the other hand, that was the way it was supposed to work. More troubling was the realization that he had done nothing to change the situation himself. In fact he had used the lack of manpower to justify doing much of the fieldwork that should have been left to Tregalles and the rest of the team. Now, he was being called on it by none other than Amanda Pierce, and he was finding that hard to swallow, especially when his inner voice was telling him she was right.

'Well, Neil?' Amanda prodded gently.

He drew a deep breath and let it out again. 'You're probably right,' he conceded as he got to his feet. 'Is that all?'

Amanda sensed resistance in the words. 'For now,' she said neutrally. 'We'll review the situation in a month and see how it's going.'

Returning to his office, Paget had only just sat down when the phone rang. 'Press office here, sir,' a young female voice said when he answered. 'Just had a call from the *Sun*. They say they've had an anonymous tip about the recent murders, and they want to know if it's true that the letter A was carved in the forehead of each victim. Our orders here are not to release that information, so I gave him the usual "unable to confirm at this time", but I got the impression they might run with it as a speculative piece anyway.'

'That wouldn't surprise me,' Paget said. 'Thanks for letting me know. I'll get back to you if there's any change.'

He had hoped to keep that information under wraps, but he'd known it would only be a matter of time before it was leaked to the press. There was always someone willing to take a few quid under the table in return for information. He thought about it for a moment, then picked up the phone. No matter how they had obtained the information, he'd better warn Amanda. Regardless of his personal feelings, they were still a team, and she had enough on her plate without being blindsided by something like this.

* * *

'Doesn't matter how she tried to wrap it up and put a bow on it, she was telling me I haven't been doing my job,' Paget concluded after telling Grace about his session with Amanda that morning. 'The trouble is she's right, but I didn't have much choice with the way things have been.'

'Which she recognized, from what you've told me,' Grace said. 'In fact, what she's suggesting sounds like a sensible solution. I know how much you like to be out there on the front line, but I'm sure John Tregalles is quite capable of doing the job, and it'll give Molly Forsythe more responsibility and a worthwhile bit of training before she moves on. And it just might allow you to have a life as well, so no matter what you may think of Superintendent Pierce, or what she did before, I think she's on the right track now.'

Amanda Pierce clicked the remote and the picture on the screen faded to black. She'd been trying to take her mind off what she saw as a disaster in the making, but it wasn't working. Coming into a new job at any time could be difficult, especially when you were competing in what was still very much a man's world, but the timing in this case couldn't have been worse. A serial killer on her patch; three people dead, all killed in the same way, yet seemingly unconnected in any other way.

As if that weren't enough, the DCI leading the investigation hated her. Not that she could blame Neil for feeling that way, but that part of her life was over now. She'd done her best to put it behind her and she had hoped – vainly now, she realized – that Neil might have done the same. Stupid of her. It had been too much to expect, given the circumstances.

Twirling the stem of an empty wine glass absently between her fingers, Amanda got up and wandered over to the window. The only light in the room came from a street lamp a few yards from the building. A desultory drizzle had begun just after nine o'clock, but it was raining steadily now and it looked as if it had settled in for the night. Normally the street was busy until midnight, but by now the traffic had all but disappeared, and there wasn't a pedestrian to be seen. Not a night to be out and about.

Behind her the mantel clock chimed eleven. She should go

to bed and try to sleep, but she knew it would be pointless. Amanda moved to the table and picked up the half-empty bottle of an Australian Riesling she'd discovered recently, and refilled her glass. Too many things to think about; too many memories buzzing around inside her head as she settled into the armchair and wrapped the darkness around her.

FIFTEEN

Tuesday, 25 October

Following the briefing next morning, Molly Forsythe and DC Maxwell were given the task of going through the files and loose papers in the box taken from the storage locker, which included several old chequebooks. Maxwell had only recently rejoined the team after spending a year with the fraud squad on white collar crime, where he'd acquired some accounting skills. So anything to do with money, bills, invoices, credit cards, bank statements and so on, was to be turned over to him.

'As for the rest,' Ormside told Molly, 'files, papers, letters, whatever else is in there, go through them carefully. We still need that connection between the victims.' He sat down at his desk and turned his attention to Tregalles. 'You said something during the briefing about talking to one of the salesmen at Bridge Street Motors last night,' he said. 'What was that about?'

'Just a bit of fishing, that's all,' Tregalles said. 'I just happened to be down near there last evening, and I saw the salesman, a chap by the name of Leyland, who was there the day Paget and I went to see Mike Fulbright. So I stopped in and asked him if he'd been there when Whitelaw had gone in to see Fulbright, and he said he was. Then he said, "You mean the day they had the argument?"

'He said he was outside, but he could see them through the window. Whitelaw was waving his arms about, and their voices were raised, but not enough that he could hear what was said. But one thing's for sure,' Tregalles ended, 'whatever they were arguing about, I'll lay odds it wasn't about a non-existent Nissan X-Trail station wagon.'

Paget pulled a folder from the in tray and opened it. He looked at the date and mentally winced. Two months old, and he'd barely looked at it in all that time. Fortunately, timing wasn't all that important in this case, but it did serve to remind him that he had not been giving his full attention to this part of the job. He just wished it had been someone other than Amanda Pierce who had pointed that out to him.

The ringing of the phone interrupted his train of thought.

'I have an outside caller asking to speak to you, sir,' said a female voice when he answered. 'She says her name is Valerie Alcott.'

Valerie! Alcott's youngest daughter. 'Yes, by all means, put her through,' he said.

'Valerie,' he said when he heard her voice. 'How are you, and—'

'Sorry to trouble you at work, Mr Paget,' Valerie cut in apologetically, 'but I thought you would want to know. My father died last night.'

'Oh, Valerie, I'm so very sorry. Is there anything I can do? Is anyone with you? Is your sister with you?'

'Celeste?' Valerie was trying hard to control her voice. 'No. I phoned her, of course, but she . . . she won't be coming. She and Dad never . . .' She drew a deep, shuddering breath. 'It's just that it was a shock, even though I was afraid it might happen this way. He didn't want to live any more, Mr Paget. He hanged himself.'

Her voice caught, and it was a moment before she could go on. 'It's just that he always spoke so highly of you, and you were so helpful when he went missing, I thought . . .' She broke down and began to cry.

'Where are you, Valerie?' he asked. 'Are you at home? Would you like me to come over?'

'No, no thank you. I'm all right, really I am. I've been handling Dad's affairs since he went into . . . into hospital, and his solicitor has been very helpful, so he's coming round to help me sort things out. He said there will have to be an inquest.'

The full impact of what Valerie had said finally sank in, and he felt as if he had been kicked in the stomach, followed closely by an overwhelming feeling of guilt. He'd been meaning to visit Thomas Alcott ever since he'd been transferred to the psychiatric long-term care unit in Tenborough. But that was two months ago, and somehow the time had slipped by and he'd never made it.

'Are you still there, Mr Paget?'

'Yes. Yes, I am, Valerie. It's just that I don't know what to say. I liked your father very much, and I'm so sorry to hear he's gone.'

'He blamed himself, you know.' Her voice was firmer now. 'Blamed himself for my mother's death. His second-hand smoke. He never got over it. But he's at peace now, and I have to accept that.' She drew a deep breath. 'Sorry to go on like that, but I think you understand.'

'I do,' said Paget. 'And I mean it: if there's anything I can do, please don't hesitate to call me. The funeral . . .? I suppose that will depend upon the inquest?'

'That's right. But I will let you know, and it'll be in the paper, of course. Goodbye, and thank you again, Mr Paget.'

He hung up the phone. His vision was blurred and his nose wouldn't stop running. He opened the bottom drawer of the desk, took out a couple of Kleenex and blew hard.

The phone on Ormside's desk rang. The blinking light indicated a call from the front office.

'There's a woman by the name of Davies out here at the front desk,' he was told when he answered. 'Says she used to be Mrs Whitelaw. She says she's come up from Cardiff to ID the body.'

'Right,' Ormside said. So she had decided to come after all. Perhaps it was the offer to pay her way that had changed her mind. 'Hold her there and I'll have someone come for her in a few minutes. Be nice to her. Offer her a cup of tea and a biscuit.'

He dropped the phone back on its rest, then got up and went down the hall to the room next door where Molly and Maxwell were working their way through Whitelaw's effects.

'Sorry to drag you away, Molly,' he said, 'but I've got a job for you. Bronwyn Davies, Whitelaw's ex-wife, is here to ID his body. She's at the front desk. I'd like you to take care of her, then bring her back here, because Mr Paget wants to talk to her himself.'

Bronwyn Davies was a small, dark-haired woman, who told Molly that she was only there because she feared there would be 'consequences' if she didn't comply. When Molly asked what she meant by that, what she got in return was a disdainful toss of the head, and, '*You* know very well what I mean, so don't pretend you don't!' The remark made no sense whatsoever to Molly, but, wisely, she let it go.

During the short drive to the mortuary, Bronwyn Davies complained bitterly about the inconvenience of having to come back to Broadminster to identify her former husband, when, as she said, 'Any one of your lot could have done the same, because he spent more time at work than he ever did with me.'

They'd done a pretty good job on his face, considering its appearance on the night he died, but it was still not a pleasant sight. Bronwyn showed no emotion as she looked down on her former husband, then turned away without saying a word.

'This *is* Gavin Whitelaw?' Molly prompted. She wanted to get it right this time.

'Of course it's bloody Gavin Whitelaw,' Bronwyn snapped. 'Can we go now?' She looked at her watch. 'How long is this interview thing going to take?'

'I shouldn't think it will take very long,' Molly said, hoping that she wouldn't have to take part. She was finding it hard enough to be civil to the woman as it was, so the sooner she was rid of her the better. She checked herself. Perhaps she was being unfair. Bronwyn Davies had been reluctant to come to ID the body of her former husband, but she had come. So, perhaps, in spite of everything that had gone on before, there were some deeply hidden feelings beneath the hard and brittle exterior she was presenting to the world.

Impulsively, she said, 'I'm sorry you had to come all this way to do this, Ms Davies. It's never a pleasant duty under any circumstances, so thank you.'

Bronwyn shot a sidelong glance at Molly, then shook her head. 'You really mean that, don't you?' she said as if in wonder. 'After what he did to me, the only reason I came back here today was to make sure the bastard was dead, and if you think I'm going to help you find who killed him, you can forget it.'

'How is she?' Paget asked as he and Tregalles prepared to talk to Bronwyn Davies. 'Things go all right at the mortuary? Any emotional problems?'

'Depends what you mean by emotional problems, sir,' said Molly drily. 'After she viewed the body, she said the only reason she agreed to come was to make sure that Whitelaw was dead. And she made a point of telling me she wasn't prepared to help us find his killer.'

'She actually said that?'

'She did, sir. And I'm sure she meant every word. She's a very bitter woman.'

Paget thought about that for a moment. 'In that case,' he said, 'since she already knows you, perhaps it would be best if you sit in with me rather than Tregalles. All right?'

Molly groaned inwardly, then said, 'Certainly, sir,' and tried to sound as if she meant it.

Bronwyn Davies sat straight and rigid in her chair, lips pursed, eyes narrowed suspiciously. She looked up just long enough to register who was coming into the room, then looked away again. Paget introduced himself as he and Molly took their places facing her across the table, and said, 'I believe you already know Detective Sergeant Forsythe.'

The woman stared at him, but gave no sign that she had heard what he'd said.

'I know that coming here today must have been difficult and stressful for you,' Paget continued, 'so this is an informal interview, and I'll try to keep it as short as possible. As you know, we are investigating the murder of your former husband, so any help you can give us regarding his activities before you parted company and moved away would be very much appreciated.'

Her eyes shifted to Molly, then back again to Paget. 'Didn't she tell you I'm not interested in who killed him?' she said. 'He stole ten years of my life and I'm glad he's dead. He deserved it, so why should I help you catch his killer?'

'I'm sure you have your reasons for saying that,' said Paget, 'but two other men have died at the hands of the same person, both good men according to those they left behind, and I'm very much afraid there could be more victims if we don't find the killer soon. So, much as I might regret your former husband's treatment of you, I cannot let that stand in the way of finding his killer before he kills again. Do you understand me, Ms Davies?'

Cold, unblinking eyes continued to stare at him from beneath half-lowered lids. But Paget's eyes didn't waver, and it was Bronwyn who looked away and said, 'What do you want to know, then?'

'First of all, did you ever hear him mention a man by the name of Billy Travis? He was a photographer. Or Dennis Moreland? He was a butcher.'

'I don't think so,' she said slowly, 'but then we were hardly on speaking terms the last couple of years before the divorce. He came and went, and Megan and I did our best to steer clear of him when he was home.'

'Can you tell us anything about who his friends were? I haven't read the details of the divorce, but was there ever any suggestion that he might have been involved with criminal elements?'

Bronwyn stared at him. 'You're asking *me*?' she said contemptuously. 'He *worked* for you, for twelve years, for Christ's sake, and you let him get away with murder. It's no wonder people don't have much faith in the police any more, when you let someone like Gavin do as he pleases. Drinking on the job, skiving off to go and screw one of his fancy women while his partner sat outside in the car twiddling his thumbs. And you want me to help you?'

The woman shook her head in disgust. 'God knows Gavin was bad enough, but what about his sergeant, eh? I haven't heard of anything happening to him, have I? Drinking together at all hours, womanizing, fiddling the overtime. Gavin used to boast about it. He'd make more in overtime some months than his regular wage, and he'd never worked a bit of it. Not that I ever saw any extra money. He'd sooner spend it on drink and betting and other women than let me see any of it.' Bronwyn sniffed contemptuously. 'And that sergeant's still there, isn't he? Protect your own, no matter what. Isn't that it? Lie, cover up, whatever it takes. You're all the same. Well, we'll see about that!'

Her eyes glittered as she leaned forward and jabbed an accusing finger at Paget. 'That man destroyed our lives,' she said softly, 'and you and all the rest of you are responsible. So you can stew in your own juice, as far as I'm concerned, because I'm not the least bit interested in helping you find the person who killed Gavin. Good luck to him, I say.'

Bronwyn Davies picked up her handbag and got to her feet. 'I'm going home now,' she said, 'and I don't want to hear from you ever again. And I'll be sending you a bill for every single penny I've spent coming here.' She walked to the door, then paused to look back at Molly. 'You seem like a decent sort,' she said, 'so let me give you a bit of advice. Get the hell out of here while you can. This is no place for the likes of you.'

She flicked a glance at Paget as he got to his feet. 'And I don't need you to see me out,' she said coldly. 'I'm sure I can find my own way, thank you very much.'

'Superintendent Alcott died last night,' Tregalles said as he hung the damp tea-towel up to dry. He leaned against the counter while Audrey put the last of the dinner plates away. 'Paget told me this afternoon. Valerie Alcott rang to tell him this morning.'

'Died?' Audrey said. 'I didn't know he was ill. I knew he was in that care place in Tenborough, but I thought that was because he had a breakdown after his wife died. What happened? How did he die?'

'Suicide, according to his daughter. He blamed himself for his wife's death from his second-hand smoke. She had emphysema if you remember.'

'Oh, dear, I am sorry to hear that,' Audrey said softly. 'How awful for the poor man, and for his family. I remember you used to go on about him, but I think you liked him, didn't you, love?'

'I did,' Tregalles said. 'He had a sharp tongue, and he was always in a hurry, always looking for a quick solution, but he always came round in the end, and he stood up to Brock for us on a good many occasions. He and Paget used to go a few rounds every now and again, but I know Paget was sorry to see him go, and he was sorrier still to hear the news this morning.'

'How's Mr Paget getting on with his new boss, then?'

'Superintendent Pierce?' Tregalles pursed his lips. 'I don't really know,' he said slowly. 'He hasn't said much to me about her, but he's been in a sort of funny mood ever since she came.'

Audrey sniffed. 'Hardly surprising, since she took the job that was his by rights.' Audrey had always been a big fan of Paget's.

But Tregalles was shaking his head. 'I don't think it's that,' he said. 'I know they've run into each other before, years ago in the Met, and I don't think they like each other very much, but he hasn't said anything against her. And considering the lack of progress we've made on these murders since she came, she's been pretty decent about it. Alcott would have been screaming bloody murder by now, but she sits in on the briefings and seems to understand the problems we're facing. Though God knows what she tells Brock.'

'You've changed your tune,' Audrey said. 'You were dead set against her before. What happened?'

Tregalles frowned into the distance as if thinking hard. 'I think it's those long legs,' he said slowly. 'And she's got a gorgeous fig—' He yelped and scooted away as Audrey chased him out of the room snapping the tea-towel at his behind.

SIXTEEN

Wednesday, 26 October

Tregalles looked at the clock. Twenty past ten. When he had asked Mike Fulbright to come in to make a statement, Fulbright had said he would be there at ten. He'd asked if he needed to bring his solicitor, and Tregalles had said, 'By all means, if you think you're going to need one.'

He had hoped that Maxwell or Molly might find something in the material taken from the storage locker that would tie Whitelaw to Fulbright, but no such luck. Confirmation of the sale of the Nissan X-Trail some six months ago was found among the papers, which gave the lie to Fulbright's story, at least as far as Tregalles was concerned. 'The man was not only broke after the divorce,' Maxwell said, 'he was in debt up to his ears. He was in a court-ordered debt reduction programme, but it would have taken at least three or four years to pay it all off had he lived. And that's assuming he didn't incur any more debts along the way. Which might explain why he was living in the cheapest place he could find down on Prince Street.'

Molly had nothing better to offer. 'The only things left from the locker are a couple of old biscuit tins full of odds and ends,' she said. 'Mostly junk as far as I could see when I took a quick look last night, but you never know, so I'll go through them as soon as I get a chance and let you know if I find anything important.'

Mike Fulbright was forty minutes late, and he arrived without a solicitor. 'Sorry if I held you up,' he said breezily as they took their seats in the interview room, 'but things to do, you know. Can't just leave them, can we? Specially when you're the boss.'

'This interview will be recorded,' Tregalles said, then went on to explain the procedure to Fulbright, and nodded for Maxwell to start the recorder. He'd intended to have Molly sit in, but, having mentioned the biscuit tins, Molly said she'd like to go through them and get them out of the way.

'Is there a problem?' he asked when he saw Fulbright frowning at the recorder.

'No. No. None whatsoever,' Fulbright said expansively. 'I'm here to help in any way I can.'

'Good, I'm glad to hear it,' Tregalles said, 'so perhaps you can begin by telling me why you felt it necessary to lie to DCI Paget and me when you said Gavin Whitelaw had come in to talk to you last week about trading in his car.'

Fulbright scowled. 'I certainly did not lie!' he said indignantly, 'and I didn't come here this morning to be treated like this. Gavin said he was thinking about trading his car in on a newer model, and we talked in general terms about that. As I told you, he was trying to get me to commit to a firm price for his car, but I told him I couldn't give him that without seeing it.'

'Did he say he would bring it in?'

'He said he'd think about it.' Fulbright did his best to look sad. 'Unfortunately, he never had the chance, poor devil.'

'And the make and model of the car you were discussing, sir, was a five-year-old Nissan X-Trail. Is that right?'

'That is what I said, Sergeant,' Fulbright said tightly.

'Did you talk about anything else?'

'Oh, for God's sake, man, where is all this leading?' Fulbright demanded. 'Yes, I suppose we talked of other things. I don't remember exactly.'

'Including the recent murders of Billy Travis and Dennis Moreland?' Tregalles prodded.

Fulbright hesitated. 'Why would we be talking about them?' he asked cautiously.

'You tell me,' Tregalles said, 'and please try to make what you tell me more believable than the load of bollocks you've been giving me about Whitelaw trading in his car.'

Fulbright's eyes narrowed. 'I did not come here to be insulted, Sergeant,' he said thinly, 'and I will not tolerate being spoken—'

'It's not an insult when it's the truth,' Tregalles cut in, 'so let's stop playing games and get to the truth, Mr Fulbright. You see, I have trouble believing you when I know that Whitelaw sold his car months ago to pay off debts. He was broke, he was living in a flea pit, and the furthest thing from his mind was buying a car. He couldn't afford a car of any description while he was still paying off debts. So I'll ask you again, what did you talk about?'

Fulbright stared hard at Tregalles. His jaw was set, but the slow rise of colour in his face betrayed him. 'I don't know what you're talking about,' he said belligerently. 'Why would he come in then?'

'Exactly my question,' Tregalles told him. 'Why, when he hadn't the faintest hope of buying a car, would he come in to talk to you? And it wasn't just talk, was it? It was a heated discussion, possibly even an argument. We have a witness who claims there was a lot of arm waving and shouting, and Whitelaw didn't look happy when he left. So I suggest we forget the load of crap you've been feeding me, and you start telling the truth. Which reminds me: where were you between midnight and three o'clock last Thursday morning?'

'Courses,' Amanda announced briskly. 'I've been looking at the record of the courses taken by all members of our staff in the past three years, and it appears that more than half of them were cancelled at the last minute. That's not a good sign, and I would like to correct that if I can, Neil. Apart from the odd case of sickness, I take it the rest of the cancellations were because of workload?'

'That's right,' he said. 'You've seen the figures, so you know what it's been like. You can cut staff and delay filling vacant positions, but there's always a price to pay, and one of the easiest things to cut back on is training. We budget for so many hours a year; we submit names and a proposed schedule, and Training uses that to allocate places. But when the time comes for that man or woman to go, all too often we simply can't afford to let them go for a week or sometimes two, so we cancel. It's a waste of our time making up a schedule we know we won't be able to keep, and it makes thing difficult for Training, because others are doing the same. And in some cases, a course has to be cancelled because it's not worth running for two or three people. So even the ones who *could* have gone lose out.

'Not only that,' he continued, now in full flight, 'most of our courses are taken at the West Mercia Training Centre in Hindlip Hall, and if we commit to a certain number of places, they have every right to charge us for those places if they aren't filled. If they have to cancel the course itself, it throws their scheduling out, and it leaves them with instructors idle for days or even weeks. Now, I'm sure West Mercia has similar problems, but it doesn't make for very good relations between the two regions. The result is, we're wasting time and money all the way up and down the line, and our people aren't as well trained as they should be.'

Paget settled back in his chair. 'God knows Superintendent Alcott and I tried to get Mr Brock and others to see that, but it was like talking to a brick wall for all the good it did. So I wish you luck, Amanda, I really do, because I think it's important, but I suspect you'll find the door is also closed on that one.'

Amanda Pierce nodded slowly. 'I suspected as much,' she said, 'and I'm sure you're right, but I'm wondering if we can't overcome some of the obstacles by doing some in-house training.' She slipped on her glasses and picked up a file. 'I see that you spent some time as an instructor at Hindlip Hall yourself, so I thought—'

Whatever Amanda was thinking was cut off by the ringing of her phone. She hesitated for a moment, then picked it up and said, 'Yes, Fiona?' She listened for some time, then said, 'Thank you, Fiona,' and put the phone down.

'It seems Fiona has developed something of a quiet relationship with Mr Brock's secretary, Claire Raeburn,' she said, 'and Claire phoned to let us know that Bronwyn Davies went over to New Street after she left here yesterday, and insisted on delivering a letter personally to the chief constable. She must have prepared it beforehand, because she repeated much of what she told you about her ex-husband and his sergeant, and said that, unless action is taken against the sergeant and *his* superior within the next thirty days, she'll go to the media with her story. Needless to say, it had the desired effect; there will be an internal investigation, and it sounds as if everyone in that section is already scurrying for cover.' The muscles around her mouth tightened, and her eyes were flinty as she said, 'It would have been nice if Mr Brock had told me that himself, but perhaps it just slipped his mind when we spoke earlier this morning. Anyway, I suppose I should be grateful that Whitelaw was in Uniforms under DS Grimshaw and not one of ours.' Amanda took in a deep breath, let it out again slowly and said, 'Now then, training. Where were we . . .?'

Picking through the contents of old, rusting biscuit tins was not Molly Forsythe's idea of how a newly minted detective sergeant should be spending her time. But, regardless of her feelings, the job had to be done, and as DS Ormside had pointed out, it should be done by someone who was familiar with what had been found among the possessions of the previous victims.

She looked at the list she'd been compiling as each item was removed: a fountain pen that used real ink, two pencils, a four-inch-wide paint brush that had never been cleaned and should have been tossed long ago; string; a pair of horn-rimmed glasses, a half-used packet of corn plasters; two batteries, corroded . . . Really! What was the point, she wondered as she put everything back and opened the second tin. More of the same by the look of it. God! The things people collected! Sticky tape, brittle with age; bits of cloth; more string and rubber bands, odds-and-sods of every description. Something in an envelope at the bottom of the tin. Photographs. She shuffled through them, counting as she went. Twenty-two of them, some fairly old, judging by their subject matter, and they were all of Gavin Whitelaw, from the time he was a boy of ten or twelve, to when he was about twenty. Pictures of him astride a motorbike, at the wheel of a car, on a beach with a group of young men waving bottles of beer about. Clearly, the man had thought a lot of himself, she thought as she studied each one.

She stopped at a group picture, a little different from the

rest. It was a picture of a choir outside a church. Adults, male and female, in the back row, teenagers in the middle row, small boys and girls in the front row. Molly recognized the church: All Saints on Riverview Road. And there was Gavin Whitelaw in cassock and surplice in the middle row. Thinner in the face and with hair brushing his shoulders, he'd been quite a good looking kid. Hard to think of him as a choir boy, but there he was, grinning at the camera.

A memory stirred in the back of her mind. A snapshot of an angelic looking Billy Travis in cassock and surplice. She stared at the picture in front of her. Yes! There was Billy at the end of the row. Older in this picture – sixteen or seventeen, perhaps? He was so slight and small compared to the other boys, it was hard to tell his age.

Molly sat back in her chair. So the two boys had been in the same choir back then, but did that mean anything? She opened a desk drawer, took out a magnifying glass and bent closer to examine each face, but if Dennis Moreland was there, she couldn't see him. She set the picture aside and dug back in her notes for Joan Moreland's telephone number.

Joan answered on the third ring. She sounded cheerful enough when she first answered, but her voice became guarded when Molly identified herself. 'Dennis? In the choir at All Saints?' she echoed when Molly asked the question. 'Oh, no. He didn't belong to any church when I first met him. It took me quite a while before I could persuade him to come to mine, and then it was only because of the children and Sunday school. What's this all about anyway?'

'We're still trying to find the reason for your husband's death,' Molly told her, 'so we have to look at every possibility, no matter how improbable. Sorry I had to trouble you again, Joan.'

'It's . . . it's no trouble.' Joan Moreland's voice had softened. 'And I'm sorry if I was short with you the other day. I know you were only trying to do your job. So if there is any way I can help, I don't mind if you call.'

So that fence was mended, thought Molly as she put her phone away, but she was still no further ahead. She sat looking at the photograph, then made up her mind. It might not come to anything, but it was better than what she was doing. She shuffled through the remaining pictures. All the rest of them were of Gavin Whitelaw mugging for the camera in his younger days, and none included Billy Travis.

All Saints church was set well back from the road on the corner of Riverview and Rutland. Its high, square tower of weathered stone was a landmark in the town; it could be seen from almost any point of the compass, and was frequently used as a point of reference when giving directions. When comparing it to the photograph of the choir, the church itself was unchanged, but the grassy bank and shrubbery that had served as a background were gone, replaced by a paved car park. Another mark of 'progress', Molly thought wryly. On the other hand she would have had to feed the meter if she'd parked on the street, so perhaps she should be grateful for small mercies.

There were two other cars in the otherwise empty car park, an ancient Volvo and a bright red Mini Cooper. Molly had always liked the look of Mini Coopers, in fact she might have owned one if it weren't for the price. She gave the car an affectionate pat on the roof as she went by.

Molly climbed the steps, opened the heavy, iron-bound door and went inside. She hadn't been aware of the street noise outside until the door closed behind her, and suddenly there was silence. She stood there for a moment, looking down the long centre aisle to the chancel, choir stalls on either side, and the altar beneath a stained glass window. It had been chilly outside, but it seemed even colder inside. Cold and still. Molly shivered . . . then jumped when a voice beside her said, 'Can I help you? Oh, dear, did I startle you? Sorry. I didn't mean to.'

Molly turned to face the speaker, a small, round-faced woman with a kindly smile. 'I'm Esther Phillips, the vicar's wife,' she said, extending her hand.

'Molly Forsythe,' Molly said automatically as she took it. 'I'm looking for your husband. Is he here?'

'He's in the office. If you'd like to come with me?' Esther Phillips set off down the aisle. 'I don't believe I've seen you here before,' she ventured. 'New to the parish, are you, Molly?'

Molly produced her warrant card. 'Actually I'm here on business,' she said. 'Detective Sergeant Forsythe, and I'm looking for some information from your husband.'

Esther Phillips stopped to turn and look at Molly. 'To do with Brian? Or the church?' she asked anxiously.

Molly smiled. 'It's nothing like that,' she said. 'I just need to ask him about some old records. It's to do with a case we're working on, and he may be able to help.'

'Oh, that's all right, then,' Esther said as she set off again, turning at the chancel steps to lead Molly through a door into a corridor, at the end of which was another door bearing a brass plate that said *Office*.

Esther tapped gently then opened the door and poked her head inside. 'I have a visitor for you, Brian,' she announced, opening the door wider. 'A Detective Sergeant Forsythe. Can you spare a minute?'

The Reverend Brian Phillips was a ruddy-faced man in his sixties. Grey hair and thick, bushy eyebrows, roughly hewn features, he wore a heavy woollen cardigan and baggy trousers, all of which made him look more like a farmer than a man of the cloth. He rose to his feet and came out from behind a small desk.

Slightly stooped, he waved a dismissive hand when Molly asked if she was interrupting anything important. 'Nothing that can't wait,' he said. 'Besides, I could use a break. Would you like a cup of tea . . . umm, Detective?'

'I would,' said Molly. 'Thank you. And since I'm not here to arrest anyone, just Molly will do for now.'

'Well, that's a relief,' he said with a chuckle. 'Detective Sergeant did sound a bit intimidating. Now, what's this about?'

Molly brought out the picture and showed it to him. 'I'd like to know if you could identify the people in this picture for me. I know a couple of them, but not the rest.'

Phillips looked closely at it, then shook his head. 'I'm sorry,' he said, 'but this was taken long before my time here. I've only been here three years. But you could ask Theodore. Theodore Fulbright. No doubt he would know who these people are. He was the pastor here before me. He lives with his son and daughter-in-law now. Interesting chap. He's also an excellent miniaturist. Makes doll's houses and miniature furniture and that sort of thing. Took it up as a hobby some years ago for relaxation. Shame, though. He has Parkinson's disease. Early stages, but it doesn't bode well for that kind of work, I'm afraid.'

Fulbright. Coincidence? Not likely. 'Is his son's name Michael?' Molly asked. 'Sales manager at Bridge Street Motors?'

'That's the one,' Phillips confirmed. 'I can give you his home address if you like.' He didn't wait for an answer but went to his desk and leafed through a leather-bound phone book, then scribbled the address and gave it to Molly. 'Anything else I can do?' he asked.

'Can you tell me if any of the people in the picture are still in the choir? Do you see anyone you recognize?'

Phillips studied the picture again. 'That's Mike Fulbright,' he said, pointing to a tall lad in the middle row. 'I didn't realize he'd been with the choir that long. He's still with us, of course. Excellent baritone. You could ask him. Oh, yes, and there's Meg Bainbridge. Pretty girl, wasn't she, back then? She has a good voice as well.'

'What about this boy?' Molly pointed to the lad at the end of the row.

Phillips peered closely at the picture. 'Billy Travis! Oh, my goodness! There's another one who—' He stopped abruptly. 'So *that's* why you're here,' he said softly. 'I was absolutely stunned when I heard he'd been killed. Terrible! Absolutely terrible. I can't say I knew Billy very well, but he seemed like a nice little chap. As a matter of fact, he was sitting next to me on the bus a few weeks ago on our way back from the choral festival in Chester.'

'What about Gavin Whitelaw? Was he still a member of the choir as well?' Molly pointed him out in the photograph.

Phillips looked closely at the picture, then shook his head. 'No, I don't recognize him or the name, although . . .' He paused. 'Isn't that the name of the fellow who was killed the other night?' He looked hard at Molly. 'Are you suggesting that these recent deaths have something to do with the choir?'

Molly shook her head. 'Not necessarily,' she said, 'but we're looking for a connection between these men, and it's beginning to look as if they did know each other when they were young. Does the name Dennis Moreland mean anything to you?'

Phillips shook his head. 'Afraid not,' he said. 'Sorry. Perhaps Theodore will be of more help.'

'What about the choirmaster?' Molly asked. 'Is he . . .?' She stopped. Phillips was shaking his head and smiling ruefully.

'Gone as well, I'm afraid,' he said. 'Moved to Market Drayton. He has family there, I believe. Peter Jones is the choirmaster now. Has been for the last couple of years.'

'Tea and biscuits,' Esther announced as she came through the door, bearing a tray, then turned a baleful eye on her husband. 'Shame on you, Brian,' she said tartly. 'Standing there all this time. Why ever didn't you offer Molly a seat?' She set the tray down and picked up the teapot and milk jug. 'Milk in first, is it, Molly?'

SEVENTEEN

Back in the office, Molly sought out Tregalles and told him about her conversation with the Reverend Phillips. 'The trouble is,' she concluded, 'all it tells us is that Billy Travis, Gavin Whitelaw and Mike Fulbright knew each other back when this picture was taken. And Whitelaw went to see Fulbright a couple of days before he died, but I don't know if that's significant or not. Did you get anything out of Fulbright this morning?'

'No. He's sticking to his story about Whitelaw talking about trading in his car, and says Whitelaw must have been playing some sort of bizarre game. He even suggested that Whitelaw had committed suicide and wasn't murdered at all.'

'With his hands bound and an A carved in his forehead?' said Molly. 'That's a bit of a stretch, isn't it? Could Fulbright be our killer?'

'I suppose it's possible,' Tregalles said slowly. 'He's big enough and strong enough. But those killings were planned very carefully, and Fulbright doesn't strike me as a planner. He strikes me as the sort who makes it up as he goes along. Like this morning. I know he was lying, but he'd made up that story and he's sticking with it. He claims he was at home in bed on the nights all three men were killed, and says his wife will confirm that. Another possibility is that he's a potential victim, because I know I hit a nerve when I mentioned Moreland and Travis. He tried to hide it, but he's definitely worried about something.'

'So, what's next?' Molly asked. 'I haven't seen DCI Paget today. Is he away?'

'No, he's here,' Tregalles told her, 'but it looks as if he's going to be spending more time upstairs until DS Pierce gets up to speed.'

Molly pushed her chair back and stood up. 'In that case,' she said, 'I think we should go and talk to Mrs Fulbright about her husband's alibi, and find out if Fulbright's father can identify the rest of the people in the photograph of the choir.'

'You really think there's a connection?'

'I have no idea,' said Molly, 'but it's all we've got at the moment, so why don't we go and find out?'

'Can't,' Tregalles said. 'At least not until tomorrow morning. Ormside's away this afternoon. Dental appointment, so I'm filling in for him. But I could use your help. I'm behind on my daily reports, and Paget's not too pleased about that, so would you do me a favour and transcribe them for me? I've got three days of notes to write up, and you can type a hell of a lot faster than me.'

Connie Rice looked at the clock for perhaps the tenth time in the last five minutes. Her feet were killing her, and all she wanted to do was go home and crawl into bed. She hated to admit it, but the decision to buy the new shoes had been a bad one, and an expensive one as well. Even worse was her decision to wear them to work. They'd looked so neat in the shop, and she'd felt so sure that they would be all right once they'd been worn a bit, but she was wrong on all counts. She could have taken them off while she was serving behind the bar, but she was afraid she wouldn't get them on again. Besides, she was short enough as it was, which was why she'd been tempted to buy three-inch heels in the first place.

She looked at the clock again. Twenty more minutes to go. She could have gone half an hour ago for all the trade there was. Old George Peacock was still there in his corner. A mate of his from the residence up the road had just left, but not George. George would be there until he was walked to the door by Vic, and gently but firmly pushed out into the night. The ten or twelve members of the family who had been celebrating some sort of lottery win had gone, and the couple who'd been drinking shorts all night were getting up to leave.

Her thoughts skipped to the man who had come in just after ten. A stranger, broad-shouldered, good looking, who'd propped himself up at the end of the bar and started chatting to her. Fortyish, smartly dressed; grey roll-neck pullover and dark slacks. Longish hair that could do with a bit of a trim, but it looked good on him, so forget the trim. Nicely spoken, too. Didn't sound like he was local. Chatted a bit about the weather to start with, then on to a few comments about the place. Commented on the silver charm bracelet she wore. Asked her if she'd worked there long, and she'd begun to think she was in with a chance. He seemed so nice, and it had been such a long time since she'd had a real date.

He'd stayed for about an hour, drinking halves, then looked at his watch and said he had to go. 'I enjoyed talking to you,' he'd told her as he set his glass down, and she'd held her breath, expecting – or at least hoping – that he would ask her for a date. Instead, he'd shrugged into his coat, wished her goodnight, and left.

Connie winced as she shifted from one foot to the other and looked at the clock again. The hands had hardly moved at all. Oh, to hell with it! She should just go. She began to undo her apron, then stopped. It would mean an argument with Rick, and you could never win with him. As far as Rick Crowley was concerned, her hours were five till midnight. The place could be empty, but that wouldn't make a scrap of difference to him, so why risk the hassle for the sake of a few minutes? She'd thought he would cut her a bit of slack after she'd slept with him a few times, but business was business and pleasure was something else as far as Rick was concerned.

'Better get those glasses stacked if you want to get off on time, Connie,' he called from the other end of the bar. It was as if he had been reading her thoughts. 'Up yours!' she muttered beneath her breath as she picked up the glasses.

Midnight at last. Connie hobbled into the office to get her coat. It had been raining on and off throughout the evening, so she put on a plastic rain hat and tied it loosely before stepping out into the night. The rain had almost stopped, but Connie hurried along the gravelled path to her car. It was parked at the very end of the small car park under the trees. Normally it would be the only one there at this time of night, but tonight there was another one just a few yards away from her own. She wondered about it in a vague sort of way as she swept leaves from the windscreen before getting in, but she was so anxious to get home and put her feet up that it didn't really register. She was opening the door when she heard the sound of a footstep on gravel behind her. Suddenly fearful, she started to turn. She caught a movement out of the corner of her eye. She opened her mouth to scream . . . Her head seemed to explode; she fell against the car, and her legs buckled beneath her.

Thursday, 27 October

The sky had cleared overnight. The temperature had dropped dramatically, and there was a hint of frost in the air, but the sun was shining and it was a beautiful morning.

'Seems like you're always driving into the sun this time of the year, no matter which way you're going,' Tregalles grumbled as a shard of light half blinded him when he turned into the driveway leading to Fulbright's house. 'Just look at that, will you? Look at that house. I always knew there had to be good money in cars, but I wouldn't have thought a sales manager could afford something like this.'

'Rachel Fulbright has money,' Molly told him. 'Have you not

heard of her? She's quite well known for her metal sculptures, and there's an example.' She pointed to a free-standing sculpture of a tree, its limbs bare and graceful as it might appear in winter. 'Didn't you notice the one on the sign at the bottom of the drive as well? This is called Beech Tree House.'

'Can't say I did,' Tregalles said as they got out of the car. 'Not exactly my thing, metal sculpture. Audrey likes it, but it doesn't do a thing for me. Half the stuff I've seen looks like the leftovers from a scrap iron merchant, and they charge the earth for it.'

It was a big house. There was nothing particularly notable about it, other than its size, but in this part of town on this amount of land, it had to be worth a lot of money. Red brick, two storeys. Probably something like four or five bedrooms. The very tall chimney stacks were an odd feature, and yet they seemed to go with the house. Tregalles mounted the two shallow steps to the front door and rang the bell. Chimes sounded faintly inside, but there was no response. Tregalles pressed the bell again.

Molly stood back from the house, head on one side, listening. 'Hear that?' she asked. 'Hear that banging?'

Tregalles came down to stand beside her, listening. 'Back of the house,' he said. 'Let's take a look.' He led off with Molly following.

There was a large, square, brick building, half hidden by a stand of trees on the far side of the lawn and tennis court behind the house, and the sound of hammering was coming from inside. There was no point in knocking, so Tregalles tried the door and found it unlocked. He poked his head inside, then pushed the door open and stepped over the sill. Molly moved in behind him and closed the door.

A slim figure in overalls and goggles was hammering away at a piece of red hot iron on an anvil. Tregalles and Molly moved closer. 'Mrs Fulbright?' Tregalles called loudly, trying to time it between strokes. The woman kept on hammering. 'Are you Mrs Fulbright?' he called louder.

'Yes, I'm Rachel Fulbright, and I heard you the first time,' she shouted back, 'but whatever you want will have to wait a minute. I can't leave this now.'

It was a full five minutes before the woman set the hammer aside, then took off the goggles, and wiped the sweat from her forehead on the sleeve of her overalls. 'You don't look like Seventh-Day Adventists or Mormons,' she said, squinting at them, 'so what do you want?'

Tregalles and Molly took out their warrant cards and displayed them. 'A few questions, if you don't mind?' Tregalles said.

'Ah, yes, Mike did say someone would be round to check up on him. Good idea. He needs checking up on from time to time. Shall we go outside? I'm sweating like a pig.'

Once outside, Rachel Fulbright led them to a metal bench. She unzipped the front of her overalls and flapped them about a bit before sitting down. 'That's better,' she said with a sigh, motioning for them to sit down as well. 'Now, what is it Mike's supposed to have done, and I'm supposed to say he couldn't possibly have done it because he was with me all day?'

'That's not *quite* the way it works, Mrs Fulbright,' Molly said gently. 'We do prefer the answers to be truthful.'

Rachel Fulbright smiled crookedly. She was an attractive woman, not much older than Molly herself. 'Now there's a novel idea,' she said, 'but I'll give it a try. What's the question?'

Tregalles gave her the times and dates of the murders. 'And Mr Fulbright told us you can confirm that he was at home in bed in all three cases,' he concluded.

'Did he, now?' Rachel pursed her lips and looked thoughtful. 'He may have been,' she said after a long pause. 'But then again, he may not. I take it he didn't mention our sleeping arrangements?'

Tregalles and Molly exchanged glances.

'No, I see by the expression on your faces he didn't,' she continued. 'What I can tell you is that he went to bed as usual on those nights, and he was there again in the morning. But we have separate bedrooms, and I sleep very soundly, so I never know which nights he remains there and which nights he pops over to sleep with his secretary and receptionist, Anita Chapman. It depends on whether or not her husband is home, so you may have to talk to her as well. Was there anything else?'

'I'd appreciate it if you would treat this more seriously, Mrs Fulbright,' Tregalles said stiffly. 'Three people have been murdered in a particularly brutal way, and we do need to know where your husband was on those nights.'

'Do you *really* think Mike had something to do with those murders?' she asked, then shook her head vigorously and said, 'I'm sorry, Sergeant, but the very idea struck me as so utterly preposterous that I couldn't take it seriously.'

'Preposterous or not, I would still like a proper answer, Mrs Fulbright.'

Rachel pursed her lips. 'What were those dates again?' she asked. Tregalles read them off. 'I don't know about the others,' she said slowly, 'but the last ones, the nineteenth and twentieth – Wednesday night and Thursday morning, right? Mike was here. Well, to be honest, he was out of it, but his body was here. We had some people in Wednesday evening, and they didn't leave until around one o'clock, and it must have been close to two before we got to bed. As I said, we have separate rooms, but he'd been drinking steadily throughout the evening, and I had to help him to bed. He was asleep the moment he hit the bed, so there's no way he could have gone out and killed Gavin Whitelaw.'

'You're prepared to swear to that, if necessary, Mrs Fulbright?' Tregalles asked.

'*If* necessary,' she said tightly.

'Did you know Gavin Whitelaw?'

Rachel Fulbright eyed Tregalles in a calculating way before she answered. 'I knew who he was,' she said carefully, 'but he was by no means a friend, if that's what you're after. He and Mike knew each other from the time they were at school together, but Mike didn't like the man, and he did his best to avoid him. But disliking a man is a far cry from killing him,' she ended.

Molly took out her notebook. 'These friends you had in last week,' she said, 'could you give me one or two names?'

'Is this *really* necessary?' Rachel asked icily.

'If we are to eliminate your husband from a list of possible suspects, yes, it is, Mrs Fulbright.'

'I'll give you two, but there's no need to go into detail

regarding why you want the information, so for God's sake try to be discreet.'

'Just one more thing, Mrs Fulbright,' said Molly after jotting down the names. 'I understand that Mr Fulbright's father is living with you. No one answered when we rang the bell, so could you tell me where we might find him?'

'He'll be in his room,' Rachel said. 'Probably had his radio on and didn't hear the chimes. Why do you want to talk to him? He can't tell you if Mike was home or not; his room is at the other end of the hall.'

'It's about another matter,' Molly told her.

Rachel continued to look at her as if expecting further elaboration, but when Molly remained silent, she reached into a pocket of the overalls and pulled out a phone, and thumbed in a number. 'He's a bit slow these days,' she said, not unkindly. 'Oh, hello, Theo? There's someone here to see you. Can you come down? We're on the seat outside the workshop. It's the police. They want to ask you some questions.' There was a pause, then, 'No, it's not about your driving licence.' She cupped a hand over the phone. 'He wants to know what it's about,' she said.

'It's a question we have about some of the people who were in the All Saints choir fifteen or more years ago,' Molly told her. She took out the picture and held it up for Rachel to see.

Rachel relayed the information, then closed the phone. 'He says you can go up, but he's in the middle of a delicate operation, so he wants you to wait outside the door of his room until he tells you to come in. As I said, his room is at the end of the hall, and it will be open.' She slipped the phone back into the pocket of her overalls and got to her feet. 'I have to get back to work,' she said brusquely, 'but since you are the police, I suppose I can trust you not to steal the silver. The back door's open, so go through the kitchen and the hall and to the top of the stairs and follow the sound of the radio.' She turned to go, then paused. 'And please don't go poking around in other parts of the house. I do know you need a warrant for that.'

They could hear the radio before they reached the top of the stairs. They turned to the right, followed the sound to an open door at the end of the hall and stopped as ordered. An elderly man, wearing corduroy trousers and a stained white smock, was seated at a trestle table. On his balding head was a magnifying visor with light attached. It was focused on something very small, held in the grip of tiny pincers on the end of a prosthetic arm, while in his right hand was a very small paintbrush. But, fascinating as that was, Molly's attention was drawn to the three beautiful doll's houses sitting on three separate tables.

'With you in a minute,' Theodore Fulbright called loudly without looking up. 'Just stay where you are.'

Two of the small houses were closed, but the third, a two-storeyed house with furnished attic, was open and lighted. 'Now that is beautiful,' Molly breathed. Tregalles followed her gaze. 'It is,' he agreed. 'Olivia had one when she was small. Nothing like that, of course, but the same idea. I made a few bits and pieces for her, but she didn't really appreciate it, in fact I spent more time with it than she did, so it ended up in the gift shop. Too bad, because I quite enjoyed working on it.'

The Reverend Fulbright sat back in his chair and took off the visor, then turned the radio off. 'Come in, come in and tell me what it is you want,' he said. 'I have to wait a few minutes for the paint to dry.'

'What are you working on?' Molly asked with a nod toward the table.

'A stained glass window for the front door,' Fulbright replied. 'You can buy them, but I prefer to do my own. Are you interested?'

'I've always loved doll's houses,' Molly confessed, 'but I'd never have the time to work on them. But this one's beautiful.' She pointed to the house that was open. 'Mind if I have a closer look?'

'Not at all.' The tone of his voice was considerably softer as he got to his feet. He raised his left arm to display the prosthesis with the claw-like pincers where a hand should have been. 'Does this bother you?' he asked. 'It does some people.'

Both detectives shook their heads, and he said, 'Good. It is interchangeable for a hand, of course, but this is what I use when I'm working. It was specially made for the work.'

Despite Tregalles's sidelong glances and shuffling signs of impatience, Molly spent the next few minutes examining the interior of the doll's house. 'Did you make everything in here?' she asked.

'Almost,' Fulbright said. 'Never found a way to make a light bulb, but I made just about everything else.'

'It's gorgeous,' Molly said, straightening up after a not so gentle nudge from Tregalles. 'You do beautiful work, Reverend Fulbright.'

He shrugged modestly, but it was evident he was pleased. 'And I prefer people to call me Theo now that I'm retired. And you are . . .?'

'Sorry,' Molly said guiltily as she produced her warrant card and introduced herself, and Tregalles. 'We're investigating the deaths of Billy Travis and Gavin Whitelaw,' she explained. 'Both were in the All Saints choir years ago, and we wondered if you could put names to the people in this old photograph of the choir.' She took out the picture once again and handed it to Fulbright.

He took the photo in his right hand and studied it.

'There's my son, Michael,' he said. 'Can't miss him, can you? He was tall for his age even then. Oh, yes, there's young Billy. Poor little devil. He was still there in the choir when I left. Still is, for that ma—' He stopped abruptly. 'I mean *was*,' he said quietly. 'When I read about him being killed, I couldn't believe it! Any idea yet who did it?' His eyes flicked from one to the other, then returned to the picture when both remained silent.

'That's Meg Bainbridge,' he said, tapping the picture. 'She's still there. In fact she's one of the few originals. The chap on the end is Fairfield, the choirmaster back then.' He indicated a heavy-set, balding man in the back row. Fulbright went on to name every one of the adults in the back row, but said they'd been gone for years. 'Trasler is dead, and Mary Monahan and her husband were living in Spain last time I heard, but that was a few years ago. I still see Preston in church from time to time, so you could try him.' Fulbright didn't sound too hopeful. 'As for the rest, I don't know if they're still around or not, but I haven't seen them lately. And as for the youngsters . . . I don't know. They came and went; I don't remember their names.'

'What about this one?' Molly pointed to Whitelaw. Fulbright looked closely. 'The face is vaguely familiar,' he said, 'but I don't remember the name.'

He started to hand the picture back, but his hand suddenly shook and the picture dropped to the floor. 'Sorry,' he said brusquely as Molly stooped quickly to pick it up. 'Careless of me. Is that it, then?'

'Can you tell us when this picture was taken?' Molly asked.

'Judging by how old Michael looks, I'd say it's at least fifteen or sixteen years old,' he said. 'But what does this have to do with Billy Travis's death?'

'To be honest, sir, it may have nothing to do with it,' Molly confessed, 'but the killings appear to have a common motive, and the only connection we've found so far is that two of the victims were in the choir when they were teenagers, and both had pictures of the choir in their possession. The latest victim, Gavin Whitelaw, was also a friend of your son.'

'Michael?' Fulbright said sharply. 'How does he come into it? Have you spoken to him?'

'I have,' Tregalles said. 'Whitelaw went to see your son shortly before he was killed, and we had hoped he might have said something that would help us, but Michael claims the only reason Whitelaw was there was to talk about trading his car for a newer one.'

Fulbright's eyes narrowed. 'Unless I misjudged your tone, Sergeant, I get the distinct impression that you didn't believe him.'

'Let's just say that it's hard to believe that story when we know Whitelaw didn't have a car to trade. In fact he sold it months ago, and he was in no position to even consider buying a car, old or new.'

'Is the name Dennis Moreland familiar to you, sir?' Molly broke in quickly before Fulbright had a chance to respond. 'Do you recall if he was ever in the choir?'

'Couldn't tell you, I'm afraid. Youngsters rarely stayed long.

They'd come in keen as mustard, but then either their voices would break or they'd get bored, and they'd be off again. Is he in the picture?'

'His wife says he isn't, but I thought it was worth asking anyway,' Molly said. 'I don't suppose you have any other old photographs of the choir tucked away somewhere?'

Fulbright shook his head. 'I presume you've spoken to Peter Jones?'

'The present choirmaster? No, not yet,' said Molly. 'The Reverend Phillips thought you might be our best bet, since Mr Jones hasn't been here very long and the previous choirmaster has moved away. But perhaps you can give us the names you do remember, and we can contact them to see if they can help us.'

Fulbright shook his head. 'Memory's not what it used to be,' he said. 'Try Michael. He might know. Or Peter Jones. Failing that, I suppose you could try tracking Fairfield down.'

Fulbright walked back to stand behind the table. 'Sorry I can't be of more help,' he said, 'but I really must get on with this, so perhaps you can find your own way out.'

'Just one question, if you don't mind, sir,' Molly said as Tregalles headed for the door. 'What happens to the doll's houses when they're finished?'

Fulbright picked up the magnifier visor and slipped it over his head. 'They go to various charities for auction,' he said. 'The one you were looking at is going to Manchester next month to be auctioned off at a charity event there.' He smiled. 'You could put in a bid if you like.' He snapped on the light and settled into his seat. 'But you'd better have deep pockets,' he called after her as she went out the door. 'The reserve price is fifteen hundred pounds.'

'Connie not in tonight, then, Rick?' The middle-aged man wearing a flat cap and tweeds was a regular in the Red Lion. 'I thought Sunday and Monday were her nights off. Not poorly, is she?' He sounded quite concerned.

'She'll be more than bloody poorly when I get hold of her,' Rick Crowley growled. 'Gone half five and no sign of her. I must have rung ten times, but she's not answering. The girl she shares a flat with said she didn't come home last night, so God knows where she is.'

'Not like her, though, is it?' the man said. 'I mean if there's one thing you can say about Connie, she's reliable.'

'Not tonight, she bloody isn't,' Crowley growled. 'All right, all right, I'm coming,' he called to the man at the other end of the bar, who was waving money about. He looked at the clock again and swore beneath his breath.

Six o'clock. Home at a decent time for a change. Molly dropped her handbag on the hall table, shrugged out of her coat and hung it up, then carried the shopping bag containing her dinner into the kitchen. Tonight it would be a chicken, vegetable and pasta dish she'd picked up at the market on her way home. If only they tasted as good as they looked on the box, she thought wistfully as she read the instructions and turned the oven on.

She wandered into the bedroom and started to undress, then changed her mind and went into the living room, where she turned on her computer. There'd been nothing from David for a week now. Nothing since she'd sent a reply last Thursday, and she couldn't help wondering whether he'd lost interest. Too many things on his mind, perhaps? Too many distractions?

She had mail. Molly sat down at the desk. It was from David! A long one.

She read it through to the end, then read it again before sitting back in her chair, her mind in turmoil. Two weeks at Christmas? He said he hadn't mentioned it to Lijuan or her grandmother yet, but he thought it might be the best way to reintroduce Lijuan to England, and they would be staying with David's aunt and uncle, Ellen and Reg Starkie. He said he was looking forward to having Molly meet his daughter and her grandmother, which was nice, but then David had gone on to say that he'd had to turn down the offer of a job at Broadminster hospital. He said he couldn't see any prospect of returning to Broadminster in the near future, so he'd felt it only fair to let them know so they could offer the job to someone else. Meanwhile, he'd taken a temporary job at the Tung Wah hospital – there was an attachment with some pictures.

Two months away. Molly felt a chill when she read that and saw the pictures. The Tung Wah hospital looked like a big one, and she couldn't help wondering what 'temporary' might mean. But two weeks at Christmas? Was it realistic to think that Lijuan would choose to live here, when her grandmother and her friends were in Hong Kong? Molly didn't think so. David had said that Lijuan was eight when she left England with her mother; and she was fourteen now. Crucial years in a young girl's life, and David had said himself that Lijuan was happy there and doing well at school. And having just lost her mother . . .

And Christmas! Maybe it was supposed to be a jolly season, with its carols and joy to the world and all that stuff, but there could hardly be a worse time to come to England. Crowded airports; cold, miserable weather. Rain, sleet or snow – it was bound to be one or the other. Dark by four o'clock; people dashing about doing their last-minute shopping . . . Lijuan was probably used to crowds, so that might not bother her, but weather-wise . . .? No, it was not a good time to come if David was hoping his daughter would opt for England over Hong Kong.

Molly turned to the computer and brought up the current weather in Hong Kong. *Eighty-two degrees and clear skies!* She listened to the sound of rain outside and groaned aloud. She typed in 'Hong Kong seasonal weather/winter'. *Ranges between fifty and sixty-two degrees. Warmer clothing is recommended.*

Molly slumped back in her chair. Oh, yes, she thought glumly, Lijuan and her grandmother would *really* be impressed. They would probably want to get on the next plane back to Hong Kong. There was no way it would be a fair test.

She was still thinking about it when she sat down to dinner. She poked at it, ate a bit, stirred it around, but finally pushed it away only half eaten. Later, when she was clearing up, Molly looked at the picture on the box before disposing of it. Good picture: it was what had prompted her to buy it in the first place. As for the product . . .? She made a face, dropped the meal in the bin and closed the lid.

EIGHTEEN

Friday, 28 October

The missing person report was logged in at 07.38, and the information was relayed instantly to the incident room, following a request by DS Ormside that he be notified when anyone was reported missing. The report was made by a Sandra Palmer of 31 Chelsea Court, a block of flats near the railway station. The person missing was her flat-mate, Connie Rice, single, aged thirty-one, who had not been seen or heard from since midnight on the previous Wednesday, when she left the Red Lion where she worked as a barmaid.

'Ms Palmer is coming in to supply more details,' Ormside told Paget when he arrived for the morning briefing. 'It may have nothing to do with the serial killing, since they've all been men so far, but the one thing that does make me wonder is the woman's age. It's in the same range as the men's. I thought it was worth checking.'

'Quite right,' said Paget. 'Who'll be doing the interview?'

'I thought you might be doing that yourself,' he said. 'Forsythe's available if you need her.'

Paget was tempted; it was hard to let go, but he had told Amanda he would give it a try, and he couldn't back out now. He'd given the matter a lot of thought recently, and he had to admit, albeit reluctantly, that he'd been too ready to jump in and take the lead, when it should have been left to others to do their job.

'Tregalles and Forsythe can take care of it just as well as I can,' he said. 'Did they talk to the new choirmaster yesterday? What's his name?'

'Peter Jones. No. They had arranged to see him this morning, but Jones is a computer tech with B and B Data Specialists, and he had to go out on an emergency call to one of the banks in Tenborough, so he's going to give us a call when he gets back.'

Paget looked at the whiteboards and decided it wasn't worth sitting in on the morning briefing. It would be a regurgitation of old material, and although he knew everyone was doing their best, there was little left for them to follow up.

'Keep me posted, then,' he said as he walked away. 'I'll be with Superintendent Pierce for most of the morning, so call me on my mobile if you have anything to report.'

Sandra Palmer was a small, plump young woman with a baby face, straight fair hair, large blue eyes, a nose-stud, and mother-of pearl fingernails that sparkled every time she moved her hands. She wore a bulky sweater and black slacks beneath a plastic mac, and carried a shoulder bag that would barely make it through most airports as carry-on luggage.

'Change of clothes for the office,' she volunteered when she saw Molly looking at it. 'I ride a bike to work. I should be there now, by rights, but I called in sick. Didn't want to tell them I was going to be talking to the police, or they might have thought all sorts of things.' She giggled self-consciously. 'Anyway, here I am, so what do you want to know?'

'Let's begin at the beginning,' Tregalles suggested. 'You share a flat with Connie Rice, right?'

'That's right. We split everything down the middle: the rent, the meals, the washing up and the—'

'Yes, yes, I understand,' Tregalles broke in, 'and according to the information you gave the officer on the phone, the last time anyone saw or heard from your friend Connie was Wednesday midnight when she finished work at the Red Lion. Why are you only reporting her missing now?'

'Because I didn't know she hadn't been home after she finished her shift on Wednesday night until Rick started calling last evening to ask where she was. See, she comes off shift at midnight, so I'm well asleep by the time she gets in – we have separate rooms, of course, in case you were wondering – and I'm off to work before she gets up, so we sometimes don't see each other for a day or two, except in passing and on weekends. So I didn't know there was anything wrong until Rick called. Rick Crowley, he's her boss, and he was in a right state. But then, Connie says he's always like that. But I wasn't particularly worried even then. It was only later, when I looked in her room and realized she hadn't been home at all, that I started to wonder. I'd left a magazine on her bed the night before for her to see when she came in, and it was still there exactly like I'd left it; it hadn't been moved.'

Sandra looked troubled. 'I tried to call her on her mobile, but got no answer. I kept trying but she obviously didn't have it on because I wasn't getting anything back at all. By the time I went to bed I was getting really worried, but then I thought maybe her mum might know something, but I haven't been able to get hold of her. She and her husband are golfers, and they travel all over the place, and it's always hard to get hold of her.'

'Where does her mother live?' Molly asked.

'Bristol. She moved there when she got married again, must be seven or eight years ago. She's Mrs Donovan now.'

'What about Connie's father? Does she have any brothers or sisters? Relatives of any kind?'

'Her father disappeared after the divorce. Mind you, he's in the navy, or he was, so he was never home anyway. She's got a sister somewhere near London; I don't remember where, but I don't think Connie's been in touch with her for years.'

'Has Connie ever done anything like this before? Disappeared without letting you know? Perhaps gone off with a boyfriend?'

'Chance would be a fine thing,' the girl said with a grimace. 'Poor old Con hasn't had a boyfriend for ages. Come to that, nor have I. Fine pair we are.' She shook her head. 'No, she's never done that before, and that's why I'm a bit worried about her.' The catch in her voice suggested that Sandra was more than just a bit worried about her friend. 'I know I should have done something sooner than this,' she continued, 'because we always said we'd look out for each other, but I really didn't know she was missing till this morning. You do think she'll be all right, don't you, Sergeant? I read somewhere that most people who go missing turn up all right. Is that true?'

'Generally speaking,' Tregalles said, then moved on quickly with another question. 'When you were talking to Mr Crowley, did he say anything that might suggest Connie had asked for time off or anything like that?'

'No. Not that she would have got it. All he was interested in was getting her in to work. He said she'd left at midnight the night before, and that was all he knew, and he seemed to think I was covering for her, because he swore at me a couple of times. So I stopped answering when he called again.'

'How does Connie go back and forth to work?' Tregalles asked. 'Does she have a car?'

'Yes, she does. Sorry, didn't I say? It's gone as well. At least Rick says it isn't there, and it isn't at the flat.' She opened her bag and started rummaging through it. 'Ah, here it is,' she said triumphantly. She handed Tregalles a piece of paper. 'Her car and her mobile phone number is on there as well,' she said. 'I thought you might need it. Oh, yes, and here's a picture of her. It's one she took of herself while she was messing about with her phone a couple of weeks back. I took it off her laptop before I came here this morning.'

'Silver 2001 Renault Clio hatchback, *and* reg number,' he observed as he handed the paper and the picture of Connie Rice to Molly. 'Very good, Sandra. Thank you. We'll get those descriptions out right away. Also, I'd like to have someone go with you back to your flat to take a look at Connie's room, her computer and other things. All right?'

'No problem,' Sandra assured him. 'I'm going back there myself.'

'Just one thing before you go,' Molly said. 'Is Connie a member of a choir? Or do you know if she was ever in a choir when she was younger?'

'A choir? Connie? Shouldn't think so,' Sandra said. 'She's never mentioned it to me, and I've never known her go to church since I've been sharing the flat with her, and that's going on three years now.'

Back in the incident room once more, Molly set the picture of Connie Rice beside that of the All Saints choir and scanned the faces of the girls. There were four of them. Three could be ruled out right away. But the fourth one . . . Molly brought out the magnifying glass. 'What do you think?' she asked when Tregalles came over to take a look for himself. 'Do you think it's the same girl?'

He bent closer to look, then straightened up shaking his head. 'Could be, I suppose,' he said, but he sounded doubtful. 'You could always run it by the Reverend Fulbright, but before you do that, perhaps we should make sure Connie Rice is really missing. I've just finished speaking to Connie's boss, Rick Crowley, and he tells me Connie was being chatted up that night by a man he's never seen before, and he left the bar not long before Connie did. So he thinks they may be shacked up somewhere, "shagging themselves blind" as he so colourfully put it.'

'Or the man was our killer and she could be dead.'

'Could be,' Tregalles conceded, 'but the other victims have all been men, and I don't see a connection. Anyway, we're wasting time here, so I think we should split up. You go and talk to Crowley, and I'll go to the flat to see if there's anything there that might tell us where Connie Rice has gone.'

It was Rick Crowley himself who opened the door. 'We open in an hour,' he said brusquely, when she introduced herself, 'so I hope this isn't going to take up too much of my time. I had to bring my day man in last night when Con didn't show, so I'll be short-handed again today. There's just Anna and me here until Cliff – he's my day man – comes in at twelve, and Anna should be back in the kitchen getting ready for the lunch crowd.' He nodded towards the bar where a young woman was setting up a menu board. 'Anyway, I told the bloke I spoke to on the phone everything I know, and I told him I think it's a waste of time. I don't think Con's missing at all. Well, not like really *missing*, if you know what I mean? I think she's—'

'Yes, I was told what you think,' Molly cut in sharply, 'but her flat-mate was concerned enough to report her missing, so we're taking that report seriously.'

The corners of Crowley's mouth turned down, 'Yeah, yeah, the Palmer woman,' he said with exaggerated weariness. 'It's like she thinks I had something to do with Con taking off.'

Crowley was short and heavy set. He stood with shoulders hunched and head thrust forward as if preparing for a fight, and, by the look of his face, he'd been in a few. His eyes were dark and probing, and they'd stripped Molly from head to toe within seconds of their meeting.

She took out her notebook. 'You said Connie left at midnight on Wednesday. What sort of mood was she in before she left? Did she say anything to you?'

'She didn't *say* anything,' Crowley said, 'but she kept looking at the clock, and when midnight came around she was off like a shot.'

'Where was her car parked?' Molly asked.

'The far end of the car park next to the fence.' Crowley indicated the direction with his thumb.

'Which means she would have to drive past the front door to get out onto the road, right?'

'That's right.'

'Did you hear or see her car go by? You must have been closing up by then.'

Crowley thought about that. 'No, I didn't,' he said. 'But then, I wouldn't, would I? I was still trying to get old George Peacock out, but he was bound he was going to finish his story about something that happened in the war. He's an old age pensioner who lives in the residence just up the road, so Connie would've been gone by the time I got him out.'

'Were there any other cars in the car park?'

'The lottery lot came by car,' Crowley said, 'but I couldn't say about the others. Not many people come by car any more, they're afraid of being breathalysed.'

'Were there other customers who left about the same time as Connie?'

'No, everybody else had gone by then.'

'Including the man you say was chatting her up?'

'That's right.'

'Can you describe him? Height, weight, approximate age?'

'Could have been anywhere from thirty-five to early forties,' Crowley said. 'Tallish. Close to six feet, I'd say. Well set up. Not fat, but solid, if you know what I mean. Looked like he could take care of himself.'

'Hair colour?'

'Sort of dark brown, I think.' Crowley's heavy brows came together in concentration. 'I remember it was long in the back, and he was wearing a pullover. One of those high-necked ones. Turtle-neck, grey.'

'Trousers?'

'He had 'em, or I would have noticed otherwise,' Crowley said flippantly, 'but I couldn't tell you what colour they were, if that's what you're after.'

'What about his facial features? Since you haven't said otherwise, I assume he was white, but can you describe him for me? Eyes? Wide set or narrow? Eyebrows? Thick? Thin? Anything notable about his mouth, nose or chin? Any distinguishing marks? Scars, moles, tattoos?'

'No, nothing like that,' Crowley said. 'Actually, he wasn't a bad looking bloke, which made me wonder why he'd be chatting up the likes of Connie. I can sort of picture him in my head, but I can't say there was anything special about him. He was . . . well, ordinary.'

Molly sighed inwardly. So much for that! 'What about his voice?' she asked. 'Did you happen to overhear any of their conversation?'

'No. Like I said, it was a quiet night. Connie was all right on her own in the bar, so I spent most of my time in the lounge. I didn't talk to him and I don't know exactly when he left, but he was gone when I looked in around half eleven. Con left on the dot of twelve, and the way she shot out of here I think she must have arranged to see him outside. That's probably why she kept looking at the clock after he'd gone. They're probably shacked up in some motel or other, and Con'll turn up all sorry for herself when he gets tired of her and kicks her out.'

'Has Connie ever done anything like that before?'

'Well, no, but she's always on the lookout for a man, and with her looks it's not as if she's going to get many chances, is it?' Crowley glanced at the clock above the bar. 'Look,' he said, 'I've answered all your questions, but I've still got a pub to run, so can I go now?'

'Just a few more questions, Mr Crowley,' said Molly. 'How long has Connie worked for you?'

Crowley squinted into the distance. 'Must be going on three years, now,' he said, sounding surprised.

'Good worker, is she?'

'She's all right. Haven't had any complaints, so, yeah, I suppose you could say she's all right.'

'And what about your own relationship with Connie, Mr Crowley?'

'My relationship?' Crowley's eyes were suddenly guarded. 'She's a barmaid,' he said. 'I'm her boss; she works for me. At least she did, but I'm not sure I'll take her back if she's going to pull stunts like this.'

'But what about your personal relationship,' Molly persisted. 'Did you ever sleep with Connie?' It was a shot in the dark, but Crowley looked the type who would think every female was fair game.

'Sleep with her . . .?' Crowley's voice rose. 'What the hell sort of question is—?' He stopped, eyes narrowed. 'It's that Palmer woman she lives with, isn't it? She told you, didn't she? She's the one who's stirring all this up. Bitch!'

Molly remained silent, but her eyes were steady on his face. 'All right, so what if I did?' he said belligerently. 'That was a while back. There was nothing to it. It was just sex. It didn't mean anything.'

'So you weren't jealous when you saw her being chatted up by another man? And a good looking one, according to you.'

'Jealous?' Crowley scoffed. 'Of someone chatting up Con? You must be joking.'

'You say it didn't mean anything to you,' Molly persisted, 'but what about Connie? How did she feel about it?'

'Grateful, I should think,' Crowley said cockily, and laughed.

Molly had to bite her tongue. She looked down at her notes. 'I need a better description of the man Connie was talking to,' she said, 'so if you could give me the names of some of the people who were in here that night, I'll see if any of them remember this man.' She stood with pencil poised over her notebook. 'What about this man Peacock, for instance? You say he lives close by?'

Crowley shook his head impatiently. 'It's no good asking him,' he said. 'Silly old bugger's out of it half the time, and he can't see more than a yard or two ahead of him.'

'So what about some of the others?'

Crowley shrugged. 'Like I said, it was a quiet night, and this bloke didn't come in till after ten, so the few regulars who were here were gone by then. As for the rest, I've seen one or two of them before, but I couldn't tell you who they are or where they live. So, sorry, can't help you. Are we finished?'

Molly closed her notebook. 'Not quite,' she said. 'I'm afraid I must ask you to come down to the Charter Lane police station to make a formal statement, and to work with one of our photofit technicians to put together a picture we can circulate. I know it's inconvenient,' she continued as Crowley started to protest, 'but considering the fact that three people have been killed in Broadminster in recent weeks, I think we should treat the disappearance of Connie Rice very seriously indeed. So the sooner—'

The sound of her mobile cut off whatever she was going to say. She looked at the screen, which showed it was Ormside calling. What now, she wondered. She excused herself and moved away from Crowley, who took that as his cue to duck into the lounge.

'We've found Connie Rice's car,' the sergeant said when she answered. 'It was parked illegally in a residents only zone in Windsor Street. Been there since yesterday morning, till someone phoned and asked for it to be removed. Are you still at the pub?'

'Yes, I am.' Molly was trying to remember where Windsor Street was.

'Good,' Ormside said, 'because you won't have far to go. Windsor Street is a little cul-de-sac one street over from where you are. A two-minute walk at best, so get over there now and keep everyone clear until I can get a forensic team down there to take over. Has Crowley been any help?'

'More or less,' Molly said guardedly.

'What about the man who was chatting up the girl just before she went missing? Can he give us a description?'

'He says yes, but he's reluctant to come in because—'

Ormside snorted. 'Never mind reluctant,' he said. 'It's not his call. We need that description, and we'll need a statement from him. And with the car being found so close to the pub, he could be a suspect as well.'

NINETEEN

Tregalles and Molly arrived back at Charter Lane within minutes of each other. 'Lots of books and magazines,' Tregalles told Ormside, 'but I'm afraid Connie Rice wasn't big on committing things to paper. We found an old diary of sorts, but it stops in March 2009, and it made pretty boring reading anyway. No personal letters, and as Sandra Palmer told us, not so much as a suggestion of a boyfriend.'

'Any indication of a lesbian relationship?'

Tregalles shook his head. 'Not if the magazines she likes are any indication,' he said. 'The team's still over there, but I don't think we can expect much from them.'

Ormside turned to Molly. 'What about your man?' he asked. 'Is he cooperating?'

'I had to almost drag him here,' she said. 'I think he sees Connie's disappearance as nothing more than an inconvenience to him. I don't think he could care less about what might have happened to her.'

'Do you believe his story about a stranger chatting up Connie?'

'Yes, I do,' said Molly. 'I don't think he's lying about that.'

'Right. In that case, I'll have Maxwell take his statement, but I want you to read it over and see if there are any discrepancies or deviations from what he told you. And get Keith Morran together with Crowley to see if they can come up with a credible photofit. He may or may not have anything to do with Rice's disappearance, but the sooner we find him and talk to him the better.'

'Right.' Molly was about to turn away, but Ormside stopped her.

'Almost forgot,' he said. 'Peter Jones, the choirmaster, is in room three. He came in looking for you and decided to wait when I told him you were on your way in.' Ormside glanced at the clock. 'He's been there close to half an hour now, so better go and talk to him.'

Peter Jones was older than she had expected. Late fifties, maybe sixty. Not very tall but solidly built. Short grey hair, broad forehead, steady grey eyes, strong facial features, and you knew he was paying attention when he looked at you.

'It was very good of you to come in, Mr Jones,' said Molly as she sat down facing him across the table. 'Sorry you had to wait. It's been a bit of a busy day.'

'No problem,' he said. 'It's been that sort of day for me as well, or I would have been here earlier. But when a bank calls and says it's urgent, we have to respond immediately. Fortunately, it didn't take long to fix the problem.'

'I wish I could get that kind of response when my computer crashes,' said Molly, 'but then, I'm not a bank.'

Peter Jones took a card from his pocket and handed it to Molly. 'Try us next time,' he said. 'You may not be a bank, but we do pride ourselves on our response time.'

Molly looked at the card. 'I will,' she said, 'and thank you.' She looked at the card again and said, 'Percival Street? Is B and B fairly new in Broadminster?'

A rueful smile tugged at the corners of his mouth. 'So much for advertising,' he said. 'We've been there almost three years, which is when I moved here. I used to work for Danforth DataCom as a technical programme manager in Wolverhampton until they were taken over by an American firm. I could have kept my job with the new company, but it meant moving to America, and I didn't want to do that. Fortunately, Bill Bristow, who owns B and B Data Specialists, is a personal friend; he was about to open a branch in Broadminster, and he offered me a job. So I moved here and I'm glad I did. I like Broadminster, and I've made quite a few friends here.'

'Through the church, I imagine,' Molly said. 'And now choirmaster. You must have a good voice.'

'Only fair,' he said modestly, 'but I do have a degree in music. I used to teach it many years ago, but I couldn't make a decent living at it, so I went back to university and found my niche in electronics. But I do enjoy the choir, so when no one else would take on the job of choirmaster when Adam Fairfield left, I volunteered.'

'Which brings me to why we're here,' Molly said, taking out the photograph found among Gavin Whitelaw's possessions. 'I know this was taken years before your time here, but I'm wondering if Mr Fairfield left any pictures or a record that might tell us the identity of the junior members of the choir in this picture?'

Jones studied the photo, then shook his head. 'I'm afraid not,' he said, 'and I can't say I'd given it any thought until you rang. But there must be some sort of record of those times.' He eyed Molly levelly. 'I take it this is to do with the tragic death of Billy Travis,' he said quietly, 'but I don't understand what it has to do with the choir. How is it involved?'

'We don't know that the choir's involved at all,' said Molly. 'We have reason to believe there's a common purpose behind the killings, but the only link we've found so far between the victims is that two of them were in the choir when they were teenagers, and one of those victims contacted an existing member of the choir shortly before he was killed.'

Frowning, Jones looked at the picture again. 'So that was Billy back then,' he said soberly. 'To be honest he wasn't the greatest of singers, but he enjoyed being in the choir and he was rarely absent or late, even for rehearsals, which is something that can't be said for all members, I'm afraid.'

He tapped the picture. 'Mike Fulbright, the tall chap at the back, has probably been with the choir longer than anyone, so he might remember who they all are. Have you spoken to him? His father was the minister there for years.' He leaned closer and said, 'Good Lord! Is that Meg Bainbridge when she was young?' He shook his head. 'She's still with us, you know. Lovely voice. She could have gone further with training. Pity.'

He handed the picture back to Molly. 'Thank you for showing me that,' he said. 'Where did you get it?'

'It belonged to one of the victims,' said Molly, 'and one of the others had a picture of himself in cassock and surplice that was taken around the same time.'

'So what is it you're looking for, exactly?'

'This picture's estimated to be something like fifteen years old,' said Molly, 'and while only two of the victims appear in it, some of the other youngsters in the picture may be able to tell us if the other victim was ever in the choir.'

'I suppose I should have asked Adam Fairfield about that,' he said, 'because the book I have was fairly new when I took over. Why not put the picture in the local paper? Some of those kids are probably still living here.'

'We thought of that. But it was felt that, since the connection is so tenuous, and we could be wrong, we didn't want to start rumours and speculation about the choir without more evidence.'

'Then why don't I contact Adam Fairfield and see if he can help? He may have taken some of that stuff with him. He must have kept some sort of records over the years. He doesn't have a computer, but his daughter does, and I've been in touch with him through her before. I don't remember the e-mail address offhand, but if I could have a copy of that picture, I'll send it off tonight and explain what it is you want. Even if he can only identify a few of the people in the picture, that could lead to others.'

The team of detectives and uniformed constables making door-to-door enquiries around Windsor Street and the Red Lion were kept going until ten o'clock that night before Paget told Ormside to bring them in. 'But I want them back at it first thing tomorrow morning,' he said. He kept reminding himself that Connie Rice's disappearance probably had nothing whatsoever to do with the killings of three men, but he couldn't shake the feeling that it just might.

Surprisingly, once he'd stopped complaining, Rick Crowley had become interested in the process of building a picture of the man he claimed had been talking to Connie, and by three o'clock that afternoon, he declared the result 'a pretty good likeness'. Warned of the consequences if he was misleading them, he stuck to his guns. 'That's him!' he declared. 'It might not be *exactly* right, but it's as near as makes no difference. So, now I've done your job for you, can I go and get on with *my* job?'

Paget had ordered the picture to be given to the media, together with the usual request for anyone who had seen the man to contact the police. Four people had called in by late evening, and those leads were being checked out.

One of the searchers in the Red Lion car park found a good-luck charm in the shape of a shamrock half embedded in the gravel some distance from where Connie usually parked her car. 'It was about twelve feet away,' the man told Ormside. 'Thing is, it was nowhere near the line she would normally take between her car and the door of the pub, but it could have come off if she were being carried or dragged to another car. I've shown it to the staff in the pub, and they say they're sure it came off her bracelet. We don't know *when* it was lost, but they said Rice was always fiddling with the bracelet, and she would have said something if she'd lost it earlier.'

Connie's car had been towed in for further examination, but the initial report from forensic was that there was no obvious evidence of a struggle.

'So it looks as if she was attacked in the car park and dragged over to another car,' Ormside said. 'Her attacker then drove her car out of the car park to make it look as if Connie had gone home. He parked it close by, then went back and drove away with the girl.' The sergeant's eyes were bleak as he looked at Paget. 'Which would mean she would have to be unconscious or incapacitated in some way while he moved her car . . . or dead.'

TWENTY

Saturday, 29 October

Windsor Street was a cul-de-sac consisting of eight houses on each side, with three forming a semi-circle to close off the end of the street, and every one of them had been visited, without result. Some residents said they'd seen the car there, even noticed that it wasn't one they'd seen in the street before, but hadn't thought much about it at the time. Others said they hadn't noticed it at all. Even the woman who reported it said she hadn't noticed the car in front of her house until midday on Thursday. 'I thought it must belong to someone visiting,' she told Tregalles, 'so I left it, thinking it would be gone by evening. But when I saw it still sitting there this morning, I reported it and asked to have it removed.'

'They're mostly older people in that street,' Tregalles explained to Ormside. 'In fact I think half of them were on their way to bed by the time we packed it in last night. But even if they had been looking out, what could they tell us? Connie Rice didn't leave the pub until midnight; it was dark; there was no moon, so whoever drove her car around to Windsor Street wasn't taking much of a chance.

'We've questioned most of the people on the route between the pub and Windsor Street. We stopped people out walking their dogs, people on their way through on bikes and in cars, and we're no further ahead than when we started. To be honest, Len, I think we're all wasting our time going out there again this morning.'

'So what do you suggest we do?' Ormside asked.

'I don't know, and that's the trouble,' Tregalles said wearily. 'Even if we assume Connie Rice was taken by the same person who killed the other three, we still don't know what connects the victims.'

'Forsythe seems convinced there's a connection through the All Saints choir,' Ormside said. 'Both Travis and Whitelaw were in the same choir, and Whitelaw did go to see Mike Fulbright, another member of the choir, shortly before he died. And you said you don't believe that Fulbright was telling the truth when he said all they talked about was cars.'

'I'm sure he wasn't,' Tregalles said, 'but the fact that some of them were in the same choir ten or twenty years ago, doesn't mean much in a town this size. I know Molly's got it stuck in her head that there's a connection, but I can't see it myself.' He frowned as he looked around the office. 'Where is she, anyway?' he asked.

'Where you'd better be if you don't want Paget on your

case,' Ormside said. 'She's been out there since seven o'clock this morning, talking to anyone she happens to meet.'

Tregalles looked at the clock. 'It's only just turned eight now,' he said. 'What the hell is she trying to prove?'

'I don't think she's trying to prove anything,' Ormside said, 'or needs to for that matter. I suspect she believes, as you do, that all this knocking on doors and stopping people in the street is a waste of time, but she's slogging through it because she knows it has to be done just in case. So why don't you go out there and give her a hand?'

The morning sun felt warm against his face as he drove along the top of the quarry, but once he dropped below the lip of the giant excavation, the sunlight disappeared, and he was reminded that it was late October, and summer was long gone. He shivered, but not so much from cold as from the memory of his last visit here. He felt guilty about slipping out of the house and leaving Jimmy behind, but Alice had flatly refused to let the boy return to the quarry. He'd agreed to skip coming here last Saturday, telling Jimmy that he had other things to do, but he knew his son had been looking forward to coming with him this weekend, and he wished now that he'd insisted on bringing him.

'He didn't actually *see* anything,' he'd reminded his wife, 'so there's nothing for him to be frightened of.'

But Alice wouldn't budge, and he'd finally given in and stopped arguing. Maybe later, when all the fuss had died down, Alice might change her mind and he could bring the boy here again.

Descending to the quarry floor, Ron Jackson stopped the pickup close to what looked like a fresh fall of stones. Sometimes the rains did that, and some of the stones looked to be about the size he was looking for. He stuck the goggles on his head, then took the sledgehammer and the largest of the cold chisels from the box in the back of the pickup, and set them on the ground. Then, head down, he began to pick his way carefully through the smaller stuff to reach the larger stones. He was wearing boots, but it was all too easy to turn an ankle, and having done that once, he'd learned to be careful.

He found a flat spot and stopped to look for just the right stone to start on. Some would split well, while others would either refuse to split, or suddenly shatter into a thousand pieces and leave you with—

'Oh, Jesus!'

Ron Jackson felt as if his blood had turned to water. He couldn't believe his eyes. He kept telling himself it was some sort of distorted mental image, an hallucination left over from the time before; it couldn't possibly be real.

But it was real, all too real. His stomach churned and suddenly he was on his hands and knees, spewing out his breakfast.

'Looks like the ground broke away beneath her when she reached the edge up there,' Paget said, 'and the whole lot came down with her. Her hands are bound behind her back, her mouth is taped just like the others, and the letter A has been carved in her forehead. God only knows what their killer thinks these people have done that they need to die in such a cruel and sadistic way.'

He was speaking to Amanda Pierce, who had just arrived at the scene. 'Starkie estimates that she's been dead for more than a day, possibly two. And if that proves to be true, Connie Rice was driven out here and killed within hours of leaving the pub – and, like the others, he believes she was alive when she went over the edge.'

There was an air of desperation in the incident room that afternoon. SOCO was out in full force at the crime scene; Connie's flat was being searched again, and her flat-mate, Sandra Palmer, was being pressured to think of *anything* Connie had said or done that might be relevant to the investigation. Five more people claimed to have seen 'the man in the picture on TV', and although Paget knew it was a long shot, he sent Molly off to ask Rick Crowley for the names and addresses, if he knew them, of the regulars who had been in the Red Lion on Wednesday. 'They may not have been in the pub at the same time as the man Crowley claims was chatting up Connie,' said Paget, 'but one of them may know the people who were celebrating their lottery win, and one of *them* may be able to tell us more about this mystery man, or at least give us a better description. And I'll get the press officer to put out an appeal for anyone who was in or near the pub that evening as well.' He was grasping at straws and he knew it, but with nothing else to work with, what was there to lose?

They had tried several times to contact Connie Rice's mother, without success, and there was no one home when the Bristol police went round to the house. 'They're off somewhere different almost every weekend,' a neighbour told them. 'They'll probably be back Sunday evening.'

Paget was staring blankly at the whiteboards when the phone on Ormside's desk rang. It sounded louder than usual in the unnatural quiet of an almost deserted room. The sergeant answered, then handed it to Paget, mouthing 'Superintendent Pierce,' and pointing upwards.

'We're on *Breaking News* on Radio Shropshire,' she said. 'They appear to have full details linking all the murders, and they used the phrase "serial killer" at least six or seven times in a two-minute clip, so you can imagine how that will go over with the public. So I think the sooner we respond the better, and I've instructed the press officer to set up a conference for six o'clock this evening, where I'll be making a statement and asking the public for their help. I'll also make another appeal to anyone who was in the Red Lion that night to come forward. And, as the senior officer heading the investigation, I think you should be there as well, Neil – so, with less than two hours to go, I'd like you to come up and help me draft an opening statement. As for the questions . . . they'll be after blood, so we'll just have to do the best we can.'

Sunday, 30 October

Mike Fulbright was still feeling the effects of last night's celebration when he came down for breakfast. The Grinders had been playing away the day before, and it had been midnight before he got home. Bleary-eyed, and with a dull ache nagging away at the back of his head, he'd given serious consideration to staying in bed and to hell with the choir this morning. But the thought of young Findlay stealing a march on him changed his mind.

'Do we *really* have to listen to the news at this time on a Sunday morning?' he asked irritably as he filled his plate. 'It's nothing but doom and gloom, for God's sake!'

'I was just listening to see if there was any update on the hunt for the serial killer,' Rachel said mildly. 'I thought you'd be interested since one of the victims was a fellow choir member, Billy Travis. And then there was the chap the police said came to see you just before he was killed. Whitelaw, was it? And now they've found the girl who was missing, in Clapperton quarry just like one of the men before her. You know a lot of women, Mike. Perhaps you knew her as well? Connie Rice?'

Hunched over his plate, Mike became very still. 'So what did they say?' he asked. 'Do they have any idea who's behind the killings?'

'It didn't sound to me as if they know very much at all,' she said. 'They were on TV last night. One of them was that chief inspector who came to see you, but neither of them said very much. Just that they're doing everything they can. They're following several leads – you know, the usual stuff – and they made an appeal for anyone who was in or near the Red Lion on Wednesday night to come forward. They spun it out a bit, but it sounded to me as if they didn't have a clue, and I mean literally!'

Rachel reached for the teapot and refilled her cup. 'You were out Wednesday evening, weren't you, Mike?' she asked innocently. 'Were you anywhere near the Red Lion?'

Sunday, a day of rest . . . for some, perhaps, but not for others, and Amanda Pierce's car was already there when Paget pulled into his parking space in Charter Lane. He'd come in this morning simply because, knowing the killer was still out there, he couldn't stay away, and there had to be *something* he could do to get the investigation moving again. But what? The question had been pounding away inside his head since last night. The press conference had been bad enough, but it looked ten times worse by the time the editors had worked it over for airing on the late evening news.

He entered the building and was heading for the incident room when the duty sergeant stopped him to tell him that Detective Superintendent Pierce wanted to see him in her office the moment he arrived.

'Sounds serious,' Paget said. 'Did she say anything else?'

'No, sir,' the man said, lowering his voice, 'but she usually says "Good morning" when she comes in. Not this morning though. Tell the truth, sir, she looked a bit grim.'

He was right. Amanda did look grim when Paget tapped on the door and entered her office. She waved him to a seat, then sat looking at him across the desk for a full half minute before she spoke.

'I received a call from Mr Brock following the press conference last night,' she said abruptly. 'To say that he was less than pleased would be an understatement, in fact he called it a public relations disaster. He told me that neither he, nor the assistant chief constable, nor the chief constable are happy with the lack of progress on these serial killings, and then went on to say he attributes that to a lack of cooperation between you and me.'

Amanda paused, eyes narrowed as if searching for something. 'I don't know where he's getting his information from,' she continued, 'but he went on to say there have been rumours – or as he put it *disturbing* rumours – that you and I are not working well together because of something in our past relationship in the Met, and because you resent being passed over by me when I was given this job. He went on to suggest that you may have been dragging your feet in this investigation because of that resentment, and said that if we can't resolve our differences and work together to clear up this case, then perhaps one or both of us should consider a transfer to what he called a "more productive environment".'

Paget eyed Amanda levelly. 'Were you given an opportunity to reply?' he asked.

Amanda looked up at the ceiling and let out a long breath. 'I was,' she said, 'and I tried to be diplomatic, but I'm afraid my tongue got the better of me. I suggested that if he had read my daily progress reports more carefully, he would see that we have followed every possible lead, but until we can establish a connection between the victims and come up with a motive, or find some physical evidence to work with, our hands are tied. In retrospect, I should have shut up then, but the man's whole attitude annoyed me, so I went on to tell him I would be more than happy to listen to any suggestions he might have regarding what we could have done differently, and I asked him to point out exactly what we've missed. I also told him I had every confidence in your work; that you've given me your full cooperation on every level and your record should speak for itself.'

The corners of her mouth twitched in what might have been a wry grin if the muscles hadn't been quite so taut. 'I'm afraid that little speech didn't go over very well,' she said. 'Hardly surprising, I suppose, considering his background. The man hasn't got a clue about on-the-job policing. I like to know the backgrounds of people I'm dealing with, so I made it my business to learn about Detective Chief Superintendent Brock's background, and, as I'm sure you know, he came up through the admin side of the service, and he's never done a day on the front line in his life.

'Unfortunately,' she continued with something like a sigh of resignation, 'he is still my boss, and he reminded me that I was very much on trial here and told me not to be impertinent. Then he switched to what he called "these rumours about the bad blood between the two of you", and demanded to know what that was all about.'

Amanda's eyes locked with Paget's own. 'So I told him, yes, there had been a bit of friction between families years ago, but you and I had resolved our differences and it was no longer an issue.' Amanda stopped speaking, but her gaze never wavered. 'But that's not true, is it, Neil?' she said softly. 'We haven't resolved our differences, at least with regard to Matthew, have we?'

'No,' he said, 'I'm afraid we haven't, Amanda, and to be honest, I don't know if we ever will. I'll continue to do my job, but every time I see you I think of Matthew and the way he died, and what that did to Jill. That was cruel, Amanda, and I can't get past that.'

'I understand that,' she said quietly, 'and I know I can't expect you to believe me, but I had to make a choice, Neil, and I did the best I could under the circumstances . . .' She broke off and made a gesture of complete helplessness, then tilted her head back and covered her face with her hands.

'God! I hate this!' she said fiercely. 'I'm so sick and tired of keeping silent; tired of being hated by the people I loved; tired of living this lie. You hate me because of what you think I did to Jill, and I don't blame you for that, but I went through hell trying to *protect* Jill, because I knew what it would do to her if she knew the truth. Jill wasn't just my best friend, Neil, she was more than that. There was a special bond between us from the very first day we met, and the last thing I wanted to do was hurt her. I grew up in foster homes, Neil. I never knew my mother and father. I had no relatives. Nobody cared about me but Jill . . .' Amanda swallowed hard. She was clearly fighting back tears, but she forced herself to go on. 'We were just kids, thirteen years old, but Jill took me under her wing, and for the first time in my life I had a friend. She was my lifeline. I loved her and I would never knowingly do anything to hurt her.'

'Then why . . .?' Paget began, but Amanda carried on as if he hadn't spoken.

'Jill was a wonderful friend,' she said, 'though God knows why I'm telling you that, Neil. We both loved her in our own way and I know she loved both of us. But if there was one person in Jill's life who was just that little bit extra special, it was her brother Matthew. The sun rose and set on Matthew, the big, friendly, loveable bear, the man I married, and the man who killed himself supposedly because of what I'd done.'

'*Supposedly*, Amanda . . .?' Paget's withering look said more than words, but Amanda was on her feet now and speaking again. 'I had hoped that enough time had gone by that you and I would be able to put the past behind us,' she said, 'but clearly I was wrong, and I can't go on like this. So I'm going to tell you the truth and you can believe me or not. Please lock the door.'

'Lock the door?' Paget echoed. He shot a puzzled look at Amanda. 'It's Sunday morning. There's no one else up here.'

'Humour me,' Amanda said tersely. She stood waiting.

Baffled by her strange request, but curious, he got to his feet and turned the key in the lock, then stood with his back to the door and folded his arms. 'All right,' he said coldly, 'the door's locked. Now what?'

Amanda took off her jacket and draped it over the back of her chair, then began to unbutton her blouse.

Downstairs in the incident room Tregalles picked one of the cards at random and looked at it. 'Mrs Agnes Breckenridge, The Cedars, 12 Littlewood Lane,' he said. 'Claims to have sighted our man down by the sports grounds yesterday afternoon. Saw the picture on TV last night, but didn't report it till this morning, because she thought there would be nobody here that late at night.' He groaned as he waved it at Ormside. 'You know this is going to be a waste of time, Len. Haven't you got anything better than this?'

'How do you know which one will be better than another?' Ormside countered. 'You know as well as I do that they've all got to be checked out, regardless of where they come from or who reports them.' He sat back in his chair and looked at his colleague through narrowed eyes. 'So what's your problem, Tregalles?' he asked. 'It's not just this, is it? You've been out of sorts for days.'

'It's nothing,' Tregalles said irritably. 'It's just that . . . it's like we're working blind. I mean where the hell is Paget these days? I know it's Sunday, but normally he'd be down here in the thick of things, and out there talking to some of these people himself. It's not been the same since *she* came,' he added darkly. 'It's almost as if he's left us to go it alone.'

'I should have taped that,' Ormside growled. 'You should listen to yourself, Tregalles. I never took you for a whinger, but that's what you sounded like just now. You've had it too soft all these years with Paget leading the way. He's got his work cut out bringing the new super up to speed, and doing his own job as well, so perhaps he thinks it's time you flew on your own.'

'I *wasn't* whinging!' Tregalles said heatedly. 'I was just saying, that's all. It doesn't seem right for him not to be down here the way he used to be. You know how it was, Len. We were partners. We worked like that for years.'

'Well, things change, so get used to it, Tregalles. And they're liable to change a lot more before we're done. Now, are you going out to see Agnes Breckenridge or not?'

TWENTY-ONE

Standing with his back to the locked door, watching Amanda take off her clothes, he didn't know what to expect . . . until she removed her blouse and bra and stood there, naked to the waist.

'This,' she said quietly, 'is what Matthew, that great big loveable bear, did to me, Neil. So take a good look and remember it while I tell you what happened and why I did what I did.'

The scarred tissue covered almost half of her upper body, beginning at the shoulder and ending just above the waist. The left breast was misshapen, and there were scars, faded but still ugly. He found it very hard to look at; even harder to look away.

'That is what a saucepan full of boiling soup will do to you,' Amanda continued as she put her bra and the rest of her clothes on again. He could see that the left side of the bra contained some padding and a moulded cup to cover the misshapen breast. 'Not very nice to look at, is it? And it wasn't very nice when it happened, believe me. Sorry if that was over-dramatic, but I felt I had to make sure I had your full attention, so please sit down and let's get this out of the way once and for all . . . if you're willing to listen?'

'You're saying *Matthew* did that to you? Deliberately?' he said as he moved to his seat and sat down.

'That and more. Much more. Now, tell me honestly, Neil: how do you think Jill would have reacted if I'd tried to tell her that Matthew, the brother she adored, was not only an alcoholic but a control freak, who systematically abused me, and finally did this to me?'

'She wouldn't have believed you,' he said. 'And neither would I without proof.'

'Exactly. And if I had given her proof, you know as well as I do what that would have done to her. She would have been devastated. As I said, I loved Jill dearly, but she had a blind spot when it came to Matthew. He could do no wrong in her eyes.'

'I'll concede that Matthew had his faults,' Paget said, 'and I know he used his charm and good nature to gloss over the fact that he'd never quite grown up. In and out of university; changing courses; in and out of jobs; and you're right, Jill thought the world of him. But as for being an alcoholic, it was only after you left him that he began to drink heavily – and it was drink that led to his death in the end. As for the rest, in all the years I knew Matthew, he was always pleasant and easy-going to a fault.'

'That was the problem,' Amanda said. 'Everyone who knew Matthew would tell you the same thing, so I don't blame you for doubting me. The thing is, are you willing to listen to what I have to say before you judge me?'

The scars she had shown him were real. He couldn't deny that. He nodded slowly and said, 'Go ahead, then, I'm listening.'

'Thank you.' Amanda drew a deep breath. 'Then the first thing I have to tell you is that no one knew, except perhaps for a few bartenders, that Matthew was an alcoholic, and had been for a long time before I married him. I know you'll find that hard to believe, but don't judge until I'm finished. Matthew was very good at concealing his addiction to alcohol. He could be completely drunk, yet appear to be normal. In fact he was so good at concealing it that we'd been married for several months before I realized there was something wrong.

'Even then, I made excuses for him, because he always seemed to be trying so hard, yet things never seemed to turn out right for him. I felt sorry for him. We all did, if you remember. Then there were the "migraines". Remember them, Neil? It took me months to realize they were hangovers, but he was clever enough to make sure that no one else, especially you and Jill, ever saw that side of him.

'And that side of him was pretty dark. We would go on for days leading a normal, happy life and everything would be fine. Then, suddenly, I would come home to find him in a foul mood, and nothing I could do or say would be right.'

Amanda went on to say that the first real argument they'd had was over her name. She'd kept her own name when she married Matthew, and he'd made no objection to it then, but suddenly he wanted to know why she wouldn't take his name. 'He wanted to know if I was ashamed of his name, and if I'd kept it because I didn't want the men I worked with to know I was married. It was so bizarre; I didn't take him seriously, but when I tried to make light of it, he became very angry and stormed out of the house.

'He came back around midnight. I'd gone to bed, still baffled by his strange behaviour, so I was still awake. He came in and went down on his knees beside the bed and begged me to forgive him. Over and over again he said he was sorry, he didn't know what had got into him, and he promised it would never happen again.

'But it did happen again,' Amanda said tonelessly. 'Time and time again. Everything would be fine for several days, sometimes a week or more, then suddenly it would change, and I never knew what to expect when I got home.' She went on to say that the next flare-up was over the *time* she got home from work. Why couldn't she be home at the same time every evening like other people? Did she think more of her job than she did of him?

'It finally dawned on me that what was really bugging him was the fact that I had a career and he didn't, and things became even worse when I became a sergeant. He kept hinting that my promotion must be due to the fact that I was having an affair with someone at the office, and that was why I'd been coming home late some evenings.' Her voice turned brittle. 'And, in case you're wondering, Neil, I wasn't. I earned my stripes the hard way.

'I tried,' she continued, 'I really did try to understand what was going on in Matthew's head, but it didn't seem to matter what I said or did, it was wrong, and it was driving me mad. I was losing sleep, I was finding it hard to concentrate at work.

I had to talk to someone, and who should know Matthew better than Jill? I even wondered if he'd confided in her, and maybe she would be willing to help us sort things out. I knew how sensitive she was when it came to even the slightest criticism of Matthew, so I tried very hard to be careful.'

Amanda brushed aside a stray wisp of hair; her eyes clouded, and she looked beyond Paget as if reliving a painful memory. 'But when I told Jill that things weren't going as smoothly in our marriage as I thought they should, hoping for her to respond in a way that would encourage me to tell her at least a little of what was happening, she laughed at me and told me that all married couples have some adjustments to make. She left me with the impression that she thought I was being unreasonable, because Matthew had always been so easy to get along with. I knew then that if I pushed it, there was a very good chance that it could affect our friendship, so I dropped it. And that,' she concluded, 'was when I finally had to admit to myself that no matter how much I loved him, Matthew was never going to change, and things could only get worse. So I stopped acting like a love-sick girl and started acting like a policewoman, and began to record everything, using a pen recorder I "borrowed" from work.'

Amanda reached down and unlocked the middle drawer of her desk. She took out an ordinary looking pen and a memory stick and set them on the pad in front of her. 'I still have it,' she said. 'Technically, legally, I suppose it's stolen property; it belongs to the Met, and I took it without permission, but I knew no one would believe me without hard evidence, because Matthew was so very, very good at switching roles and he could be so very charming with everyone he met.'

Her eyes shifted once again to a point beyond him, brow furrowed in concentration. 'I couldn't leave the house without Matthew demanding to know where I was going,' she continued. 'He was drinking heavily, and it was becoming harder for him to hide it, so we stopped going out and mixing socially. We were always making excuses; you must remember that, Neil? The times you or Jill would phone to ask us to join you, but we'd be busy or working, or not feeling too well?'

He did remember. There had been a period when he and

Jill and Matthew and Amanda had spent a lot of time together. Dinners, barbecues, parties, shows when they could afford them, and they'd had a lot of good times. But Amanda was right. He and Jill had put it down to the fact that with three out of the four of them moving up the ladder, working shifts and odd hours, it was becoming harder to arrange something where all four could get together. That was the way it was. Part of the job; part of the price you paid.

Amanda was speaking again. 'I know it must sound foolish, even stupid to you now, but even then, I wanted to save Matthew from himself. I kept remembering the man I'd married, and more than anything I wanted to get back to the way things had been then. If only I could get Matthew to stop drinking, everything would be all right and nobody would have to know. Especially Jill.'

Amanda grimaced. 'In hindsight, I probably made matters worse by thinking I could change things, because after every outburst, Matthew would say he was sorry and plead with me to forgive him, and he would sound so damned sincere that I couldn't bring myself to give up on him. At one point I really thought I'd made a breakthrough when he said he would join AA. I was so happy when he did that. He went off religiously on meeting nights, but I found out later that he wasn't going. Even then, idiot that I was, I still thought I could save him.'

Tears glistened in Amanda's eyes. 'Until he did this to me,' she whispered. Her hand went to her chest. 'I came in late one night. I knew he would probably start in on me again, but I took off my coat and jacket and went to find him. He was in the kitchen, standing at the stove, heating up some soup. It seemed an odd thing for him to be doing, because he didn't care for soup, but I kissed him on the cheek, then saw that the soup was bubbling like mad, so I said something like, "You should never boil soup like that, love", and started to walk away. But he called to me in quite a gentle voice, so I turned round to face him.'

Amanda sucked in her breath. 'He picked up the saucepan and flung the boiling hot soup straight at me. You've seen for yourself what it did. Most of it hit me across the chest. I'm not sure whether the shirt helped or made things worse, but it left me with what I later learned were second-degree burns.' Amanda shuddered and closed her eyes. 'The pain was excruciating. My legs went out from under me and I started to fall, but even as I was going down I saw the look in his eyes, and I knew that was no sudden, impulsive action. Matthew had known exactly what he was doing. He'd planned it in advance. I blanked out, although I don't think I could have been unconscious for more than a few seconds, but when I came round I was soaking wet, and Matthew was standing over me, holding a saucepan. But it wasn't the saucepan that had held the soup; it was larger, one I remembered seeing on the counter, filled to the brim with water.

'I have very little recollection of the next twenty-four hours, but when I did become fully conscious, I was on the bed and Matthew was standing there looking, oh, so terribly anxious and guilt-ridden. I felt as if my whole body was on fire and I pleaded with him to get me to a hospital, but he kept insisting he would look after me, and he kept apologizing for the "horrible accident", and saying how fortunate it was that he had the presence of mind to save me from worse burns by throwing the saucepan of cold water over me. He kept bringing me tea and Paracetamol tablets, and looking so worried and contrite . . .'

Amanda broke off, shaking her head as if even now she found it hard to believe what had happened. 'He phoned in to work to say that I'd had a fall and it would be a week or two before I could return. I heard him on the phone. He sounded so worried and sincere. Oh, yes, he also took away my mobile phone and disconnected our land-line, because he said he didn't want me to be disturbed, and that was when I became *really* scared. I knew then that he'd crossed the line, and if I didn't play along and agree to everything he said, I could end up dead. So I pretended to be thoroughly confused and accepted what had happened as an accident.

'I'm not sure how many days went by before I was able to get to my pen recorder and put it beside the bed,' she continued, 'but it was there when Matthew sat down one day and told me that I had to quit my job. That it was the cause of the breakdown in our marriage, and police work wasn't for married women. It was too dangerous, the hours were too long, and it was affecting our relationship. And he was dead serious. He wanted me out of there. I think his idea was that I should get a job in an office where I would be surrounded only by women. No men. I belonged to him. He made that very clear.

'So, when I was finally well enough to get dressed and go back to work, I did as he asked. I tendered my resignation. Matthew wanted me to tell them I found the job too stressful, but I was looking to the future and I didn't want that on my record, so I said there was a crisis in the family and I had to look after a relative who was seriously ill in Southampton, and I could be gone for a long time, and I had no choice but to resign.'

'Southampton . . .?'

Amanda shrugged. 'I picked Southampton because it was about as far away as possible from the place I intended to go. Once everything was done, I told Matthew it would be another two or three days before they got my pension and payout money sorted, then I went off as if I was going to work next morning. Instead, I waited for the bank to open and went in and took out half of what we had in there. Most of it was mine anyway, because Matthew hadn't had a proper job for months, but I couldn't leave him with nothing. Then I caught a train to Southampton. Once there, I had copies made of the recordings and sent one to Matthew with a note saying I had deposited copies with a solicitor, who would send them to the police and to Jill if he tried to find me or if anything happened to me.'

Amanda looked away. 'But that note I sent to Jill was one of the hardest things I've ever done,' she said softly, 'because I knew it would be the finish of us as friends. I'm sure you remember that, Neil?'

'I remember it very well,' he said. 'And to say that both of us were stunned would be an understatement. You said you were sorry that things hadn't worked out between you and Matthew, that it was your fault and you hoped Jill could find it in her heart to forgive you. Why did you send that note, Amanda?'

'Because I didn't want there to be any doubt that I'd left

of my own accord. Perhaps it was my police training; perhaps by then I was more than a little paranoid. But I didn't want anyone to start wondering if Matthew had done away with me and start an investigation. Anyway, when I left Southampton, I made my way up to Kendal in Cumbria.'

'Why Kendal?'

'It was the only place I could think of that was far enough away and where I knew someone who might take me in. I had no relatives to turn to, and the only person I knew I could trust was a woman I'd kept in touch with over the years. Lillian Taggart. She was a social worker when I was in foster care, and she was very kind to me. But she and her husband had moved to Kendal, where they managed a number of holiday cottages, so I took a chance and went up there to ask if I could stay until I could find some sort of job. Unfortunately, I'd no sooner got there when my left breast became infected. The burns had never been treated properly, because Matthew would never let me go to a hospital, so it was hardly surprising when something went wrong. I tried to hide it and treat it myself, but it got worse, my temperature went sky high, and finally things became so bad that Lillian and her husband rushed me into hospital. There were questions, of course, but I wasn't in any state to answer them. But Lillian was.' Amanda smiled thinly at the memory. 'She told them I was her niece and a worker in a mental health institute down south, and a patient had thrown a pot of boiling water over me. She said that once I'd been released from hospital, I'd come up there to recuperate. I don't know if they believed her or not, but no more was said while I was in there.'

'When did you come back down south?'

'Almost five months later. I would have preferred a job well away from London, but I was running out of money, so when I saw the opportunity with Thames Valley, I applied and got in at Oxford.'

Suddenly Amanda looked drained. 'When I read about the way Matthew died, the only thing I could think of was how Jill would feel, because if it hadn't been for me . . . It never crossed my mind that he would do such a foolish thing.'

Speaking so softly now that he could barely hear the words,

she said, 'I've asked myself over and over again if I could have done anything differently, and I still don't know the answer. At the time, I thought it better that Jill hate me rather than learn what her brother was really like. Was I wrong, Neil?'

Was I wrong, Neil? Sitting in his office later that morning, the words continued to echo inside his head as he pulled the memory stick from the USB port on his laptop and slipped it into his pocket. He would listen to the rest of it at home, but he'd heard enough to know that Amanda was telling the truth. And yet, even now he found it hard to reconcile his memory of big, affable Matthew with the picture conjured up when he listened to the recording. He could imagine how hard it would have been for Jill if she'd been confronted with the same evidence. So Amanda had sacrificed her own reputation rather than have Jill find out the truth about her brother.

He felt guilty for ever doubting Amanda. He tried to console himself with the thought that he had judged her on the evidence available at the time, but it brought him little comfort. And it was a sobering reminder that 'evidence', no matter how strong, could still be misleading.

The ringing of his phone broke into his thoughts, and he picked it up. It was Control asking if he wished to speak to a Valerie Alcott.

'Valerie,' he said when they were connected. 'What can I do for you?'

'I just wanted to let you know that the inquest was adjourned, but the coroner has issued a cremation certificate, so there will be a memorial service at two thirty next Saturday afternoon at St Mark's Memorial Chapel. Dad didn't attend church very often, but he was a good man in his own way, and I'd like to do this for him. Can you come?'

'Of course I can, Valerie,' he said. 'Is there anything I can do?'

'As a matter of fact, there is,' she said hesitantly. 'Dad didn't have many friends outside work, so I don't think there will be many people there, and I was wondering if you would say a few words?' The request took him by surprise, and he hesitated. 'But if you'd rather not, I'll understand,' Valerie added quickly.

'No, no, I'd like to,' he said. 'Really, Valerie, I would, and thank you for asking me.'

'Are you sure you want me to hear this?' Grace asked when Paget suggested they listen to the recordings together after dinner. 'I mean, this is a very personal thing for you; something that caused you and your wife a lot of pain. I really don't mind if you'd rather listen to it alone.'

But Paget wanted Grace to hear it. 'I've given you a very one-sided view of Amanda,' he said, 'so I'd like you to hear this so you'll understand, as I did, what she must have gone through. Not only with the verbal and physical abuse from a man she loved, but the decision and the sacrifice she made to keep Jill from knowing the truth about her brother. I know Jill would have been devastated. And although I'm sure Amanda thought she was doing what she did for the best of reasons, I wish there had been another way.'

They listened to the tape in silence, and when at last it came to an end, Paget slumped back in his chair and rubbed his face with his hands. 'I hear it, yet I still have trouble taking it in,' he said. 'I know that was Matthew's voice, but the Matthew Hambledon I knew was a totally different person, happy-go-lucky, fun to be with . . . although I must admit he could be irritating at times because he never seemed to take anything seriously.'

His face became grave. 'You should have seen what he did to her chest, Grace. God! How she must have suffered without proper treatment, and then later, with the infection and the subsequent operation. She's disfigured for life. And we didn't have the slightest inkling. We had no idea about what was going on in that house.'

'What about the time she was in the house recovering from the burns? She must have been out of contact. Didn't you wonder about that?'

'No, not really, because by that time we were seeing less and less of them, and it wasn't unusual to go without seeing them for weeks at a time. We worked in different boroughs;

we had no contact at work, so we didn't suspect anything was wrong.'

'So, how do you feel about Amanda Pierce now?'

'I was thinking about that earlier, and I think "relieved" would be the best way to describe it. Even when I was blaming her for causing Matthew's death, I kept remembering the Amanda I used to know, and I was deeply disappointed in her when she left Matthew and disappeared. Matthew told us she'd had a lover for some time and she'd gone off with him. We didn't know if that was true or not, but he was very convincing, and we had no reason to doubt him.' He shrugged and shook his head. 'And there didn't seem to be any other explanation at the time.'

'Will it make a difference in how you feel about working for her when the job might have been yours?' asked Grace.

He sat hunched forward, frowning as he thought about that. 'I must admit I was disappointed when I didn't get the job, and even more so because the selection committee made their choice for all the wrong reasons, but I can hardly blame Amanda for that. Anyway, it's done now, and from what Amanda told me about her session with Brock last night, we're going to have to show him we can work together, and prove him wrong. The trouble is, we're literally at a dead end, so unless the killer makes a serious mistake, I don't know how we're going to do that.'

TWENTY-TWO

Monday, 31 October

Molly checked her messages first thing Monday morning, hoping to see something back from Peter Jones, but there was nothing. She reminded herself that it had been the weekend, and that there were those who lived normal lives and took time off over the weekend. On Sunday afternoon, she'd tracked down two of the older members of the All Saints choir in the hope that they could help – they couldn't, and neither one could tell her for certain in which year the picture was taken.

'Meg Bainbridge might know,' one of them suggested. 'But she's not here this Sunday. She's gone to be a matron of honour at a friend's second marriage on the Isle of Wight, but she said she'll be back Monday or Tuesday.' Molly left a message on Meg's answering machine, asking her to contact her as soon as she returned, but she needed something now.

She went over everything again in her mind. She'd started out by speculating that the killer could be one of the people in the picture, but that wasn't necessarily so. As the Reverend Fulbright had said, younger members were always coming and going, so, assuming that all four victims were in the choir at the same time – assuming for the moment that Joan Moreland might not know *everything* her husband had done when he was a boy – it could have been in another year. Molly searched her memory. Dennis Moreland was thirty-two years old when he died. How long had the Morelands been married? Michael Moreland had said he was ten, so, assuming they were married before he was born, and assuming that Dennis and Joan had known each other for some time before that, she needed to concentrate on a period prior to twelve years ago.

But what did that prove? she thought glumly. Even if they had all been in the same choir many years ago, there was no evidence to suggest that they'd kept up that friendship. And if it turned out that being a member of the choir had nothing to do with the recent killings, then she'd wasted a hell of a lot of her time as well as that of other people.

She looked at the clock. Connie Rice's mother, now Mrs Donovan, had been contacted late last evening by the Bristol police, and she'd said that she and her husband would come up to Broadminster first thing this morning. They would probably be here by ten o'clock, and, once again, Molly had been assigned to 'do the honours', as Ormside put it, and she wasn't looking forward to it at all. She sighed. At least she'd remembered to call Dr Starkie's office to let them know that Mrs Donovan would be there this morning to identify the body.

* * *

Sheila Donovan arrived shortly before ten o'clock. A short, plump, middle-aged woman, she was accompanied by her husband, Alex, also short, but lean and wiry and deeply tanned. 'Sorry you couldn't reach us before,' he said apologetically, 'but we were in Eastbourne over the weekend. Golf tournament. We didn't know, you see. I mean, how could we?' He eased Molly away from his wife. 'You are *quite* sure it really is Connie, are you?' he asked anxiously. 'I wouldn't want Sheila . . .' He lowered his voice further. 'She's barely spoken two words since we heard last night. They didn't see a lot of each other, Sheila and Connie, but they used to talk on the phone. Is it all right if I stay with her while she . . . you know?'

'Views the body? Yes, of course, Mr Donovan. We're quite sure it is Connie, but we still need official verification.'

Sheila Donovan appeared to be calm and in control of her emotions as she stood before the window, and her voice was steady when she said, 'Yes, that's Connie,' in answer to Molly's question. But suddenly her eyes rolled up and her knees gave way and she would have fallen if it hadn't been for the quick reaction of her husband. Between them, they got her to a bench, and the attendant, who had seen it all before, was there in seconds to offer help. Sheila opened her eyes and started to cry, then buried her face into her husband's shoulder and clung to him. Cradling her in his arms, Alex Donovan spoke quietly to Molly. 'I knew it would be a shock for her,' he said, 'but I wasn't quite ready for this.' He glanced around the small room and wrinkled his nose. 'Just give us a minute or two, then we'll get her outside in the fresh air.'

'If you'd like to give me about five minutes,' Molly said, 'I'll go and get the car and bring it to the door, so your wife won't have so far to go. Can you manage on your own?'

'We'll be fine,' he assured her. 'And thank you, Sergeant.'

'Meet you outside in five minutes, then.' Molly left the room and was part way down the hall when a door opened and Dr Starkie came bustling out. He stopped in front of her, frowning as he peered at her over the top of his glasses. 'Connie Rice?' he asked cryptically. 'Who's doing the ID?'

'Her mother,' Molly told him. 'She's taken it very hard, I'm afraid.'

'It is hard on families, especially when there are injuries to the face,' said Starkie, 'but there's only so much that can be done with injuries like that.' He looked at his watch and started to move away, then stopped. 'Speaking of families, I must say I feel sorry for poor old David and the problems he's having with Lijuan. I really thought things were working out, but I suppose it's understandable if you look at it from her point of view. Still,' he continued cheerfully, 'I'm sure it will sort itself out in the end. Things like that usually do, don't they? Anyway, mustn't hold you up, and I have to get on myself. Busy day ahead.'

What would sort itself out? Starkie was fast disappearing down the hall and she could hardly call after him. Had the doctor been referring to the e-mail David had sent last week, or had the Starkies heard from him more recently? She had checked her e-mail before leaving home this morning – it was always the last thing she did before leaving for work – but there had been nothing. Perhaps David had phoned them. Ellen Starkie was his aunt, after all, so he probably called her every now and then. It was just that Molly had come to think of herself as part of . . . well, not the family, exactly – that would *really* be presumptuous – but she had become used to being included in the e-mail loop.

Molly suddenly realized that the Donovans would be coming out any minute, and she had some distance to go to where the car was parked. She ran up the steps, but her mind was still busy replaying everything Starkie had said. He *could* have been talking about the things David had mentioned in his e-mail last Tuesday, but somehow Molly didn't think so.

So what else had cropped up, she wondered. Starkie seemed to have assumed that she would know what he was talking about.

The Donovans were waiting for her when she drove up. Sheila Donovan had stopped crying, but she was leaning heavily on her husband's arm, and by the time they got her into the back seat, she was breathing heavily and wheezing.

'It's asthma,' her husband said. 'I have her inhaler here. She'll be all right in a minute. It's the stress.'

Listening to the woman's breathing, Molly wasn't so sure,

so, instead of getting into the car herself, she waited and watched while Alex Donovan coaxed his wife to use the inhaler. Remarkably, Sheila's breathing settled down within a couple of minutes, and her voice was almost back to normal when she spoke to Molly. 'It's all right, love,' she said. 'Like Alex said, it's just the stress of seeing Connie . . .' She closed her eyes and waved a listless hand as if to brush away the memory.

'You're sure?' asked Molly doubtfully. 'We're right here at the hospital.'

'Quite sure,' Sheila said. She took several deep breaths and let them out again. 'Can we go now?'

'Of course,' said Molly, 'but do you mind if I ask you a question first, Mrs Donovan?' Molly wasn't sure she should be asking the woman questions considering the state she was in, but she didn't want to let the opportunity slip away. 'It might seem a little odd to be asking this, but was Connie ever in the All Saints choir here in Broadminster when she was young?'

Sheila Donovan looked puzzled. 'What an odd question,' she said, 'but, yes, she was. But she didn't stay long; just a few months, I think it was. She was fifteen or sixteen at the time. Mad to get in, but she didn't stay long. But how did you know that?'

'It was just something that came up during the investigation,' Molly said evasively. And it could be a step forward, she thought as she got in the car. Connie was thirty-two when she died, and if she had been fifteen or sixteen when she was in the choir, that narrowed the search down to one of two possible years: 1994 and 1995. Now, if she could connect Dennis Moreland to—

The thought was cut off by Sheila Donovan speaking again. 'You said something earlier on about there being more questions at the station?'

'That's right. I know it's a difficult time, so I'll try to be as brief as possible.'

'What kind of questions?'

'Almost anything you can tell me about Connie,' said Molly. 'Friends she may have mentioned, problems she may have had, things she might have told you or discussed with you during your telephone conversations?'

Sheila looked away, then shook her head. 'The truth is, I haven't spoken to Connie for months, and I haven't been what you might call close to her for many a year. Once she got to be about twelve or thirteen, she changed. We couldn't agree on anything, and it got worse as time went on. She was never in any *real* trouble, like with the law or anything like that, but she ran with a funny crowd, and nothing I said or did made a scrap of difference. In fact, if I said one thing, she'd go out and do the opposite. It was as if we were living separate lives from then on, and when I married Alex and moved down south, she *might* call me on my birthday, if she remembered – I always called on hers – but we had nothing to talk about. So, you see, I'm the wrong person to ask. That girl she lives with can probably tell you much more than I can. Sandra . . . I forget her last name. I've spoken to her once or twice and she seems like a nice person, so perhaps you should talk to her. And to tell you the truth, I'd rather not talk about it any more. I'd just like to lie down.'

Later, as they were getting into their own car in the Charter Lane car park, Alex Donovan thanked Molly for her help. 'If you should need to talk to Sheila about anything, we'll be staying at the George until we can sort things out,' he said. 'I don't know how long we'll be here or what needs to be done, exactly. I suppose we'll have to see about things in Connie's flat, and make funeral arrangements and that sort of thing. I've not had to deal with anything like this before.'

Molly took out a card and scribbled a number on the back of it. 'This is the number to call to find out when the body will be released by the coroner's office,' she explained, 'and if you have any questions, or if you or Mrs Donovan think of anything that might help us, please call me.' She watched as they drove away, then heaved a sigh of relief as she made her way up the front steps and entered the building. It wasn't that she was unsympathetic, but if Sergeant Ormside asked her to accompany one more grieving relative – or even a non-grieving relative like Bronwyn Davies – to view a body, she would tell him to get stuffed. A tight smile tugged at the corners of her mouth as she visualized Ormside's reaction to that! Perhaps it would be better to put it another way, she decided, but the sentiment would be the same. She'd had enough. Let someone else do it next time.

As she walked down the corridor to the incident room, a young uniformed constable came hurrying around the corner. He grinned when he saw her and said, 'Good news, eh?', putting two thumbs up as he hurried past.

'Good news about what?' Molly called after him.

'Didn't you hear? The bloke you've been looking for. The one on TV. Walked in calm as you like half an hour ago. Your boss is in with him now.'

TWENTY-THREE

'My name is Edwin Redgrave,' the man said, speaking clearly and distinctly for the benefit of the recorder. 'I live in Oxford, and the reason I am here today is because my mother telephoned me last night, in a very agitated state, to say the police were looking for me. She said she remembered my mentioning being in the Red Lion last Wednesday evening, and talking to the woman behind the bar, and between that and the picture on TV, she was sure it was me you were looking for. I assured her she had nothing to worry about, and told her I would come down first thing this morning to straighten things out. So, gentlemen, here I am. What would you like to know?'

He took a card case from his jacket pocket and slid a card across the table. 'My home address and telephone number in case you should need it,' he said, then sat back in his chair and folded his arms. Dressed casually, wearing a white shirt, open at the neck, light brown pullover, corduroy jacket and tan trousers, he appeared to be perfectly at ease; in fact there was a certain presence about him. Crowley had said the man was good looking, and he was right: broad shoulders, compact frame, well-defined facial features, a loose mane of dark brown hair that made him look younger than he probably was, and calm if somewhat watchful eyes.

There was a hint of the academic about him, so Paget wasn't surprised when he read: *Edwin Redgrave, PhD.* He clipped the card to the folder in front of him. 'You say your mother rang you. She lives here in Broadminster, I take it?'

'That's right.'

'And you are admitting to being the man who was talking to Connie Rice in the Red Lion last Wednesday evening?'

'I'm not sure I like the way you use the term "admitting",' Redgrave said, 'but, yes, I was talking to Connie Rice that evening. But I had nothing to do with her subsequent disappearance.'

'What did you talk about?'

Redgrave shrugged. 'Nothing special,' he said. 'It was very quiet in there, and I got the impression that all she wanted was for the shift to end so that she could go home. We exchanged the usual observations about the weather; she did some not exactly subtle probing as to who I was; what I was doing there, and . . .' he smiled, 'whether I was married or not.'

'Are you?' Paget asked. 'Married?'

'I have a partner,' Redgrave said, 'but I'm not sure that's relevant, so why do you ask?'

'What about your side of the conversation?' Paget asked, ignoring the question. 'We've been told by the manager there that you were, in his words, "chatting Connie Rice up". So why were you in the Red Lion? Were you looking for some companionship, perhaps?'

Redgrave shook his head. 'On the contrary,' he said. 'I was looking for a bit of peace and quiet, so our conversation didn't last long, and I left after a couple of drinks.'

'By car?'

Again, Redgrave shook his head. 'I was walking,' he said. He leaned forward to rest his arms on the table. 'Perhaps it would simplify things if I told you why I was in Broadminster in the first place, and how I happened to be in the Red Lion that night, and then you can ask all the questions you like. All right?'

'Fair enough,' said Paget. 'Please go ahead, and remember that whatever you say is being recorded.'

Tregalles shot him a puzzled glance. The interview wasn't turning out the way he'd expected. The man could be the killer they'd been searching for, but it seemed to him that Paget was allowing him to run the interview. On the other hand, if Redgrave thought he was in control and became over-confident, he might very well trip himself up.

'A bit of history to begin with, then,' Redgrave said, 'Nine years ago, my father was the victim in a hit-and-run accident, and he ended up with a fractured skull and brain damage that affected his memory and his ability to control his actions. Prior to the accident, he was a maths and science teacher at Westonleigh, but the accident put paid to that. Since then, there's been a slow but steady decline in his health and in his mental state, and it's now reached the point where my mother can no longer look after him. She's ten years younger than my father, and very capable, but, much as she'd like to, she can't keep it up. He needs to be in a home where he can receive professional care. Unfortunately, it's proving all but impossible to get my father into the kind of care facility he needs, so I've been coming down here as often as I can for the past couple of months to give my mother a break. We've tried to get someone to come in to help her, but that's almost as hard as getting him into a home. God knows how she's managed to do as much as she has all these years, because I find it wearing after a couple of days.

'And that's how it was last Wednesday. My father had been particularly difficult that day, so once we had him settled down for the night, I went out for a walk. I just wanted to get out of the house for an hour or two, that's all. It wasn't really raining when I set out, but when it came on heavier, I ducked into the nearest pub, which happened to be the Red Lion. As I said, I had a couple of drinks, chatted with the girl behind the bar, Connie Rice, for a bit, then left after about three-quarters of an hour. I stayed on at the house to help my mother through the day on Thursday, but I had to be back on Friday, so I drove back to Oxford Thursday evening.'

'What kind of car do you drive?' Tregalles asked.

'A Mazda 6 TS estate,' Redgrave said cautiously. 'Why do you want to know that?'

'Where is it now?'

'Outside in the visitors' parking section, but—'

'Would you have any objection to it being taken in for a forensic examination?'

Redgrave's eyes narrowed. 'What, *exactly*, does that mean?' he asked. 'And why would you want to do that?' He turned to Paget. 'Am I a suspect in this woman's murder?'

'You were one of the last persons to be seen talking to Connie Rice prior to her disappearance,' Paget pointed out, 'and we have to look at every possibility. Did you meet anyone you knew while you were walking to or from the Red Lion that night?'

Redgrave shook his head impatiently. 'I haven't lived here for years, so the only people I know are the next-door neighbours, and then only to nod to.'

'Did you make any phone calls? Stop anywhere along the way?'

'No. It was late. I went straight home . . . that is, to my parents' house.'

'Which is where?'

'Cumberland Crescent.'

'That's quite a long way from the Red Lion,' Paget observed. 'Any particular reason why you went to that particular pub?'

'It's about half a mile, actually,' Redgrave said tightly. 'And I thought I had made it clear that I didn't set out to go to any specific place. I went for a walk to clear my head. In fact, if it hadn't started to rain when it did, I would never have gone into the Red Lion at all.'

'And your mother can verify when you got back?'

Redgrave hesitated. 'She'd gone to bed,' he said. 'I let myself in. I have a key.'

'I see.' Paget opened a folder and took out a sheet of paper, which he slid across the table. 'Do you recognize any of those names?' he asked.

Redgrave took a pair of glasses from his top pocket and put them on. 'Connie Rice, of course,' he said as he scanned the list. 'Whom I met for the first time last Wednesday,' he added quickly. 'As for the others, no, I don't think so.' He took off his glasses and handed the paper back to Paget.

'What about Mike Fulbright?' asked Tregalles.

'What about him?'

'Do you know him?'

'I know *of* him,' Redgrave said. 'In fact I played a bit of rugby myself when I was at Westonleigh, and later in Oxford, and I used to follow the Grinders. Is he still with them, or has he retired from the game? I haven't followed them for years.'

'Have you seen him or talked to him since you've been coming back here?' Tregalles persisted.

'I would hardly be asking about him if I had, would I, Sergeant?' Redgrave said testily.

Paget opened the folder. 'You say you've been coming back here on a regular basis these past few months, so I'd like you to give me a list of those dates so I can compare them with the dates I have here. All right?'

'Those dates being when the other people were killed, I presume?' said Redgrave.

'Exactly,' said Paget. 'And the sooner we can verify where you were on those dates, the sooner we can eliminate you from our enquiries . . . or not, Mr Redgrave.'

Redgrave hesitated, then took a Blackberry from his pocket and said, 'Right, give me the dates and I'll tell you where I was at the time.'

'Sorry, Mr Redgrave,' Paget said, 'but that's not the way it works. I'll take the Blackberry, if you don't mind.'

There were three messages waiting for Molly when she turned her computer on, but the only one she was interested in was the one from David. It was addressed to his aunt and uncle, with a copy to her. Perhaps now she would find out what Dr Starkie had been talking about this morning. She scanned it quickly, then more slowly as the gist of the message began to sink in. A cold, hard knot began to form in the pit of her stomach as she read on. David would *not* be coming back to England any time soon. That much was certain.

Lijuan, he said, had made it clear that she did not want to return to England with him. He said he'd had a long talk with her, and while she appreciated what he had done and was trying to do for her as her father, she said that after being away from England for six years, her home was in Hong Kong now. Her friends were there and her grandmother was there, and, with her mother gone, Lijuan did not want to be separated from her grandmother as well. What was also implied, if not actually spoken, was the message that, while Lijuan wasn't rejecting him outright, he shouldn't expect to walk back into her life as a replacement for her mother.

David went on to say that Lijuan's grandmother had not put any pressure on the girl to stay, but he knew that she would be devastated if she lost Lijuan so soon after losing Meilan, her only daughter. However, it was not all bad news: Lijuan had been receptive to the idea that he spend some time there so they could get to know one another better – as long as he agreed not to try to pressure her to change her mind. *It seems*, he concluded, *that her aversion is to England rather than to me, so I'm looking at that as a plus and a starting point in getting to know my daughter again. And since they can use my services here at the Tung Wah hospital for the next few months at least, I can pay my way while I'm here.*

Molly slumped back in her chair and rubbed her face with her hands. Not all bad news, he'd said. She couldn't blame him for wanting to get to know his daughter again, but if Lijuan didn't want to come to England, what if David decided to stay in Hong Kong himself? And Tung Wah hospital for the next few *months*? What if they offered him a permanent position?

Perhaps she had been fantasizing about their relationship all along, she told herself as she prepared for bed that night. Perhaps there never had been a 'relationship' as far as David was concerned. And yet Molly was sure there had been *something* between them, right from their very first meeting. But, even if that were true, how did a nebulous 'something' compete with David's need to re-establish a relationship with his daughter?

Molly got into bed and turned out the light. If he *did* decide to stay in Hong Kong, would that be the end of it, she wondered. Would she ever see him again? She lay there, staring into the darkness, trying hard to think of other things, but David's image kept getting in the way.

TWENTY-FOUR

Tuesday, 1 November

Amanda Pierce slipped into a seat at the back of the room as Paget was summing up. 'Redgrave may be telling the truth,' he said. 'Perhaps he was just out for a walk and perhaps he just happened to drop into the Red Lion. But he did talk to Connie Rice, and he was one of the last people to see her alive . . . perhaps *the* last person to see her alive. According to his own records, he was in town when Whitelaw and Moreland were killed, but there was no indication of where he was on the weekend when Travis was killed. He claims he was in Oxford, but those dates had been erased. So we are going to have to try to account for every minute of Redgrave's movements on all of those dates. That includes talking to Redgrave's mother, and possibly his father, depending on his condition. And, since Redgrave himself will probably be there, I think it best if both DS Tregalles and DS Forsythe tackle that one together.'

Molly smothered a groan. Oh, yes, good old Molly. Send her along with Tregalles. She's good at handling grieving widows or upset wives and mothers. She could just imagine how Mrs Redgrave would feel when she and Tregalles started asking her questions about dates and times, and she realized that her son was a suspect in four brutal killings.

'Forensic have Redgrave's car,' Paget continued, 'and it's being given priority, so if there is anything to be found, we should have the information by the end of the day. As for the rest, I'll let DS Ormside fill you in.' He moved aside and sat down.

'Right,' said Ormside. 'Here's what we have so far. Dr Redgrave is thirty-eight years old; he's unmarried, but he and his common law partner, Delia Cavendish, have been together for the past six years. Both have unblemished records as far as we're concerned, and Redgrave has some standing in the academic community in Oxford. He is currently engaged in a research mentoring programme, which, I'm told, means that he acts as an advisor, instructor and sort of guidance counsellor to people learning how to do actual research.'

'What field is he in?' someone asked.

'Biochemistry,' Ormside said, 'and according to the people I spoke to yesterday, Redgrave is respected in his field, and well liked.'

'Oh, jolly good,' said someone at the back.

Ormside silenced the man with a look before turning back to his notes. 'Now, regarding the hit-and-run in which his father was injured: Arthur Redgrave was knocked down on a pedestrian crossing by a car on Bridge Street one Friday evening in July, 2002. Witnesses said there were at least three people in the car. They said it was speeding and weaving in and out of traffic, and Redgrave never had a chance. The car, which turned out to be stolen, was found the following day at the bottom of Meadow Lane, its interior burned out. Forensic had it in, but any evidence that might have been left behind was destroyed by the fire. The driver was never found, and the file is still open.'

Ormside took off his glasses. 'I spoke briefly to Arthur Redgrave's doctor yesterday evening,' he said, 'and he confirmed, in general terms, what Redgrave son told DCI Paget and DS Tregalles yesterday, so at least that part is true. But there's more to be done, both here and in Oxford, and I'll be assigning one or possibly two of you to take care of that end of things following this briefing.'

'You say Redgrave's father is *Arthur* Redgrave?' Tregalles said.

'That's right,' said Ormside. 'Why? Does that mean something to you?'

'It's just that his name starts with the letter A. And you said there were several people in the car that knocked him down, so what if Redgrave found out who they were and he's been killing them off one by one?'

'It's *possible*,' Ormside said slowly, 'but Travis, Moreland, Whitelaw and Rice all together in one car, joyriding through the streets of Broadminster? I have trouble with that picture,

Tregalles. They *might* have all known each other when they were kids, although we can't be sure of that, but at least some of them seem to have gone their separate ways since then.'

'As far as we *know*,' Tregalles countered. 'Maybe they were at some sort of do together, maybe a reunion or something, and they all got thoroughly pissed. It could happen. And after what Redgrave senior's been through, to say nothing of what his wife and son have had to put up with over the years, I'd say it's worth looking at.'

'And we will,' said Paget as he got back on his feet. 'We're going to be looking at everything. Now, has anyone got anything to add?' He looked out over the group and pointed at Molly. 'Did you learn anything yesterday from Connie Rice's mother?' he asked.

'Just that Connie, like Billy Travis and Whitelaw, was a member of the All Saints choir when she was a teenager,' Molly said, 'but I still don't know how that helps us. Peter Jones, the present choirmaster, is contacting his predecessor, Adam Fairfield, to ask if he has any of the old records, but I haven't heard back from him yet.'

'Still no connection with Moreland, then?' said Paget.

'No, sir. And, to be honest, while it's the only connection we've been able to find between the victims, I'm not sure if the information is useful or not. This isn't a very big town, so it isn't exactly surprising that some of the kids in C of E families would join the choir of the only C of E church in town.'

'Mike Fulbright's been a member since he was a kid,' Tregalles put in, 'and I still think he knows something about all this.'

'I believe he is holding something back,' Paget said, 'but it may or may not have a bearing on the case.' He turned to Molly again. 'However, since you've gone this far with it, you might as well see it through, so give Jones another call, and if he hasn't come up with anything, get onto Fairfield yourself.'

He looked around, and was about to ask Amanda if she wished to add anything, but she had already risen and was making her way to the door. 'That's it, then,' he said, 'so let's get on with it.'

* * *

Eleven o'clock, and Molly was back in the office typing up notes. She felt drained after spending more than an hour in the house with the Redgraves. Tregalles had done his best to keep both father and son occupied while she talked with Mrs Redgrave, but it had been difficult. Iris Redgrave had been cooperative to a point, but she'd made it clear that she did not appreciate the fact that her son was a suspect in the series of killings that had shaken the entire town.

'The whole idea is ludicrous,' she'd said. 'When Edwin is here he rarely leaves the house. He's here to give me a break, and it's a full-time job looking after his father. As you can see for yourself, Arthur can't be left for a moment.'

At least that part was true. Molly had expected to see a bed-ridden man, but Arthur Redgrave was up and dressed, and very, very active. 'Arthur can be as quiet as a mouse one minute,' Iris Redgrave explained, 'but the next he would be out the door if we didn't stop him. And he's strong. Sometimes it's all I can do to handle him, and I'm not getting any younger. So, when Edwin's here, he takes over to give me a break, and there's no way he would even have time to do whatever it is you're suggesting.'

The trouble was, on the nights that her son was there, Iris Redgrave had said that the one thing she really looked forward to more than anything else, was going to bed early and getting a full night's rest, so she wouldn't know if her son had left the house or not. Earlier in their conversation, Iris had mentioned that there were times when the only way to handle her husband was to sedate him. 'I don't like to do it, but sometimes it's necessary,' she'd said, so if she was in bed and Arthur was sedated Edwin Redgrave could be out all night and no one would be the wiser.

Molly looked at the clock and picked up the phone. Time to ring Peter Jones again. Three rings, then voice mail again. *Please leave a message.* It was no good; she would have to try to get in touch with Fairfield herself. She put the phone down, but had barely taken her hand away when it rang.

She picked it up again and said, 'DS Forsythe.'

'Got a woman on the line says her name's Bainbridge, Sergeant,' a young male voice announced. 'She says you left a message for her to ring you. Want me to put her through?'

Bainbridge? It took a moment to register. 'Oh, yes . . . right. Thank you. Put her through.'

'Detective Sergeant Forsythe? Meg Bainbridge,' the woman said as soon as they were connected. 'You left a couple of messages asking me to ring you when I got back, but are you sure you have the right Bainbridge?'

'If you're a member of the All Saints choir, then it's you I'd like to talk to,' said Molly.

'I am,' Meg said cautiously, 'but what's it about?'

'I just need some information,' Molly said, 'and I'm told that you might be able to help me. To begin with, do you recall a boy by the name of Dennis Moreland being in the choir back some fifteen or so years ago?'

'Moreland . . .? Doesn't ring a bell,' said Meg, 'but I could look it up if it's important.'

'Look it up?'

'In the register. If I can remember where it is. Can I get back to you? I've only just got in, and I've got a few errands to run.'

Molly gripped the phone tighter. 'Are you saying you have a register of the names of everyone in the choir, going back all those years?'

'Yes, I've got it,' Meg said. 'We had a burst pipe in the vestry three years ago and some of the books got wet, and the register was one of them. So I took it home to dry it out, and it's still here. It was around the time Adam Fairfield left, and we were without a choirmaster for a while before Peter Jones took over, so I'm afraid it was overlooked. I should have brought it back ages ago, but we needed a new one anyway, so . . .'

'Look, Mrs Bainbridge, I know you've just returned, but I would very much like to see the register for myself. Do you mind if I come round?'

'It would have to be later this afternoon,' Meg said. 'I have an appointment I can't break, but I should be back around two thirty or three. Why do you want to look at it?'

'It's part of an ongoing enquiry,' Molly said, being deliberately vague. 'Shall we say two thirty, then?'

'Make it three,' Meg said firmly. 'Wouldn't want you waiting on the doorstep for half an hour.'

Now that she knew a register existed, Molly was anxious to see it, but she supposed another half hour wouldn't make any difference, and it didn't sound as if Mrs Bainbridge was about to give ground on the time. 'Three o'clock it is, then,' she said. 'And thank you very much, Mrs Bainbridge.'

'No trouble,' the woman said, 'and the name's Meg. You know where I am, I presume?'

'Marlborough Place . . .?'

'That's right. Number ten. We're on the very end next to the fairgrounds.'

TWENTY-FIVE

Ten Marlborough Place was a neat and obviously well-cared-for semi-detached house. As Meg Bainbridge had said, it was on the end of the row, next to an open field that everyone referred to as the fairgrounds because that was where the fair used to set up every year. The fair itself had been gone for a number of years, but the name of the field remained, a reminder of days gone by.

'Can't say I miss it,' said Meg when Molly mentioned it. 'Dirty, smelly old thing, and the noise used to drive me up the wall. Five solid days of it every year. Seemed more like fifty. Nobody mentioned that when we bought the house. Anyway, come on in and I'll get that book for you.' She thrust out her hand. 'And as I said on the phone, the name's Meg. Do I call you Sergeant . . . Sorry, what was the name again?'

'Forsythe,' said Molly, 'but Molly will do for now.'

'Right. So what's this all about?' Meg asked as she led the way to a small room off the hallway. 'This is my office,' she explained before Molly could answer. 'I'm an independent insurance adjuster. I work for several companies on contract, and working from home allows me to set my own hours.' She walked over to her desk and picked up an old-fashioned ledger. 'So, what *is* this all about?' she asked again.

'So what you're saying,' said Meg, when Molly had finished

her explanation, 'is that you think these murders we've been hearing about have something to do with the choir?' She shook her head. 'Can't see it,' she said flatly. 'It's got to be a coincidence. Still, I suppose you have your job to do, so what was the name again? Moreland, was it?' She opened the book. 'Do you know the year?'

'Nineteen ninety-four or five,' said Molly, and showed Meg the picture. 'I'm not exactly sure when this was taken, but Billy Travis and Gavin Whitelaw are in it, and so are you.'

'Right. There's me,' Meg said, pointing to a dark-haired girl in the second row. 'I must have been about fifteen then. God! Look at that. I had big knockers even then. See? Stuck out like doorknobs under the surplice.' She chuckled. 'Very proud of them back then, I was. None of the other girls my age even came close, and I never had any trouble attracting boys. Oh, yes, there's Mike Fulbright – he was one of them, boys, I mean – and there's Mr Trasler,' she pointed to a much older man – 'he wasn't, of course.' Meg went on to name several others before Molly was able to get her attention again.

'Right. Moreland,' she said briskly as she started flipping through the pages of the book. 'Here we are. 'Ninety-four.' Meg ran her finger down the list of names. 'No, no Moreland there, so let's try 'ninety-five.' She hummed a little tune as she turned the page. 'Moreland, Dennis,' she announced triumphantly. 'January 'ninety-five.' She frowned. 'Funny, but I don't remember him at all. Anyway, does that help?'

'It certainly does,' Molly said. 'What about Connie Rice? Is she in there? According to her mother, Connie must have joined about the same time, but she didn't stay very long.'

'Yes, she's here. Joined in May. Come to think of it, I remember her. Chubby girl, boy mad. Anything else you need to know?'

'I'd like to confirm that all those who have been killed were there at the same time,' said Molly. 'Can we take a look?'

'That won't show up here,' Meg told her. 'This registers when they first joined, and they didn't all join in the same year. What you want is the attendance record for that year.' She grinned when she saw the look of concern on Molly's face. 'Fortunately, it's in the same book,' she said, lifting a tab and turning to another section. 'So let's see if they were all there that year.'

'Tell me,' said Molly, 'would the Reverend Fulbright have known about the register, and that you'd taken it home after the pipe burst in the vestry?'

'Of course he would. In fact he was the one who said that the church wasn't the best place to dry the book out, so I volunteered to take it home. The trouble was, it took months to dry properly – you can't rush something like that – so we started a new one.'

'I wonder why he didn't mention it when we spoke to him,' said Molly, more to herself than to Meg.

'Who knows?' Meg said offhandedly. 'Always has been a bit of an oddball, has Theo. He builds doll's houses. Did you know?'

'Yes, I've seen them,' Molly said, then pointed to the book. 'But could we . . .?'

'Of course. Sorry.' Meg began searching through the pages. 'Ah! Here it is.'

According to the attendance record, Dennis Moreland joined the choir in January and left it at the end of October. Connie Rice joined in May of that year and left in September. 'Of course, the two boys in your picture, Billy Travis and Gavin Whitelaw, were there that year as well. So, for what it's worth, all four were there at the same time,' Meg concluded, 'but I don't see what that has to do with them getting killed. Mind you, I can't say I'm all that surprised about Whitelaw. I remember him. Couldn't keep his hands to himself. Tried it on with all the girls. Not that it got him very far, not with Mike around. They all wanted to be like Mike – the boys, I mean, because he knew how to pull the girls, and I think they thought some of the attraction might rub off on them. He had quite the little gang there for a while. Oh, but he was a handsome boy, Molly. That picture doesn't do him justice at all.' Meg sighed. 'Brings back memories, this does,' she said wistfully.

Molly stared at the open book. 'Speaking of memories,' she said, 'do you recall if anything significant happened that year?'

'Like what?'

'I don't know . . . Something involving the boys? You said there was quite a gang of them.'

Meg shook her head. 'I didn't mean a gang in that sense,' she said. 'I just meant they trailed around after Mike. I mean he was *the* man at that time, both for the boys and the girls, and he made the most of it. He was always a bit of a show-off, still is for that matter.'

'I'd like to take that book with me,' Molly said. 'I'll give you a receipt.'

'Just as long as I get it back,' Meg said. 'It's an official record, so it really should go back to the church.'

'Nineteen ninety-five,' Meg said pensively as she accompanied Molly to the door. 'You know, there was something happened that year,' she said slowly. 'At least I *think* it was that year, but not the sort of thing you were talking about. I'm almost sure that was the year the girl who was visiting committed suicide. Jumped off the tower. God! That was awful. It was her last day with us. Nobody had an inkling. Shook her poor aunt Edith up. I don't think she ever got over it. Edith Compton had been in the choir forever, but she never came back after that. She's dead as well. She used to have the Hillside llama trekking farm out at Monksford Cross. It's gone now. She worked very hard to make a go of it, but she couldn't compete with the one in Hereford. Died while she was feeding the animals, they said. Just dropped dead, and she was only in her early sixties.'

'The girl who committed suicide,' Molly said. 'Would she be in this book? What was her name?'

'No, she's not in the book because she was never a regular member of the choir,' said Meg. 'She was staying with Edith during the summer holidays, helping her on the farm. I don't think Edith was her actual aunt, but the girl called her Aunt Edith. Anyway, Edith brought her along to choir practice, and when she told Fairfield that the girl was training to be a singer – she was only sixteen – Fairfield said she could sing with us while she was here. Nice kid, too. Pretty, blonde, blue eyes, and a voice like an angel, so pure and clear.' Meg looked off into the distance. 'Funny in a way,' she said quietly. 'I haven't thought about her in years, but I remember thinking at the time how appropriate her name was. Angelica. That was her name.'

* * *

'No one in the street saw or heard anything on those nights,' Tregalles was saying when Molly entered the incident room. He was speaking to Paget and Ormside. 'I spoke to a Mrs Bagshott, who lives two doors down, and sometimes sits with Arthur Redgrave when Mrs Redgrave has to go out to the shops, and she told me that she's a very light sleeper and she would have heard if Redgrave had started his car in the night.' He made a face. 'In fact, she was pretty annoyed with me for even asking questions about him. She said he's wonderfully patient with his father, and he's been a great help to his mother in trying to get a place for his father, and she wouldn't hear a word said against him.'

'Perhaps he's exactly what he says he is and just happened to be in the Red Lion the night Connie Rice disappeared,' Paget said. 'We'll have to see what turns up at the Oxford end.' He turned his attention to Molly as she approached. 'You're looking rather pleased with yourself,' he said. 'Did you hear back from Jones?'

'No, I didn't, sir,' said Molly, 'but that doesn't matter now, because I've found the register of everyone who was or is a member of the All Saints choir, and Travis, Whitelaw, Rice *and* Dennis Moreland were all there at the same time in the spring and summer of nineteen ninety-five.' Molly held up the book. 'It's all in here, sir. One of the choir members, Meg Bainbridge, had it.' She went on to explain how the book had come to be in Meg's possession, ending with, 'And both Mike Fulbright and his father must have known about this book, but neither of them said a word to us about it.'

'And Jones? Did he know as well?'

'Meg says they'd started another book by the time he took over, so he may not have known about it, or perhaps thought Fairfield had it. But there's something else, sir. Meg told me about a sixteen-year-old girl who committed suicide by jumping from the church tower in August that year. Meg couldn't remember her last name, but her first name was Angelica. I don't know if it's significant, but Angelica does begin with the letter A.'

'I had noticed,' Paget said drily. 'However, point taken.' He turned to Ormside. 'If the girl went off the church tower, we must have been called to the scene, so there should be something in the files, and the local paper should have something in their archives as well, so get someone started on that right away. I think it's time we had another talk with Mike Fulbright, Tregalles, and ask him why he never mentioned the register. And we can ask him what he knows about this girl's suicide as well.'

'I know he's been holding something back,' Tregalles said, 'but do you think he could be our killer?'

'I rather doubt that,' said Paget, 'but he is a big man, so just in case I'm wrong, take someone with you.'

'I'd like to go, if that's all right, sir?' Molly said quickly. 'One thing Meg Bainbridge said was that the boys used to try to hang around Mike Fulbright. In fact she said he had quite a gang around him for a while, so I think he could be involved in some way.'

'That makes two of us,' Tregalles said grimly, 'so let's go, Molly. You can tackle him and hold him down while I caution him.'

'I'm afraid Mike's gone for the day, Sergeant,' Anita Chapman said. 'He left here about half an hour ago. He said he had things to do at home. Is there anything I can do for you?'

A couple of things crossed Tregalles's mind, but he resisted the temptation to voice them, and shook his head. 'It's not important,' he said. 'I'll drop by tomorrow.' He didn't want Anita to let Fulbright know that they were coming.

'You've been quiet,' he said to Molly as they got back in the car. 'Penny for them?'

'It's just that I keep wondering if anyone else in the choir could be involved in all this, and why Mike's father didn't tell us about the register when he knew we were looking for the information. I don't think it's the sort of thing that would have slipped his memory.'

'Seems to me a few things have slipped people's memory,' Tregalles observed caustically as they pulled out into Bridge Street.

Tregalles rang the bell three times before the door was opened by Theodore Fulbright. 'Oh, it's you again,' he said with barely concealed displeasure. 'What do you want now?'

'We'd like to talk to Mike, if you don't mind, sir,' Tregalles said. 'May we come in?'

'*Michael*,' Fulbright said with emphasis on the name, 'is not here.' He started to close the door, but Tregalles stood firm with his shoulder against it. 'We were told he was,' he said, 'so I would like to verify that for myself.'

But Fulbright wasn't giving an inch either. 'I told you he isn't here,' he said. 'He was here, but he went out again.'

'Can you tell us where he went?'

Fulbright shook his head impatiently. 'I don't ask my son where he's going every time he goes out,' he said coldly. 'You'll have to come back later if you want to talk to—'

Tregalles's phone buzzed insistently. Without moving from his position against the door, he glanced at it then handed it to Molly, mouthing 'Ormside' before turning his attention back to Fulbright. 'I'm sorry,' he said in a conciliatory tone, 'but we do need to talk to Michael, so if you have any idea where he might have gone—'

He stopped as Molly grabbed his arm to get his attention. 'They've found the obituary,' she said breathlessly. 'The girl's name was Angelica Jones, and heading the list of surviving relatives is her father, *Peter Jones of Wolverhampton*! The choirmaster was her father!' Molly's voice suddenly rose. 'Mr Fulbright . . .?'

Theodore Fulbright was clutching the door for support, and every hint of colour had drained from his face. 'Jones,' he said shakily. 'Peter Jones was her father? Oh, God, no! Michael . . .'

'What about Michael?' Tregalles asked sharply. 'Where is he? What do you know about this?'

'He had a phone call. Michael said Jones had changed his mind about the solo in the Christmas anthem, and he wanted Michael to do it instead of Findlay, so he asked him to go over to do a run-through before choir practice tonight.'

'At the church?'

Fulbright nodded as he fought for breath. 'I have to talk to Jones. He doesn't know . . .' He was gasping for air. 'He'll kill Michael.'

'Doesn't know what?' Tregalles demanded, but Fulbright

shook his head. 'We've got to stop him,' he said. 'Got to get to the church.'

He started forward but Tregalles stood in his way. 'We'll take care of it,' he said. 'You stay here and try to get him on his mobile.'

But Fulbright wasn't to be denied. 'I *have* to be there,' he insisted. 'I have to talk to Jones, to make him understand.'

'Understand wha—?' Tregalles began, then decided he was wasting time. 'Oh, for God's sake come on, then,' he said. 'You can tell us on the way.' He took Fulbright by the arm and hustled him down the steps and into the car. 'You can try calling him as we go,' he said. 'And get hold of Paget,' he told Molly, 'and tell him that Mike and Jones are at the church, and we're on our way there now.'

Mike Fulbright was feeling very relaxed. He raised his glass and winked knowingly at Peter Jones. 'Great stuff, Dalwhinnie,' he said. 'Good choice. Best single malt in the Highlands. Drink it myself all the time.'

'I know,' said Jones. 'The first time I tasted it was at that party you gave last year, and I've developed a taste for it myself. Which is why I bought a bottle to celebrate my birthday today. I thought I was going to have to drink to it on my own, so I'm glad you're here to have one with me before we get down to business.'

'Happy to oblige,' Mike said, grinning broadly. He'd never known a single drink of Dalwhinnie to make him feel like this. Must have been a particularly good year. 'Which one is it?' he asked. 'Birthday, I mean.'

Jones hesitated. 'Sixtieth,' he said. 'A milestone in my life.' He looked around the vestry. 'Hardly the place to celebrate a sixtieth birthday, though, is it Mike? A dingy old vestry. I'd like to do something really special to mark the occasion; something *different*!' He frowned as if thinking deeply. 'Tell you what,' he said abruptly. 'Let's go up the tower and have a drink up there. That would be different; something to remember and mark the occasion. Just the one drink, though. I want you in good shape for your solo.'

But Mike was shaking his head. 'Don't like the tower,'

he muttered. He held out his glass. 'Let's have another one here.'

Peter Jones frowned at him. 'I never would have believed it,' he said as if surprised. 'Mike Fulbright, afraid of heights? Well, well, well. Do your mates in the Grinders know about this, Mike?'

'I am *not* afraid of heights,' Mike said heatedly. 'It's just . . .' He seemed to be searching for words of explanation, then shrugged as if the effort were too much for him.

'Just what, Mike?' Jones seemed to be genuinely puzzled. 'I mean, I am doing you a favour, and I'm not asking much in return. I'd just like to make this birthday a bit memorable, that's all. But I suppose, if you have trouble with heights—'

'I do *not* have trouble with heights!' Mike insisted, 'so don't keep saying that!' He grinned weakly, and his tone was more conciliatory when he spoke again. 'Look, if it's that important to you, Pete, I'll come up and have one drink with you. We'll drink to your health and tell the whole world you're sixty. Just one drink, though, then we'll come down and get to work. All right, Pete?'

Jones nodded slowly as he picked up the bottle. 'Believe me, Mike,' he said, 'you'll never know how much I appreciate this. Lead on. I'm right behind you.'

TWENTY-SIX

'That's Michael's car,' Theo said as they drove into the car park outside the church, 'and that one belongs to Jones.' Tregalles swung into a space next to Mike's car. He had just opened the door when another car swung in behind them and Paget got out.

'Please stay where you are,' Tregalles said to Fulbright as he got out of the car, but he might as well have saved his breath, because Theo was already scrambling out. There was no time to argue. Tregalles ran up the steps and pulled the door open. Molly darted past him and headed for the vestry, but a shout from Fulbright stopped her.

'The tower!' he called, pointing to a curtain pulled aside to reveal an open door. 'They'll be up there.' He started running, but Paget, half a step behind him, grabbed his arm and swung him round. 'Stay here,' he said. 'This is our job.'

'You don't understand,' Fulbright protested hoarsely. 'He'll kill my son. I have to be there . . .' But Paget was already moving up the steps, and Fulbright's words were lost as the others crowded through. The climb was steep and the steps were worn, but when Molly glanced back, she saw Fulbright close behind her, panting hard but gamely coming on.

The door at the top was open. Paget stepped out cautiously, eyes searching for Jones and Fulbright, but the roof appeared to be empty. He heard a noise to his left and turned to see the two men standing with their backs to one of the openings in the crenellated parapet, and he caught his breath.

Mike Fulbright's wrists were bound behind his back with cable ties. A short, thin rope led from his wrists to a noose around his neck, forcing him to hold his hands high against his shoulder blades to prevent the noose from choking him. If he so much as relaxed his arms, the noose would cut into his throat and strangle him. His ankles were tied together loosely so that, at best, he could only shuffle. Duct tape covered his mouth, and a white dressing on his forehead was held in place by another strip of duct tape. Standing beside him, Peter Jones had a firm grip on Mike's collar.

Behind him, Paget heard Theo Fulbright suck in his breath.

'Stay where you are!' Jones called sharply. 'One move towards me and he goes over.'

'We're not moving,' Paget said quietly, 'but I'd feel a lot happier if you would move away from the parapet, and loosen the rope around Mike's neck.'

'I'll bet you would,' said Jones. 'And who the hell are you?'

'Detective Chief Inspector Paget. I can understand—'

'How I feel? Is that what you were going to say, Detective Chief Inspector Paget? You don't understand anything about me.'

'Perhaps not,' Paget conceded, 'but don't you think there have been enough killings? Have any of them taken the pain away? I don't think so,' he continued, 'and neither will killing one more.'

Peter Jones shook his head slowly from side to side. 'You're right about the pain,' he conceded, 'but you're forgetting satisfaction, and killing every one of them has given me a great deal of satisfaction.' His eyes flicked back and forth across the group. 'I hadn't anticipated an audience for this final act,' he said. 'This was to have been a quiet affair between Mike and me, but now you're here, I want you to know the truth about the way my daughter died. Sixteen years old,' he said softly, 'and this pitiful specimen of manhood and his gang of followers set out to rape her. Up here on this very roof.'

Mike started to make choking noises, but Jones jerked the rope and said, 'Keep your hands up! I haven't finished with you yet.'

'You can't know that—' Paget began, but Jones cut him off with a wave of his hand and said, 'I *wouldn't* have known it if it hadn't been for Billy Travis sniping at Mike on the bus coming home from Chester the other week, then having an attack of conscience and spilling his guts out to Phillips. But Phillips had had a bit too much to drink, so he fell asleep and didn't hear what Billy was saying. But I did. I was sitting in the seat behind them, and I heard enough to make me want to know the rest.' He paused, and his eyes drifted for a moment as if he were looking at a scene from the past. 'I was never satisfied with the coroner's verdict,' he continued. 'I knew Angelica could never have killed herself, so when I heard Billy talking about what *really* happened, I wanted to know everything. That's why Billy was the first, and he did tell me everything before he died. He told me how Mike boasted he'd have my little girl, and told Billy and the others to come and help hold her down, and then they could have her as well when he'd finished with her.'

Jones pulled savagely on the rope. A horrible gurgling sound tried to break through the duct tape, and Mike's knees started to buckle, but Jones jerked him upright again.

'I got them all,' he continued. 'Travis, Moreland, Whitelaw and Rice.' The names rolled off his tongue like a judge pronouncing the death sentence.

'But Rice?' Paget said, looking desperately for a way to keep the man talking and a way to distract him. 'Even if what you say is true, what did Connie Rice have to do with any of this?'

'Oh, I'm so glad you asked that,' Jones said quietly, 'because I want Theo to hear this. Connie was the Judas goat. Mike, here, promised to have sex with her if she would get Angelica up here for him and the others. Billy said he even lied about that. He said Mike couldn't stand the girl, but he could get her to do anything for him.'

His voice rose. 'Take a good look, Theo,' he shouted. 'This is the son you were so proud of. This is the piece of shit who drove my daughter off this tower, just as I'm going to do to your son, Theo.' Standing as he was, inches from an opening in the parapet wall, it was only Jones's steadying hand that prevented Mike from going backwards over the edge.

Paget made to step forward, but Theodore Fulbright put out an arm to stop him. 'You're wrong, Peter,' he called. 'Mike didn't do that. He wasn't even here when Angelica went over. It was me. I did it. I didn't mean to; it was an accident, but she wouldn't stop screaming, and—'

'Aha-a-a-a!' The sound coming from Jones was like a long drawn-out sigh. It seemed to hang in the air between them. 'I wondered if you would have the guts to admit that,' he said softly. 'Billy told me you came up and caught them and chased them all down. So what happened, Theo? Run in the family, does it? A taste for under-age girls?'

'It wasn't like that,' Theo said wearily. 'I caught Connie as she came down the tower. I knew she was up to no good, so I made her tell me what was going on, and she said the boys were up there "having a bit of a game with Angelica", as she put it.' Theo closed his eyes as if trying to shut out the past. 'I went up to stop it. I was trying to *save* your daughter. I sent the boys down, and I tried my best to calm Angelica down, but she was hysterical. She wouldn't listen to me. She kept screaming that she was going to tell everyone about Michael. I tried to reason with her, but she wouldn't listen. She would have destroyed Michael. We struggled . . . I hit her; hit her with this.' He held up his prosthetic arm.

'I knew I'd killed her,' Fulbright continued. 'There was no

pulse. There was nothing I could do for her. But I couldn't leave her there. There would be questions, an investigation, so . . .'

'So you threw her over the wall,' Jones finished for him. His voice hardened. 'She was sixteen years old, Theo, and you threw her off this roof like a piece of garbage. Did you go to the inquest?' he asked abruptly, then answered his own question. 'No, you did not! But I did, and I remember your name being mentioned as the pastor of this church, and, according to the statement read into the record, you told the police you'd already gone home for the evening and had no idea that Angelica was still in the church when you left.

'So you didn't hear the two women who were in the graveyard at the time testify that they heard Angelica scream a second or two before she landed on the pavement below. She was alive, Theo. My daughter was *alive* when you threw her off this tower to save your son's worthless skin. Angelica died screaming, Theo,' he said softly, 'just as your son will die screaming when he follows her.'

Jones tore the tape from Mike Fulbright's mouth in one swift movement, then, almost casually, placed a hand on his face and pushed. It was over in seconds . . . the bone-chilling scream and then silence.

'Now you can suffer as I have, Theo,' said Jones, then he, too, was gone.

TWENTY-SEVEN

Theodore Fulbright, aided by Paget and Tregalles, made it to the bottom of the steps before he collapsed. Molly called for an ambulance and a response team, then stayed with Theo until the ambulance came, while Paget and Tregalles went out to await SOCO's arrival. Fortunately, the bodies lay on the graveyard side of the church, shielded from the street and passers-by. Except for necessary instructions, no one spoke. It was as if the shock of what they had witnessed had overwhelmed their senses, each replaying the scene over and over again in their minds.

'I keep thinking there had to be *something* I could have done to save them both,' Paget told Grace later that night, 'but Jones had Mike standing in one of the openings right on the edge, and the only thing stopping him from going over the edge was Jones himself. The distance between us was just too great to attempt to rush him. There was *nothing* any of us could do.'

'And, from what you've said, I don't suppose Mike Fulbright could do anything to save himself, bound the way he was?'

Paget shook his head. 'Not only that,' he said, 'but I suspect he was drugged as well. Jones used Rohypnol on some of the others, so Starkie ordered tox tests to be done before the drug has a chance to disappear.'

'At least it's over, and the man responsible for all those deaths is dead,' Grace said, looking for something positive she could say. 'And there are times, Neil, when there *is* nothing you can do. You said it yourself: rushing the man was out of the question. He was determined to play things out his way right to the end, and there was nothing you or Tregalles or even the Reverend Fulbright could have done to stop him.'

She didn't like to see Neil like this. His face was beginning to show some colour, but it had been grey when he arrived home, and there was still a haunted look about the eyes.

But he seemed to want to talk. 'There will be an inquiry,' he told her. 'This thing could drag on for months. Once I'd briefed Amanda, she took things in hand and did everything by the book. That's why I'm so late home. We all had to write our separate reports, each in a separate room under supervision to make sure there was no cribbing, and I expect there will be recorded interviews tomorrow.'

'Bit of a shake-up for the new sergeant,' Grace commented. 'Poor girl. How did she take it?'

'She stood up well. She did her job and I'm proud of her.'

'Still, something like that can hit you later,' Grace said, 'so . . .'

'I'll be keeping an eye on her,' Paget promised, 'and if I see any signs that it's bothering her, I'll send her off for counselling.'

'What about you?' Grace asked, 'and I'm not being facetious. That sort of thing can get to you.'

For the first time since coming home, Paget smiled. 'I've got you,' he said as he put his arms around her and pulled her to him, 'and you're better than any counsellor I've ever met.'

Theodore Fulbright was being kept in hospital overnight for observation, but he would be arrested and charged with the killing of Angelica Jones once he was released. But, terrible as his crime was, Paget couldn't help wondering what good it would do to lock the man up, other than to satisfy the law of the land. 'He'll spend the rest of his life in prison,' he told Grace, 'but I suspect he's already as good as dead inside.'

The next few days were a blur to all of them. Everything had to be documented, checked and double checked for the Crown Prosecution Service, who would be putting together the case against Theodore Fulbright, although the word was that he had said he intended to plead guilty and wasn't interested in defending himself. But, as Amanda pointed out, he could change his mind, so the rules had to be followed, tedious as they might seem.

'I feel as if it's us who are under investigation,' Tregalles complained to Molly. 'Next time, I'm going to carry a video camera, and they can see and hear what happened for themselves.'

'I hope to God there never is a next time, not like that,' said Molly. 'I keep seeing those two men every time I close my eyes, and I can't help thinking—'

'That there was something you could have done?' Tregalles broke in. 'There wasn't, Molly. You know it and I know it. If we'd made a move towards him, the result would have been the same. There was no way Jones was going to be talked down. He'd made up his mind that Mike Fulbright must pay for killing his daughter, and once that was done, he had no reason to live himself. If you hadn't come up with the connection to Angelica Jones's death, he might have got away with it. But with us there, he knew he was finished. The fact that it turned out it was Mike's father who killed her, made no difference to him in the end.'

EPILOGUE

Saturday, 5 November

St Mark's Memorial Chapel was a small brick building on Wentnall Street. Paget, in dress uniform, arrived early, together with Grace, and Valerie Alcott was there in the lobby to greet them. Paget introduced Grace, and they chatted quietly for a few moments, but Valerie was obviously on tenterhooks and kept looking at her watch.

'As I told you on the phone,' she said, 'I don't expect more than a handful of people will be here, and I do appreciate your agreeing to say a few words about my father, Mr Paget.' She looked at her watch again and was about to say something when the door opened and Fiona McRae came in. Paget was about to make introductions, but Valerie shook her head and said, 'It's all right, Mr Paget, we've met, and thank you so much for coming, Fiona. Dad would be pleased.' Blinking back tears, Fiona embraced the younger woman, and then stood back.

Valerie sighed and looked at her watch again. 'I know it's not quite time, but perhaps we should go in. I don't think there will be any more com—' She stopped speaking as the outer door opened and Superintendent Amanda Pierce, in full dress uniform, entered, followed by a line of uniformed officers filing in behind her. Amanda paused to be introduced to Valerie and to offer her condolences, then moved on into the chapel. Ormside, Tregalles and Molly Forsythe, all in uniform, paused as well, while the rest filed quietly by to take their seats inside. Twenty-one of them, Paget counted as they went past.

There was no sign of Brock. Amanda had sent the chief superintendent a memo, and Paget had hoped that someone from head office would attend to mark and show respect for the passing of a colleague. But no . . . Perhaps that was just as well, he thought, because the people who were there had come because they wanted to pay their respects.

Paget turned to Valerie to suggest that they take their places. Tears were streaming down her face, but she was smiling. 'They remembered him,' she said. 'Dad would have been so pleased.' She touched Paget's arm and said, 'I think I'm ready to go in now.'